**Tori left the pub and kept walking.**

Mark's gaze burned into her back as she tried to stop smiling. The man's piercing blue eyes, his deep, calm voice and care for his daughter had drawn something out of her she hadn't known existed.

Need.

God-awful, unwanted, deeply feared need for someone to care for her. For so long, Tori had kept Melissa and their parents at arm's length to prove to them, and herself, that what Brian Appleton did to her hadn't defined her.

Yet, in the pub with Mark, something had momentarily shifted, scaring her so much, she'd quickly slammed in place an attitude of being in charge. When in truth, it had been Mark in the driving seat from the moment he'd confessed his love and fears for Olivia.

She risked a look behind her. He'd gone.

She released a shaky breath. Whether Mark Bolton realized it or not, she'd not only agreed to him helping her with the investigation, he had slipped a little way under her personal defenses too. Time and again during the hour they'd been in the pub, she had waited for an annoying comment to come out of his mouth. Waited for him to make a move or say something disparaging about the case or even about something she said. Anything to put her off him, to give her reason to kick him to the curb as she'd warned she would.

Nothing. Nada.

The man was nice. Really nice.

_To Sephi,_

_Congratulations!_

_Rachel Brimble x_

# If I Want You

## by

## Rachel Brimble

**If I Want You**

Cover Art by *Kim Mendoza*

The Wild Rose Press, Inc.
PO Box 708
Adams Basin, NY 14410-0708
Visit us at www.thewildrosepress.com

Publishing History
First Crimson Rose Edition, 2017
Print ISBN 978-1-5092-1804-2
Digital ISBN 978-1-5092-1805-9

Published in the United States of America

## Dedication

To my many loyal readers
who have followed me from my first book in 2007
to my nineteenth book in 2017.
I thank you all from the bottom of my heart!

Chapter One

Tori Peterson shifted farther back in her car seat and glanced from the open e-mail on her laptop toward the gates of her niece's school. No sign of any kids. No ringing of the bell. If she could just get this copy back to her editor while waiting for her niece to get out of school, she could swing Georgia home to her mum, beat a hasty retreat and succumb to a rare and enforced early night.

She lowered the window. The late October air blew gently against her skin and Tori breathed deep.

"Are you okay?"

Her colleague's question from the passenger seat refocused Tori's lagging attention. She faced Cally and sighed. "I'm fine. Just tired."

Cally frowned. "Well, I'd be tired too if I worked continual ten hour days. You need to take some time off. Have some fun."

"And what is this *fun* you talk of?"

"How about this for starters?" Cally grappled in her bag for God only knew what. The girl had endless enthusiasm even if she could be annoyingly excitable sometimes. "Ta da." She brandished what looked suspiciously like an invitation and thrust it toward Tori. "Here."

Tori slowly took the invitation. It winked and sparkled in a garish blend of black and orange.

Halloween party. *No thanks*. She handed it back to Cally. "Thanks, but no thanks. I have my own plans."

"What plans?" Cally's eyes filled with disappointment as her smile vanished. "You never see anybody."

"Yes, I do."

"Who?"

Irritation prickled and Tori refocused on her laptop. "People. Lots and lots of people."

The ensuing silence spoke volumes and guilt edged into Tori's conscience. How was Cally meant to understand that, for Tori, parties meant little more than people getting drunk, out of control and looking for a quick escape from their problems? Something as dangerous as it was idiotic. People should keep their guard up and their senses clear.

Danger lurked everywhere. Even at social get-togethers.

So did loneliness…and loneliness sucked.

She sneaked a look at Cally. She appeared to have forgotten their conversation. She sat a little straighter in her seat, her head shifting left and right as she considered the nonexistent activity along the street, her eyes wide and alert. Tori looked again toward the school gates. Maybe she *should* start mixing with her colleagues out of the office. Start inching out her hand toward friendship. Who knew? Sooner or later she might think of going even further with someone…some day.

The only problem being, a full, loving, relationship with commitment and promises was a step too far. Relationships meant compromise and trust. Neither was in her makeup and she wasn't sure they ever would be.

She hastily added a few more words to her e-mail and pressed send just as the school bell rang. Cursing, she shut her laptop and fumbled to close the window. Leaning through the gap between the seats, she pushed her laptop onto the back seat and glanced through the rear window.

She froze. "What the…"

A few meters away, a man gripped a young girl's arm as he roughly pulled her toward the open back door of a car. He wore a baseball cap low, a scarf pulled high, all topped off with mirrored sunglasses. The getup more or less completely concealed his face and escalated Tori's suspicion. She stared at his nondescript black jacket, jeans, and boots before snapping her gaze to the child.

The expression on the girl's face was not that of a tantrum, but of fear and uncertainty.

Memories surged Tori's mind and adrenaline burst like fire inside her. "What the hell do you think you're doing?"

"What is it?" Cally gripped her arm. "What's wrong?"

Tori yanked her arm from Cally's hand and pulled on the door handle. Leaping out of the car, she raced toward the man. "Hey, what's the problem? Hey!"

After shoving the child inside the car, he slammed the back door. He glanced back, his gaze briefly locking with Tori's, then at her car, before he hurried to the driver's seat, deftly sliding behind the wheel and pulling away with a screech of tires.

"Hey!" Tori slapped her hand on the car's rear fender, but was forced to leap backward by the near swipe of the car. She stared after it, her heart thundering.

The little girl's face was etched with terror as her gaze met Tori's through the rear window, her small palms slapping the glass over and over. No seat belt, no care. Only the person in the driver's seat knew the severity of his most ugly intentions.

Tori shoved her hands into her hair.

The number plate was covered with dirt, nothing visible. A dark Ford Focus.

On trembling legs, she ran back to her car. Cally stared after the car carrying the little girl, seemingly paralyzed.

Tori stared at her. "Did you see the driver? A registration plate?"

"What? No, I…" Cally's eyes were wide with panic, her face flushed. "I didn't know… I didn't see."

Cursing, Tori reached into the passenger foot well for her bag. She snatched out her phone and slammed the door closed, her mind a mess and her heart racing. She would hazard a guess at the guy being six foot one or two. Overly long strands of dark blond hair had grazed his collar and he was of average build.

He'd looked straight at her as though she was meant to see what he was doing. Was she mad to think such a thing? Surely her thought processes were merely a symptom from her own kidnapping years before.

She dialed 999, her gaze on Cally's.

Cally was rigid, her hand gripped to her throat. "What shall I do? Tori, talk to me. What shall I do?"

"Nothing. If you didn't see anything, you'll be no more use to the police than me."

"The police? You don't think—"

Leaving Cally to do whatever she wanted, Tori

sped for the school entrance with her phone pressed to her ear and cursing her high heels. This wasn't about her. This didn't mean history would repeat itself. A child's screech of laughter ripped through the air, raising every hair on Tori's body.

"Emergency services. Which service do you require?"

*Georgia. I have to find Georgia.*

"Hello? I need the police. I think I just saw a child being taken from outside Barlington Primary. Someone needs to get down here. Now."

"May I take your name, Miss…"

"Tori. Tori Peterson. Look, please send someone down here. I need to collect my niece."

She ended the call and tore through the school gates, running toward the rows of open classroom doors at the rear of the building. Kids and parents parted around her as Tori shouldered through the oncoming sea of people. She burst around the side of the school and onto the playground. She darted her gaze left and right looking for Georgia.

Groups of mums and dads chatted with one another, the world continuing to turn as though nothing was sickeningly wrong.

Running forward, Tori approached the waiting parents, her heart beating hard. "Help me. Will someone please help me?"

"Auntie Tori. Auntie Tori!" Georgia emerged through the line of waiting parents, her six-year-old arms outstretched.

Relief pushed the air from Tori's lungs as she scooped up her niece, settling her onto her hip. "Thank God." She pressed a kiss to Georgia's temple. "Thank

God you're all right."

"Why are you crying?" Georgia's eyes widened with fear. "What's wrong?"

Tori raised her fingers to her cheeks and swiped at the tears she didn't know she wept. Weakness threatened and she shoved it purposefully aside. She was stronger than this. What happened to her had made her stronger...*he'd* made her stronger.

Dragging her gaze from the worried stare of her niece, Tori looked to the parents again. "I think a little girl has just been taken from outside the school. We need to do something."

Time stood still as a wave of terror swept over the mass of faces around her.

Moments passed and then parents torpedoed closer in a horrified reel of hysteria. The ensuing yelling and panic shoved Tori's fear into overdrive. She held Georgia closer and turned in circles, looking for a calm face.

Questions flew at her from every direction. This was her fault. Whatever happened next was down to her not being quick enough, for concentrating on her work, on her damn life...

She snatched her gaze from one terrified face to the next. "A little girl was just forced into a car outside. I called 999. We have to help her."

Phones were pulled from pockets. Some parents pressed buttons while others stood back, one hand over their mouths as they gratefully clasped the shoulders of the safe sons and daughters beside them.

Georgia started to cry. Tori closed her eyes and pressed another kiss to her niece's hair. "It's all right, sweetheart. Everything's going to be all right."

"Excuse me…excuse me. Hey, let me through, will you?"

Tori opened her eyes and looked into the face of the man who'd emerged from within the crowd of panicked parents. His concerned gaze locked on hers, his brow creased. He gently curled his fingers around Tori's upper arm.

She pulled back. "Hey, what are you doing?"

He immediately released her and raised his hands. "Trying to help. What happened? Are you okay?"

Uncertainty and suspicion rose, but Tori forced her habitual rejection of another's help into submission. This wasn't about her; it was all about that little girl. She shook her head. "No, I'm not. A little girl…he took her. She's gone and I couldn't do anything to stop it. It all happened so fast."

His jaw tightened and he looked over her head toward the school gates, while pulling a phone from his inside jacket pocket. He pressed the keypad three times and he held it to his ear. "Did you get a look at the person who took her?"

"It was a man. Maybe six foot one or two. He wore a red and gray striped scarf, black coat and a baseball cap. Dark blond hair. Sunglasses."

He held up his finger to stop her. "Hello, yes, police, please. A little girl has possibly been abducted from outside Barlington Primary."

Tori swallowed the bitter taste of guilt as it coated her throat. "I couldn't see… I didn't see…"

His gaze held hers as he slipped his hand around the shoulder of the young girl next to him. She had the same dark hair and blue eyes as her dad. If Tori hadn't noticed a child who stood right in front of her, how could she be sure she noticed anything about the man who pushed the girl into his car?

Panic threatened and she snapped her focus back to the man talking to the police.

"I'm here with a witness. She thinks it was a man, six foot one or two…"

The parents gathered around them stood in stunned silence, their focus honed entirely on the man who'd come to Tori's aid. He succinctly repeated her description of the suspected kidnapper into the phone. What choice did she have but to accept his help? To trust he had no other agenda but to help find the missing girl. *Is she missing? Or am I getting this all wrong? Maybe the man was her dad?*

Tori's stomach knotted with dread and self-doubt. If she'd made a mistake and alarmed all these people unnecessarily just because of her history, what then?

The man nodded, still speaking into his phone. "Someone's on the way now? Right. Yes. Mark Bolton. I'll be here. Yes…" He pulled the phone from his ear and met Tori's gaze. "The police need your name."

She tightened her hold around Georgia's shaking body. "Tori Peterson. I called it in a few moments ago. As soon as I saw her taken."

He nodded. "The witness' name is Tori Peterson. Yes, I'll stay with her." He slipped the phone into his pocket and stepped closer, releasing his daughter to hold her hand out to Tori before dropping it to his side. He gave a tight smile. "The police are on their way. You saw and did everything you could, okay?" He raised his eyebrows, his eyes intense on hers. "Okay?"

Swallowing the denial, the need to scream out loud she saw nothing that would do any good, Tori forced a nod.

He opened his mouth as if to say more, when the shout of a female voice reverberated in the distance. "Abby? Has anyone seen Abby Brady?"

The crowd parted.

The woman looked just a few years older than Tori, her face stricken and pale as she whipped her head back and forth, sending her auburn ponytail swaying, her eyes wide with confusion.

Sickness rolled through Tori on a cruel wave just as Cally appeared at her side. Her colleague's full skirt brushed against Tori's hip as Cally snaked her arm around Tori's waist. Tori focused on the panicked woman in front of her as a horrible, eerie silence fell on the playground.

If this was the little girl's mother, Tori would not allow her to fall apart in public like people said Tori's mother had. She would not allow her to hear the pitying murmurs and see the terrified glances when, deep inside, Tori knew each and every parent was really just relieved someone else's child had been taken and not theirs. She would be this woman's friend when everyone else was too scared, or ashamed, to look her in the eye and found they had no words of comfort, only empty promises.

Pulling away from Cally's arm, Tori stepped forward but Mark Bolton approached the woman first. "Mrs. Brady?"

The woman faced him, her gaze frantically moving over his face. "Have you seen Abby?"

He hesitated and shot a glance at Tori.

She tilted her chin; he didn't have to do this. "Let me."

He frowned. "What?"

"Let me. It was me who saw her…"

"Saw who?"

Tori and Mark simultaneously turned to the woman. Her gaze darted between them. "You've seen my daughter? Where is she?"

Georgia continued to tremble in Tori's embrace as futile sympathy slammed into her chest, making her breath catch. She stepped closer to Abby's mother. "I'm not sure."

The woman's gaze shot manically over Tori's face. "You're not sure? Have you seen her or not?" She turned from Tori and swept her gaze over the silent crowd around them. "What's going on here? Why are you all looking at me like that?"

Tori swallowed. "What does Abby look like?"

"Dark red hair, blue eyes…" Mrs. Brady frowned. "Will you just tell me what's going on?"

The missing girl's face loomed like a photograph in Tori's mind. Dark hair…dark eyes… It hadn't been clear enough inside the car to be certain of hair or eye color. "I think I just saw her get into someone's car. I think—"

"You *think* you saw her? You *think* my baby's been taken?"

The woman slapped Tori's cheek with such force she teetered backward, barely managing not to drop Georgia to the ground. Tori's skin smarted from the impact, heat ballooning toward her ear as shock clogged any further words in her throat.

Cally shot forward. "Hey! What do you think you're doing?"

Before Tori could intercept Cally's angry defense

of her or even think, Mark wrapped his arms around the now hysterical mother, pinning her arms to her sides. "It's okay. We'll find her. This isn't Ms. Peterson's fault."

The woman flailed against him as he held her tight in his arms, his gaze on Tori's.

"My baby. Someone has my baby. Do something. Do something now."

Mrs. Brady's hysterical cry sent Tori's blood icy-cold to burning hot. Unable to bear looking at Mark or the woman he so capably held, Tori turned to Cally. "Why don't you go back to the office? The police will be here soon—"

"I'm staying with you." Cally plucked at the spotted scarf at her neck with trembling fingers, as she continued to glare at the distressed woman in Mark's arms. "She hit you. She actually hit you."

"Cally, look at me." Tori grasped her colleague's hand. "Go back to the office. Tell Neil what's happened and that I'll be in as soon as I can, okay?"

Cally flitted her gaze to Tori's cheek. "Are you sure you're all right?"

"I'm as good as I can be. Now go. Please."

Inhaling, Cally flicked another glance at Mrs. Brady and Mark before she shouldered her way through the crowd, her jaw tight.

Mark's voice drifted above the soft murmurings of the parents gathered around them. "The police are on the way, Mrs. Brady. They'll find her. We'll find her."

Tori glared at him as buried memories cracked wide open and spread through her soul like poison. This guy had no idea what he was talking about. He had no right to promise this mother anything. Her child was gone, who was to say she would ever be rescued as Tori was? Who was to say she would be strong enough to take the sickness her captor bestowed on her over and over…

Tori blinked as a fire she hadn't known for many, many years ignited inside her once again.

****

Mark continued to hold Susan Brady even as her legs gave way and she slipped to the asphalt. He sat on his haunches and cradled her in his arms, his gaze never leaving Tori Peterson. A barrage of emotions swept through her green gaze. Anger to fear. Determination to sympathy.

Hushed voices floated around him, sporadically broken by a stifled sob or a child's innocent laughter. What now? What the hell happened next?

"Dad?"

Mark started and looked up into his daughter's terrified face.

Olivia glanced at Susan Brady. "What shall we do?"

"The police will be here any minute, sweetheart." He forced a small smile. "It's okay. I want you to stay here. Right by me, okay?"

Olivia nodded.

Mark looked to a father standing a few feet away, his son in his arms. "Hey, would you find the principal? She should be out here by now." The tremor in his voice belied his anger and frustration. "Ask her if she has a school photo of Abby. We need to be certain it was her Tori saw get into that car."

The man gave a curt nod and took off toward the school.

Susan Brady emitted a long, unbroken wail that sliced through Mark's thoughts and tore at his soul. He tightened his arms around her as words of comfort and reassurance dissolved on his tongue. The wail softened to a keening mew, rippling through the air and burrowing deep into Mark's gut. It was a sound he remembered only too well.

It had passed through his own body and out into the world when the police knocked on his door and told him his wife's broken body had been found hundreds of feet down the side of Barlington Downs.

Since that day, he'd vowed to do anything and everything he could to keep Olivia safe from harm. Yet, here he was, unable to do anything to reassure his daughter or the woman he held.

A rustle of clothes behind him was followed by the soft, musky scent of perfume. Despite her high heels and pencil skirt, Tori Peterson lowered to the ground on the other side of Susan, her expression etched with pain and sympathy. Respect and admiration swept through Mark as Tori maneuvered her daughter comfortably onto her lap and used her free hand to grip Abby's mother's knee in a show of support, her cheek still blazing red from the seemingly forgotten and forgiven assault.

He stared at her distinct, thick mane of red hair and wondered why he hadn't seen her at the school before. Olivia was eleven and hated him picking her up from school so, more often than not, he waited outside the school's gates but still, he was pretty sure he would have noticed this woman. He glanced at Tori's daughter as she slid her thumb in her mouth, her dried tears shining silver on her flushed cheeks.

Forcing his focus to Susan Brady as she trembled in his arms, he was about to whisper some words of support when the crowd parted to reveal male and female police officers, Principal White, and the guy Mark had asked to track her down.

"Mrs. Brady?" The principal came down to their level and stroked her hand over Susan's cheek. "It's Principal White. Can you stand for me? These police officers need to speak with you. Come on now, we can do this together. Okay?"

Susan made no move to release herself from Mark.

He addressed the principal. "We need to make sure the girl Ms. Peterson saw is actually Abby."

Principal White swept the bangs of her dark blonde bob from her eyes. Her hand shook. "Of course, of course." She thrust a photograph toward Tori. "Is this her? Is this the girl you saw getting into the car?"

Tori took the photograph and her jaw tightened before she handed the photo back to the principal. "Yes."

Principal White briefly closed her eyes. "Mrs. Brady? Come on now, the sooner we speak to the officers, the sooner we can find Abby. You have to be strong. *We* have to be strong. Okay?"

Susan didn't move. Shock had clearly given way to paralysis. Mark met Tori's eyes. They had to move her. They had to get this mother doing something before she fell apart completely. Tori nodded and together, he and Tori eased Susan to her feet before the female police officer and Principal White took over. Each with an arm around the mother's shoulders, they led her into the school building.

Before Mark could gather his senses, much less

calm the torrent of trepidation and questions storming his mind, the male police officer cleared his throat. "Are you Mr. Bolton? The man who made the call to the police?"

Mark wiped his hand over his face before planting his hands at his waist. "Along with many others, I imagine."

The officer turned to Tori. "Tori Peterson?"

She nodded, her gaze steady and her shoulders high. "Yes."

He poised a pen over his notepad. "Mrs.? Miss?"

"Miss."

He made a note. "I'm Sergeant Jansen. I'd appreciate it if you both came into the school. I need to ask you a few questions."

"I need to call my sister." Tori glanced at her little girl in her arms, her bright eyes cautiously watching the officer. "She needs to take Georgia home."

"Your daughter can stay with you. It's not a problem."

"I'm not her mum. She's my niece. She should be with my sister. She should be at home where she's safe."

Olivia stood beside him and Mark slipped his arm around his daughter's shoulders, relieved she was right there where he could see, touch and smell her. He cleared his throat. "If you give me the number, I can call your sister if you like?"

Miss Peterson turned from the police officer. "You don't need to keep offering to do things for me. I'm perfectly capable."

Considering what she'd seen, what she'd been through, it showed her strength that she was still standing, let alone strong enough to call him out. He raised his hand. "Fine."

She glared at him and Mark exhaled, hating his perpetual need for control but unable to lessen it when this heinous situation was still so uncertain. "Look, it's what I do, okay? I look after people, situations. Whatever needs to be done, I like to be the one to do it."

She raised her eyebrows. "So you've got yourself marked as some kind of superhero? For the record, they don't exist."

The police officer stepped closer. "Miss Peterson, this is hardly the time—"

"Hey, my dad might be overprotective, but that's the way he is. He has good reason and he can't help looking after people. Let him call your sister. She needs to get Georgia."

Undeniable pride mixed with Mark's knee-jerk obligation to chastise his too-often forthright daughter. He waited for Tori Peterson's response. Rightly or wrongly, Olivia had told this stranger the truth. The seconds beat out between them as Tori flitted her gaze from Olivia, to him and back again. Hitching her niece to her other hip, she blew out a breath. "Fine."

Mark drew his phone from his jacket pocket. "What's the number?"

Ignoring him, she looked to the police officer, annoyance clear in the hunch of her shoulders and the flush of color on her cheeks. "If I didn't think having a police officer call her would completely freak her out, I'd have you call my sister rather than Noble Mark and his sidekick here."

She turned and narrowed her eyes at Mark.

He waited.

She virtually spat each digit of her sister's number at him. "Tell her Georgia is all right and won't leave my side until she gets here."

Mark punched in the number and the phone rang in his ear. "What's her name?"

"Melissa."

Sergeant Jansen coughed. "We really should get started, Miss Peterson."

"Sorry, of course." She turned away, glancing once over her shoulder at Mark before following the police officer toward the school.

"Hello?"

Mark snapped his gaze from Tori's turned back. "Hello, is this Melissa?"

"Yes."

"Hi, my name's Mark Bolton. I'm one of the dads from the school. There's been an incident." An incident? God, could he be more dismissive? This wasn't a damn *incident*. This was a living nightmare. "What I mean is—"

"What's happened? Is Georgia okay? My sister was supposed—"

"She's fine. Tori's with her."

Her shaky exhalation rasped down the line. "Thank God. For a moment there…the tone of your voice…"

"You need to come to the school straight away and collect your daughter. Tori witnessed a suspected child abduction. She's with the police right now and—"

"What?"

"I said—"

"A child's been taken? Tori saw this happen? Oh, my God. Not again. Did she see whoever took the child? Was it a little girl?"

Mark gripped the phone tighter and glanced in the direction Tori and the police officer had walked. "What do you mean *again*? Has Tori seen another child taken?"

"I need to be with her. She can't deal with this. This will kill her. I'll be right there."

The line went dead.

Mark stared at the phone, his mind racing with questions. *Not again. This will kill her.*

He ended the call and slowly slid the phone into his shirt pocket.

"Dad? What is it?"

He blinked and met Olivia's concerned gaze. "Nothing. Come on, the police need to talk to me too."

He steered Olivia toward the school, all too aware how she constantly lifted her head to look at him. Mark struggled to keep his face impassive as he purposefully looked ahead. How could a person witness more than one abduction? How could Tori Peterson have been that unfortunate? He walked through the double doors at the front of the school, his mind's eye filling with her terrified face when she'd ran onto the playground.

Whether she—or he—wanted it, Tori Peterson had just become a part of his life. He couldn't walk away without doing all he could to bring Abby Brady home and finding out what Tori's sister had meant by her words. No one should have to deal with what Tori Peterson had seen alone. More than that, he was a father, and he could no more stand by and do nothing for Abby than he would for Olivia.

Chapter Two

Having never stepped foot inside Georgia's school, Tori fought the need to bounce her foot on the principal's office floor. Everything about the room notched her already stretched nerves to breaking.

She didn't do authority and, with the exception of Georgia, she purposely didn't do kids. With kids came responsibility, love and a whole lot of fear and danger. Who in their right mind opened themselves up to possible heartbreak should their child go missing, get seriously sick or end up marrying the parents' idea of Freddy Kruger?

Look what had happened today. A little girl. Taken. Afraid. Scared. Alone…

She glanced to the corner of Principal White's wide oak desk where Georgia sat happily drawing a picture, her tongue stuck to her bottom lip in concentration. Tori's heart swelled with love for her niece. The fact Tori was snatched and held captive for days had tainted her rationale and ability to give love, which led to the obvious decision that all kids were better off without her.

Tears burned and Tori faced Principal White.

The woman stared at her, concern clearly reflected in her eyes. "Are you all right?"

Tori sat straighter, embracing what control could under the circumstances. "As much as I can be.

What do you think happens now?" She glanced toward the closed office door. "Where are the police? Sitting here doing nothing isn't going to get Abby Brady home."

Principal White's dark, brown eyes glinted with sympathy. "Sergeant Jansen stepped outside to relay the details you've managed to provide about the car and the man who took Abby. I'm sure he'll be back shortly. Do you want coffee or tea? You're clearly in shock."

The urge to snap at her battled on Tori's tongue, and she briefly closed her eyes, fighting her normal defensiveness. There was nothing normal about this day. In fact, she suspected the scars she carried would very soon be slashed wide open once more. She could not leave finding Abby Brady to the police and the police alone. She had more personal experience of what that girl might, or might not, be going through than most and she would use that knowledge to do some good.

"I'm fine. Where's Abby's mum?" She touched her fingers to the tender spot on her cheek, still raw from Mrs. Brady's slap. "Maybe I should go and offer her my other cheek. I'd want to hit something too if someone had taken my child."

Principal White rose from her chair and walked to the window, her back to Tori. "The female officer took Mrs. Brady to the cafeteria. I didn't get the officer's name. I hope to God she doesn't think plying the poor woman with tea will be any sort of balm to the anguish she'll be going through."

Tori relaxed her shoulders. Anger she could deal with. Frustration she could relate to. It was kindly eyes and gestures that got to her. Her mind turned to the way

Mark Bolton had intercepted Mrs. Brady when she had focused her panic on Tori. Time and again, she'd caught him watching her. The intensity of his study had alerted her to his over-interest. Whatever his intentions to help, she'd soon set him straight if he thought he could stick his nose into her life.

Gallantry was often marred with uninvited purpose. Purpose to mess with a woman's mind and heart. She'd learned that lesson well at ten years old—and been reminded again the rare times she'd risked a date.

The silence pressed on her patience and Tori's body hummed with the need to move, to do something about finding Abby before God only knew what happened to her. As soon as her sister arrived, Tori was out of there. She would do what she could to find Abby, whether alone or with someone's help. She was a journalist for goodness sake, she had resources and contacts others wouldn't.

"I was pleased to see you with Mark Bolton when I came onto the playground. He's a good man to have been there to help you and Mrs. Brady."

He *had* helped. More than Tori liked to acknowledge.

Yet, her habitual self-preservation once again whipped up a storm of suspicion and distrust. "How well do you know him?"

The principal turned, her gaze steady. "Why do you ask?"

Tori shrugged. She had to play this right or her innate skepticism was likely to rouse Principal White's distance. The lines of communication between Tori, the school and the police needed to stay open if she had any chance of being involved in the search to find Abby.

"After the way he came to my rescue, I owe him my thanks. There's every chance I would've been the cause of mass hysteria if he hadn't been there. He's got a strange way of calming people."

Principal White studied Tori for a moment before settling against the low windowsill behind her. Her fingers curled around the wood. "Mark Bolton's one of the good guys. Popular with the mums. Quiet. Handsome. A kind and talented carpenter."

Tori frowned. "He didn't strike me as the type to be alone in his work. His assistance to Mrs. Brady and me, made me assume him to be a people person. Carpentry has to be a pretty solitary occupation."

"Once upon a time, he was extremely sociable and outgoing, but since his wife died, his only concerns seem to be his daughter and his work."

Sympathy squeezed at Tori's heart and a little of her doubt toward Mark Bolton slipped away. "I'm sorry to hear about his wife. Do you know what happened?"

"A walking accident. She was a keen hiker but something went wrong and she apparently fell over a cliff at the tip of the Downs."

"Apparently fell?"

Principal White nodded. "The inquest confirmed an accidental death."

"Poor man."

"Indeed, but he has Olivia and he's happy in his work. In fact, he's working on a bureau for me right now."

Tori nodded, unsure what to say or how to react to the inappropriate gleam of pride shining in the principal's eyes. At the end of the day, it didn't matter how nice Mark Bolton was, or how the man had probably suffered an unbearable loss that left him raising his little girl alone, after today he and Tori would go their separate ways.

Glancing toward the closed office door once more, Tori shifted in her seat and crossed her legs, her impatience growing with each wasted second. She looked to Principal White. "I have to be honest with you, I have zero intention of waiting for the police to assemble teams and put up the red tape of protocol and bureaucracy that will prevent me from doing all I can to get Abby back to her parents."

"You need to leave the police to do their job, Miss Peterson."

"I'm a journalist. I have ways and means of uncovering things it's unlikely the police will."

"How is that possible? The police have access to—"

"I've learned over the years that people—especially bad people—tend to be a lot more open to talking to the press in the hope of gaining five minutes of front page fame than they are the police. A criminal's narcissism makes it possible for the press to help where they can."

"I still think you need to leave the police to do their job. One wrong move and you could ruin the whole investigation."

"That won't happen."

"You have no idea what type of person this man is. He could be dangerous, irrational…mentally unstable. Do you have experience of people like that?"

What happened to her as a child hovered over Tori like a phantom's wings. The monster was back. He was deep in her head, and no matter how much she tried to fight him, the horror and memories forged in her body and mind had gripped her once more.

"Miss Peterson?"

Tori blinked.

"You're not alone if you feel partly to blame for Abby's disappearance. My mind is turning over and over with what I could've done differently. How maybe it shouldn't just be the first and second year students who have to have their parents collect them from the classrooms, but all the classes." She shook her head, tears glinting in her eyes. "Any blame could just as easily fall on me."

"This is nobody's fault but the bastard who to—"

There was a knock at the office door. Tori turned as it opened. Sergeant Jansen entered, closely followed by Mark Bolton and his daughter.

Tori focused on the police officer. "What's happening?"

"We've put your descriptions out to all units, as well as having other officers study the coverage from the public cameras along the street outside the school." He turned to Principal White. "We need to look at all your CCTV footage throughout the school and grounds as soon as possible."

"I'll get my secretary to sort that out for you right away."

As she left the room, Mark's stare bored into Tori's temple and she turned. He studied her with undisguised interest. His gaze ran over her hair and face as though absorbing every strand and feature. Self-consciousness rolled through her in a way that was unwanted, inappropriate and entirely discomforting.

"So…" Sergeant Jansen moved behind Principal

White's desk and sat in her high-backed leather chair, dropping his notepad onto the desk. He looked first at Tori, his dark gray eyes assessing her. Saying nothing, he turned to Mark and glanced at his daughter, who had remained standing. "Is there anyone who can take your daughter for a while, Mr. Bolton? This might not be the best conversation for either of these children to hear."

Mark shook his head, his eyes determined as he slid his arm around Olivia's shoulders. "There's no one. She stays."

Tori looked at Olivia. No one? Didn't Mark have parents? Friends? Brothers or sisters? *None of my business.* Suppressing the sympathy that edged into her heart, Tori faced Jansen.

He stared at Mark. "I would prefer Olivia sat with a teacher while we discuss things further." He stood. "I'll go and find someone."

Momentary silence fell as the sergeant left the room.

Mark slid onto a seat next to Tori, his hand still around his daughter's. Tori glanced at him and he smiled softly. "How you doing?"

"Not great." She sighed. "How about you?"

"Not great either."

Tori looked at Olivia. "Are you okay?"

She nodded, her lips pursed.

Sergeant Jansen reentered the room, a teacher Tori hadn't met behind him. Their presence abruptly broke the strained silence as he addressed Mark. "If it's all right with you, Ms. Chalfield will sit just outside with Olivia in the waiting area."

The silence stretched long enough for Tori to sneak a glance at Mark. His jaw was tight, his irritation clear in his dark blue eyes. "Fine." He tipped his head back to meet his daughter's steady gaze. "I'll be as quick as I can, okay?"

"Okay." Olivia's hand slipped from her father's and she walked slowly from the office with Ms. Chalfield.

When the door clicked closed behind them, Jansen retook his seat in Principal White's chair and looked at Tori. "Your sister shouldn't be too long now."

He glanced at Georgia who continued to draw her matchstick men, oblivious to the evil that had chosen today to visit her school. Chosen to come the day her Auntie Tori was responsible for keeping her sister's most precious possession safe from harm.

Tori pulled back her shoulders. "I need to do something, Sergeant. I was the last one to see Abby. I can't just sit here waiting for news. Her mother…" She took a breath and the remembered sting of Mrs. Brady's slap seared her cheek once more. "She blames me."

"To focus blame on an innocent witness is a perfectly normal reaction. In time—"

"In time, she'll forget all about it?" Mark huffed and stood, walking to the window. He crossed his arms and glared at Jansen. "That mother will never forget this, whether you find Abby or not."

The exact same words had hovered on Tori's tongue, but he'd got there first. She had a horrible feeling Mark Bolton was about as likely to sit by and do nothing to help find Abby as she was. Tori had real-life experience, professional experience. What did a widowed carpenter think he could bring to the investigation?

Jansen cleared his throat. "That's not what I was

going to say, Mr. Bolton. I was going to say blame is always misdirected in abduction cases. The same as it is in murder investigations. Mrs. Brady's reaction was nothing more than a human one."

Tori stilled, waiting for Mark's retaliation. He held the sergeant's gaze, before his bright blue gaze met Tori's.

Her heart beat a little faster and she looked away. She needed to get out of there. She needed to work. The room grew heavy with unspoken trepidation. The walls drew in a little closer. The familiar tightening started in her chest as the threat of claustrophobia, her biggest failing, the one she fought daily, crept to the surface.

She stood and the floor shifted beneath her feet.

Mark was immediately at her side, his hand at her elbow. "You okay?"

*Hold on, Tori. Hold on goddamn it.*

The door burst open and the air rushed from Tori's lungs as her sister stormed into the room. Melissa barely stopped as she pressed a kiss to Georgia's bowed head before striding forward and pulling Tori into a tight embrace. "I'm here. Everything's going to be all right." She pulled back and put her hands to Tori's jaw, looking deep into her eyes. "I've got you, okay?"

Tori's waited for the floor to open up and swallow her whole. What did Melissa think she was doing? She might as well have come in with a placard across her breasts saying, "My Sister Was Abducted As a Child."

Tori darted her gaze around the room. Jansen and Mark stared back, concern and maybe even suspicion lingering in their eyes. Her cheeks burned and her eyes stung, but Tori dug deep and, regaining self-control, lifted her face from Melissa's hands. "You haven't got me. *I've* got me. For goodness sake, Melissa, a little girl is missing."

"I know. I thought—"

"Why don't you take Georgia home where she belongs?"

The room chilled as Melissa's gaze and expression changed to something infinitely more sisterly and, if Tori was honest, easier to deal with. Her sister's eyes flashed with hurt and anger. She raised her hands. "Fine. Do this your way. You don't need me, just as you don't need anyone, right? Well, good, because I have Georgia to worry about. I can't deal with your need to be so bloody self-sufficient all the time. Newsflash, Tori, we need people. Everyone needs someone. Including you."

Tori crossed her arms to hide her trembling.

Melissa tossed Tori a glare before bending down to Georgia. "Ooh, is that for Mummy? It's lovely. Why don't we leave Auntie Tori to speak with the policeman on her own, huh?"

Tori stood stock still, Mark's gaze burning into one temple and Sergeant Jansen's into the other. *Why do I have to be such a bitch? I need you, Melissa. I really do.*

As if Melissa had read her mind, she hefted Georgia onto her hip, slung her backpack onto her free shoulder and stepped closer to Tori. Her sister's eyes shone with tears as she smoothed her hand up Tori's arm. "I love you. I'm going to expect you at my house as soon as you finish here. No arguments. You're staying with us tonight."

"But—"

"But nothing. You do this or I'll just come to your

place and camp outside your front door until you let me in. Understand?"

Tori slumped her shoulders. "Fine. Have it your way. I'll be over as soon as I can."

"Good." Melissa nodded to Sergeant Jansen and Mark. "Nice to meet you. I hope…" She shook her head and closed her eyes. "I just hope…"

Once the door had closed behind Melissa and Georgia, Tori looked at Jansen and tried to ignore that Mark still stood so close to her, barely a puff of air separated them. "So, Sergeant, what happens next?"

\*\*\*\*

Mark crossed his arms as Tori sat beside him and reiterated again to Sergeant Jansen what she had already told the police over an hour before. Mark waited for her to say something about another abduction, or at least explain why her sister had said, "Not again" over the phone.

She only repeated what had happened earlier that afternoon.

Curiosity battled with his frustration. Tori's past was none of his business, yet he had a gut feeling Abby Brady's abduction affected her more deeply than it would anybody else who'd been forced into such a horrible situation.

Jansen tapped his pen on his notepad. "I can see how shaken you are, Miss Peterson. Try to relax and see if you can remember any other details. Part of the registration plate, maybe a facial scar or a significant way the abductor walked or moved…"

"It happened so fast." She pushed the hair from her eyes, holding the strands in a fist. "I'm worried if I say a number or letter and I misread it, it will be my fault you've been looking for the wrong vehicle. The plate was caked in mud, whether purposely or not."

"Were you alone?"

"I'm sorry?"

"Were you alone? When Abby was taken?"

"I was with a colleague, Cally Seymour."

He scribbled Cally's name on his notepad. "Did she see anything?"

"No, she didn't get out of the car until after the driver had taken off." She exhaled. "Have you contacted Abby's dad? Has he arrived to be with Mrs. Brady?"

"Yes and yes." Jansen's gaze cooled. "If you're thinking what I suspect you are, Mr. Brady has an alibi at the time Abby was taken and the parents' relationship is perfectly stable. There's no suspicion that either of them have anything to do with her disappearance. So back to the question of the vehicle…"

Irritation simmered in Mark's gut. While he was there and sat right beside Tori, there was no way Jansen would bully her into saying anything she wasn't one hundred percent certain of. The man needed to back off. Give her some space.

"What good is it to badger the only witness you have?" Mark leaned forward in his seat. "Wouldn't it be better use of police time if you spoke to the parents you have outside this office waiting to return home to their families? Surely one of them saw something. The responsibility of this abduction should not solely fall to Miss Peterson."

Jansen's eyes turned steely. "I don't need you or anyone else telling me how to do my job, Mr. Bolton.

We have plenty of officers in the hall talking to parents, the staff and the workmen mending the roof. Trust me, we want to ensure Miss Peterson isn't the sole witness as much as anyone else. My job, my paramount concern, is helping Miss Peterson remember every tiny detail." Jansen leaned his forearms on the desk. "Now, you've told me everything you know and I appreciate your cooperation. I have your contact details if we need to speak with you again. You're free to leave and take your daughter home."

Frustrated and clearly dismissed, Mark turned to Tori. "I'll go, if that's what Miss Peterson also wants."

She snapped her head around. "What?"

"Do you want me to go? Because I won't leave if you'd rather I stayed."

He didn't want to leave her with Jansen and wouldn't unless he was forced to. The fear and confusion that had been in Tori's eyes when they were outside remained branded on his memory. There was no chance he'd let her reject his support in what he suspected would be her own investigation into Abby's whereabouts. If, by some miracle, she succeeded in shaking him off, then he'd do what he could to find Abby Brady alone.

The implications of this whole, sickening day extended so wide, it chilled his soul. Who knew what Abby's kidnapping was about? Who knew if she was a sole target—what if her abduction was just the beginning? He had to protect Olivia.

Tori's suspicious gaze wandered over his face, lingering at his mouth just long enough for a bolt of unexpected attraction to skitter over Mark's usually numb nerve endings.

She flicked her gaze to Jansen and back again. After a moment, she exhaled a shaky breath. "I want him to stay."

Relief eased the air from Mark's lungs and satisfaction unfurled in his gut as he faced the sergeant.

Jansen's jaw tightened, his annoyance clear. "This is a child abduction case. You need to leave it to us to find Abby and bring her home. I suggest you go to your sister's and try to get some rest. I've seen the same look on yours and Mr. Bolton's faces a million times before. Heading off on a vigilante crusade will not help Abby."

The shared tension emanating from Mark and Tori permeated the room and the sliver of space between them. The diabolical circumstances that had brought them together also bound them in unspoken agreement. The determination in her rigid body and the undisguised rage in her eyes left Mark in no doubt she had equally as much intention of making her own discoveries into Abby's disappearance as he did.

"Fine." Tori pushed to her feet and hitched her purse onto her shoulder. "You'll call if you find her?"

Jansen nodded. "Of course."

"Thank you." She opened her purse and extracted a handful of business cards. She laid them on the desk. "Here are my details. Give them to a few of the investigating officers. I'm a journalist. There must be some way the press can help. A write-up or a call for help? Anything has to be better than keeping us out of this. The public has a right to know what's happened. Barlington is a good town where people look out for one another. You won't be able to keep this to yourselves for long."

"I'm well aware of that, nor will we want to. We'll

need the public's help if Abby remains unfound. What we don't want is to panic her abductor into doing his worst or attempting to flee the country with her. We've alerted the train stations and airport, but sometimes these people get away." Jansen picked up one of her cards. "Be sure to call me if you think of anything else."

"I will."

"I'll see you out."

As Jansen led the way to the door with Tori following, Mark stood and swiped one of her cards from the desk. He quickly slid it into his jeans pocket. One way or another, he would see Tori again, and having her contact details would make that all the easier. Nodding to Jansen as he passed him at the open door, Mark followed Tori into the foyer.

As soon as Olivia saw him, she rushed from a corner seating area where she'd been waiting with Ms. Chalfield. "Are you finished?"

He glanced at Tori, surprised she stood beside him rather than rushing to the door as he'd thought she would. He slid his arm around Olivia's shoulders, drawing her close. "For now. There's nothing else we can do but leave the police to do their job. How about we go for a burger?"

Olivia faced Tori, her brow creased. "Are you coming too?"

Mark waited, once again, welcoming his daughter's ability to say just what she wanted, when she wanted.

Tori stared at Olivia. "Um, no. I was just going to thank your dad…" She lifted her gaze to Mark's. "Thank you. For everything you did today."

"You're welcome."

Mark stared as his interest in her deepened. Her clear vulnerability after her bouts of sass intrigued him. Why hadn't he met this woman before today? Why had such a heinous crime brought them into each other's paths? Was it fate? Or something else? She concerned him. Something was very wrong in her life if the wariness in her study was anything to go by.

He cleared his throat. "You sure you don't want to join us?"

"I need to get to my sister's before she has a meltdown and sends out a search party. I'd rather the only search party put together is for Abby, not me."

"Will you at least let us walk you to your car?"

She hesitated and glanced at Olivia. "Sure."

Ignoring the weight of Olivia's stare, Mark gestured for Tori to lead the way. They walked out the school gates, the fading evening sun turning her long, red hair bronze. Her back was ramrod straight and her shoulders tense beneath the emerald green shirt she wore.

He clenched his jaw as his thoughts turned to Abby. Where might she be? Worse, who was she with? And what might the man who'd taken her be subjecting her to?

Tori stopped beside a white Peugeot. "This is me."

Her eyes were shadowed and her complexion pale whereas when they'd been in Principal White's office her eyes were wide with eagerness, her color high. He frowned. "Are you sure you're okay?"

"I'm fine."

"You don't look fine."

Annoyance darkened her eyes. "Well, I am. Look,

I'd better go."

It was no good. He had to know more. "Only, I can't help being concerned about what your sister said."

She stilled. "Melissa?"

He nodded. "When I told her you'd seen a little girl taken, the first thing she said was, 'not again.' Why did she say that?"

"I don't know." She drew her keys from her bag and jangled them. "I have to go."

She walked around the hood and opened the driver's door.

He frowned. "Tori?"

She met his gaze across the car roof, her face set. "What?"

"Who else have you seen taken?"

"Nobody." Her cheeks flushed. "Can I give you a bit of advice? Look after your daughter. She should be your only concern after what happened today. I'm counting myself fortunate that I don't have kids, otherwise I'd be going a little insane. The piece of sh…" She glanced at Olivia before meeting his gaze once more. "The man who's taken Abby? He took her for a reason. Sooner or later, I'll find him and make sure he pays for laying a single finger on her."

Tension inched across Mark's shoulders. "*You'll* find him."

"Yes, Mark. *I'll* find him."

She got into her car, put on her seatbelt and pulled away without looking at him again. Her car disappeared around a corner at the end of the street.

"Dad?"

He dragged his gaze from the end of the street and faced Olivia. "You okay?"

"She's not worth it."

Mark forced a smile. "Who?"

She rolled her eyes. "Tori."

"Ah. Tori's not worth what?"

"Your superhero act."

He bit back a smile at the somberness in his worldly wise, eleven-year-old daughter's eyes. "My superhero act?"

Olivia shrugged. "If she can't see a good thing when it's right in front of her, she needs glasses. Anyway, you've got enough to deal with looking after me." She slipped her hand into his. "Come on, I'm hungry."

As Olivia led him to his car, Mark couldn't help thinking the same thing he always did—his daughter was growing up way too fast and one day, no matter how he fought it on a daily basis, he'd have to let her find her own way. Alone. Without her dad watching her every move, intent on keeping her safe from the bogeyman.

A bogeyman who had found the confidence to come out of his lair and hunt outside a school's gates. To capture and take a child…take someone's heart and soul and do whatever the hell he wanted with it.

## Chapter Three

*One of my greatest heroes, the great Frank Sinatra, sang of obsession. I, too, know what it is to sacrifice anything to have you near…*

*You will be mine, sweet Tori.*

*Your hair is like a sheet of rubies melted under a summer sun; your eyes as green as emeralds.*

*Yet you are so teasing, so sexual, but frustratingly aloof…. like a just out of reach screen goddess. I love you, Tori.*

*I had to get you to notice me because every day you do not see me. You will come to love me as I do you. I almost thought my plan would fail. The friend who took little Abby couldn't be certain you were watching. He thought you were too busy looking at the wrong thing…too busy not noticing. You did see her though, didn't you? You're such a good girl.*

*You will come to understand why she had to be taken; understand why it has to be you who discovers the coincidences. I don't want anyone else involved, but you and me. Always.*

*The girl is sleeping on our bed. She cries and cries for her mummy but I will not hurt her. I promised her so. She is so much like you at the same age. I know, I've seen the pictures. Please believe I didn't just borrow any child—I took her because I know you, Tori. You will soon see she could almost be you. Not just in looks, but in every way. Abby will keep me company until I have you for the rest of my days. I will clothe her in the prettiest dresses and the most beautiful ribbons. She'll be my dolly until I have you, Tori, until I can hold you in my arms and love you to the very marrow of your bones...*

\*\*\*\*

Tori lay on her back, clutching her phone to her chest as she stared at the ceiling in her sister's guest room. Behind the thin floral curtains, the morning sun had slowly drifted from one side of the bay window to the other. The bed was as soft as duck down beneath her, but it might as well have been hardwood for all the sleep she'd managed.

Sighing, she tapped her phone's screen and brought up the latest news bulletin...again. She'd been awake since three-thirty, waiting for news to break over Abby Brady, yet her phone remained ominously silent and the news updates revealed nothing.

It had been almost sixteen hours since Abby had been taken and Tori had yet to hear from Sergeant Jansen or anyone else. Paranoia threatened and the fear Abby's abductor might strike again lingered.

Although plagued with bad sleep, zero appetite and a constant stream of possible scenarios running through her head, nothing compared to what Abby's parents must be going through. Tori gripped the duvet, about to toss it aside when fear of failure, or that her suppositions or ideas might be wrong, gripped her once more.

She turned over onto her side, thumped the pillow a couple of times and stared at the wall ahead of her. The niggling possibility that the abductor might have orchestrated her seeing Abby being taken prodded cruelly at Tori's consciousness. The prospect badgered her like sharpened talons, clawing at her courage over and over.

He had looked straight at her; looked at her car as though he'd known she'd be there.

*Has Brian Appleton come back and taken another little girl to show me he can steal someone else's child over and over again, no matter that I escaped?*

Tori squeezed her eyes shut, her heart thundering. She wanted to put the nonsensical contemplation down to her fear of history repeating itself, but how could she, when ignoring the possibility might lead to her missing a vital link?

Opening her eyes, she tightened her grip on her phone and battled the urge to call Sergeant Jansen. Should she tell him about her history? Let the police persuade her that no connection existed between her kidnapping and Abby's?

Or maybe she should call Mark Bolton.

The man had barged into her thoughts throughout the night. Whether she welcomed it or not, he'd been thrown into her path under the worst of circumstances and if the way his intelligent blue gaze had held hers was anything to go by, there was every chance she would see him again.

As unnerving as his interest was, she couldn't deny the inexplicable affinity she felt toward him.

He had the same rigid set to his spine as she did; the same way of watching and waiting for whatever came next. He clearly anticipated bad things happening and seemed determined to sweep in and save others from the evils in the world.

Just like she did.

It was perfectly plausible, through the tragic loss of his wife, that he'd known the same soul-changing pain she had.

Had it just been Melissa's words that provoked his interest? Or could he know more about Abby's kidnapping than he appeared to know? Nausea rose bitter in Tori's throat. What if he was a part of this?

Impossible. The possessive love in his eyes whenever he'd looked at his daughter was unmistakable. He loved her, adored her. There was no way Mark Bolton could take part in another child's abduction.

Loss of control raced through her. She had to either stop considering the chance she was meant to witness Abby being taken, or else prove the coincidence had no merit. She also needed to stop looking at suspects that weren't suspects.

Common sense told her to stay out of the police's way. If she made one wrong move that brought harm to Abby…

But what if Abby's abductor was of the same ilk as Brian Appleton?

His temper quick and his punishments harsh.

He might not beat Abby; he might not sexually assault her. Instead he might shut her in the cupboard with the dolls. He might sit outside and sing softly until he groaned in a way that no little girl would, or should, understand.

Tori's throat swelled with a trapped sob, and she clamped her hand to her mouth. She could not freak out. Not now. Not after all this time.

There was a soft tap at the door and she quickly

swiped her fingers under her eyes and sat up against the headboard. "Come in."

The door opened.

"Are you awake?" Melissa edged into the room, carrying a breakfast tray.

"I've been awake for hours."

Melissa walked farther into the room and placed the tray on the side table by the bed. "I brought you a cup of tea and your favorite apple and cinnamon pastry. Not the healthiest breakfast, but I'll try anything to get you to eat today. You'll be wasting away if you carry on like this." She frowned. "Have you been crying?"

"No." Tori took the offered cup of tea. "And there's not much chance of me wasting away. I'm a size ten, not two."

Melissa's eyes darkened with concern. "How are you feeling?"

Tori sipped her tea and forced it down despite the immediate urge to gag. "Well, Abby's still missing and I'm still the last person to see her alive, so, not great."

"This must have brought everything back for you. Talk to me. You have to share this stuff. I'm not going to sit by and let you try to deal with your memories alone like you did when we were kids."

"I'm fine."

"That's impossible."

"Okay then, I'm as far from fine as anyone could be if they were me right now." Tori lifted an eyebrow. "Better?"

Melissa sighed and squeezed Tori's leg through the quilt. "No, not better, but at least you're telling the truth."

"I haven't slept all night, my head feels like it has a

jackhammer constantly beating at it and this tea tastes like I'm drinking rusty nails. Here." Tori passed the cup to her sister, flung back the covers and got up. "It's time for me to get out of this bed and do something."

"Do something? As in something about Abby? Tori, no. You can't get involved in this."

Tori spun around, adrenaline speeding her heart. "Why not? It was me who saw her taken, Melissa. I can't sit around doing nothing. Her face in the back of the car is constantly in my mind. I refuse to let another hour go by without at least trying to stop anything else from happening to her. I was the sole witness and we've not heard anything further from the police. This investigation could drag on for days."

Melissa stood. "You don't know that. Who's to say someone else hasn't come forward since last night? Who's to say they haven't already found her?"

"I've been checking and rechecking the news on my phone. If she'd been found, it would've been reported by now. She's still missing and I have to find her. It's too much like what happened to me. What if…" Tori exhaled a shaky breath. "What if I was meant to see Abby taken? What if this was some kind of message to me? I could be the link the police need to find her."

Melissa's eyes softened. "You're not thinking straight."

Tori battled the humiliation the pity in her sister's eyes unwittingly provoked. "*I'm* not thinking straight? How do you think her family is thinking right now? This isn't about me or you. It's about that little girl and her family."

"You are not strong enough to do this."

Tori glared, hurt that Melissa believed her so weak. "The hell I'm not. I have to use what happened to me to help. I saw Abby's face. I saw her terror…" Tori blinked against the sharp sting of tears. "I saw that man bundle her into a car with as much nonchalance as Brian Appleton did me. I can't stand by and not do anything. If you can't bear to watch me, then I'll get out of here this morning and not come back until I'm done."

She trembled. Of all the people who should understand the strength of purpose running through her blood, it should've been Melissa. Night after night, her sister had held Tori through her recurring nightmares, through the cruel reruns in her head of Brian Appleton's grinning face, his insane eyes.

Melissa's heavy exhalation broke the tense atmosphere and she crossed her arms. "What are you going to do?"

Tori held her sister's gaze. That was the million-dollar question. She had no idea. Turning, she marched in her pajamas toward an overnight bag in the corner of the room. "I don't know. At least not yet." She whipped clean underwear out of the bag and pulled the blouse and pencil skirt from the wardrobe door that she'd hung there the previous night.

She clutched the clothes to her chest and turned. "I'd love nothing more than to go to the station and demand an update from Sergeant Jansen, but I have a feeling he's as likely to talk to me today as I am to Abby."

"This is the policeman who spoke to you yesterday? Then leave things be, Tori. Please."

"No."

"Listen to me. You came out of your ordeal alive. All we can hope is that the same will be true for Abby."

"All we can *hope*?" Tori's frustration escalated, her body tense with suppressed anger. "Hope has nothing to do with this. We have to take action. Coming out alive isn't the be all and end all, you know. There's no way I'm *hoping* anything. *Doing* is what matters. Six days, Melissa. Six days I was with that man, playing an unwilling participant in his sick existence. He talked to me as if I was his possession. He brushed my hair and dressed me up…" She cursed the crack in her voice and lifted her chin. "If I can do a single thing to ensure Abby doesn't endure anything like that, I will."

Melissa's eyes glinted with tears. "I haven't got a chance of changing your mind about this, have I?"

"No. So, do I have your support or not?"

Melissa exhaled and opened her arms. "Come here."

Tori walked into her older sister's embrace and closed her eyes. "I have to do something. I need to research the family, the area, see if there are any links."

Her sister pulled back, her eyes full of sadness as she brushed some hair from Tori's cheek. "Listen to me. What happened yesterday had nothing to do with what happened to you. Why would it?"

"I don't know, but I have to be sure. If there's anything I can give the police, anything my experience might have taught me, it has to be worth sharing it with them."

Melissa's eyes shone with tears. "Okay, but for goodness sake, be careful. Anything I can do to help, I will, but Georgia has to be my priority. You understand that, right?"

"Of course I do. I wouldn't want it any other way."

"Good. Now, have a shower and get dressed. You've got work to do."

Once inside her sister's main bathroom, Tori locked the door and leaned against it, closing her eyes.

Brian Appleton's grinning face loomed and she snapped her eyes wide open.

No more thoughts about herself. No more lingering on her past. What happened to Abby was all that mattered, nothing else. Pushing away from the door, Tori embraced every ounce of her fortitude and turned on the shower.

**\*\*\*\***

Mark reached his garden gate and leaned his hand on the wall. Extending his leg, he stretched his calf muscle and then alternated to do the same to the other. The three-mile run had done little to rid his mind of Olivia, Abby Brady *or* Tori Peterson. The three females who had plagued his every waking moment and every sleeping minute for the last endless hours.

He should be in his workshop, working on Principal White's bureau, but concentration had abandoned him. Once he'd dropped Olivia at school— the playground eerily quiet—Mark had driven home, changed into sweats and ran. Ran and kept running.

Yet, he'd failed to outrun his thoughts. The suspicion something significant had happened to Tori Peterson, something along the lines of Abby's abduction, continued to badger him. Every time he'd woke during the night, he'd glared toward his open bedroom door and the study beyond, itching to fire up his computer and search her name.

But he hadn't, because he had no right.

After the media furore following his wife's death, Mark vowed he would never snoop into people's affairs as the press had his. Tori was a journalist. He should be avoiding her like the plague, yet instead, he wanted to make sure she was okay. The terrified awareness in her eyes hadn't been put there from reading a newspaper account or watching TV. Something horrible had happened to her. Yet, he had absolutely no right to edge into her private history.

All he knew, was Abby's kidnapping had further destroyed his fragile faith in humanity—and escalated his protectiveness over Olivia.

Straightening, Mark lifted his arms high above his head, stretching out the kinks and knots in his shoulders. The temptation had grown too strong. He needed to know who Tori was and what had happened to her. Her eyes told him she was scared to death by Abby's abduction…far beyond what was natural.

His wife was dead. His parents were dead. All he had was Olivia and he'd protect her with his life. Admittedly, Tori was an adult, but when he'd looked into her eyes at the school, he had never seen such a deep plea for help in his life.

He pushed open the gate and walked to his front door.

It was highly probable Tori had no idea her eyes gave away so much. Nor would she would appreciate how he'd recognized her vulnerability. If he had any chance of convincing her to let him work with her toward finding Abby, he had to tread carefully.

Maybe his deep desire to help came from his own need to feel trusted and relied upon, but that didn't mean he would turn away. He couldn't. He had to do something. He couldn't be made to feel as useless as he had after his wife died and there was nothing he could do to save her.

The silence of the house echoed with Lauren's absence and Mark breathed in her memory. For the first time since he'd lost her, there was another woman on his mind. Was he betraying Lauren by thinking about Tori? By worrying about her?

Tossing his keys onto the sideboard by the door, he walked upstairs and into his study. He dropped into the leather chair behind his desk and contemplated the blank screen of his computer. Indecision battled. Once he started looking, there would be no going back. Whatever he learned about Tori, whether good or bad, it couldn't be deleted from his memory with the press of a key.

He jabbed his finger on the mouse and the screen flickered to life. Calling up a search engine, he entered Tori's name.

Several sites appeared along with the word 'abducted'.

"Damn it." Mark leaned back and linked his hands behind his head, debating his next move. Did he want to know? He moved forward in his chair. He *had* to know. Ignoring his gut had led to Lauren walking alone without him on Barlington Downs…had led to her slipping, falling, crashing to her death.

Self-hatred clenched like a fist around his conscience. He needed to at least explore a way to find the scum who'd taken Abby so he could rest easy, at least for a while, that Olivia was safe at school. The determination in Tori's eyes had left him in no doubt that she was willing to put all she had on the line to find

Abby. Maybe together, they could do something—anything—to help the police.

He clicked on the top site and scanned the copy of the newspaper report from years before.

*"Ten-year-old Tori Peterson was abducted outside Littledale Primary School at approximately three p.m. Police speculate the possibility that Tori knew her abductor and willingly went with him. The man has been described as approximately six feet tall with dark blond hair and a beard. It is believed the man lured Tori into his car holding a black spaniel puppy. Police, friends and Tori's family have been frantically searching and appealing for her safe return for six days..."*

Mark swallowed against the dryness in his throat, his heart beating like a freight train. Ten years old. Just a year younger than Olivia. Six days. Anger tore like a hook in his chest as he curled his hands around the arms of his chair.

He stared at the words on the screen, but instead of seeing them, Tori's face loomed in his mind's eye. Her beautiful, dark red hair flowed like a fiery mane around a face that intrigued him. Now he imagined her as a scared, vulnerable child and his fury burned. Had the coolness in her wide, green eyes, the distrust and determination in the occasional way she spat words, been put there by what she'd endured at the hands of her abductor? He sensed a kindness beneath a solid and necessary veneer; a soft woman behind an enforced suit of metal armour that Tori gave no one a chance to dent, let alone break.

Mark leaned forward in his chair, his finger sliding over the mouse as he scanned each headline.

*"Found and charged—Tori Peterson's abductor, Brian Appleton, was arrested in his home in the small market town of Littledale, just a few miles from Tori's home at 7:15 a.m. this morning. A neighbour reported Appleton's suspicious behaviour and the police instigated a raid. Tori was found in a downstairs room. So far, little information has been provided of the child's physical or mental state.*

*More details will undoubtedly be divulged now that little Tori has been reunited with her relieved parents and elder sister."*

Weak satisfaction did nothing to douse his anger as Mark scrolled down farther and stopped again, a steady pulse beating at his temple. *And then they let the bastard out.*

He scanned the following article and with each word, his protective instinct rose to dangerous levels. Appleton had been sentenced to four years and served two and a half. No sexual abuse had occurred, but there were signs of physical and mental abuse. Tori had been held under duress and her abduction premeditated.

The more he read, the more Mark trembled with suppressed fury.

Appleton was believed to be living abroad with a new wife and two children. It was reported that his first wife, who Appleton was married to at the time of Tori's abduction, had moved away with their daughter when Appleton was sentenced. Names withheld.

Unable to read any more, Mark shut down the computer and rose from his chair. He paced the office, his mind whirling and his adrenaline pumping. Olivia filled his thoughts and his rage turned murderous.

He had to do something, had to make the world a

safer place. He could not risk losing the most precious person in his life. He couldn't risk anything happening to his daughter. Not ever. Olivia knew Abby. She'd seen her face at school and would, possibly soon, see it on TV and in the newspapers.

He couldn't let his baby girl be afraid, he couldn't let her down as he had her mother.

Storming into his bedroom, he picked up Tori's business card from his bedside cabinet. Only she could understand the harsh realities of the real world as he did…only she would understand and respect his motivations behind keeping Olivia safe.

Would Tori work with him? Come to see him as an ally? Or would she look at him and see a threat? Mark stared at the severe black and white print on the card, the bold and simple font bearing Tori's name and vocation. If she was ever going to trust him enough to involve him in her investigations, he needed to get a handle on his fury—on his fear.

One look in his eyes and there was every possibility the anger Tori saw there, would shut him out. Permanently. He needed to keep his anger under control and use it to focus on the task in hand. He was intelligent, strong, and got on well with people. Tori was a journalist who'd survived an unimaginable ordeal. Together, they had the potential to be a formidable team.

He took his phone from his shirt pocket and dialled her number.

Chapter Four

Tori entered the library and scanned the area around her as she inhaled the musty scent of books and paper. It was ten-thirty on a Friday morning, the library deserted—apart from the circle of kids in the children's area, playing or fussing around their mothers and each other.

A lump caught in Tori's throat and she quickly looked away. The kids' happy, smiling faces, laughter and shrieks were hard to handle. This morning, Abby Brady was most likely the furthest from smiling and laughing as any child could be.

Tori headed upstairs to the reference section, grateful the upper storey muted the noise below. She walked toward a row of microfiche readers and computers along the far wall and sat in one of the wheeled, high-backed chairs.

Running her fingers over the reader's keyboard, it wasn't long before she found what she wished more than anything she didn't need to look for—the newspapers from the time of her abduction, and the subsequent six days she was kept in captivity. The pages flickered and taunted her on the screen.

Icy-cold perspiration broke on her spine and she pushed up from her chair. Squeezing her eyes shut, Tori fought the return of the terror, the rage, the overwhelming feeling of abandonment that had consumed her throughout the hours she'd been imprisoned. What the majority of people don't know or understand, is that when a child's taken from everything they know, their traumatized emotions soon bypass the initial fear and move onto a horrible acceptance that they might never be found.

A soul destroying, deep-embedded realization that maybe their mum and dad don't actually love them as the child thought…otherwise they would come and find them.

Opening her eyes, Tori embraced the fear running through her. She needed to use its power as her motivation that would ultimately lead to finding Abby.

Tori stared at the screen. She wasn't a ten-year-old little girl anymore. She was a grown-up. A woman. Her parents hadn't abandoned her any more than Abby's parents had. They would be frantic, screaming in frustration, grasping at every possible lead and clue that would lead them back to their daughter.

Whipping back the chair, Tori sat. The chances of any further similarities between her abduction and Abby's were slim at best, yet if they were there, Tori would find them. Her thought processes were most likely based on nothing more than fear and paranoia, yet determination to do *something* past her usual reporting refused to abate.

She clicked on the first newspaper and ran through the pages of articles. It would be easier to handle if she began after Appleton's arrest rather than trawl through the pain of her abduction and the subsequent search.

Appleton's smiling face stared back at her, his huge, calloused hands clutching the shoulder of his wife on one side and the shoulder of his, then, five-year-old daughter on the other. Tori's eyes stung with tears and she blinked them back, forcing her gaze through the black and white until she clearly saw his brown eyes and dark blond hair. Hair very similar to the man who'd taken Abby. Yet, it hadn't been Appleton with his hands on her. He would be in his late forties now. The man she had seen outside the school had been at least ten years younger.

The longer she stared at Brian Appleton's image, the more she smelled him…rancid body odour, pathetically tinged with the musky scent of what she now knew to be some long forgotten cologne from decades before.

She would not falter; he would not win.

She read about his arrest and following release two and half years later. She studied pictures of her ten-year-old self being walked from his house, hand-in-hand with a female police officer. Remembered relief swelled Tori's heart as though she'd been transported back in time to the hammering at Appleton's front door, the fierce shouting and then the crack of splintering wood as the stomp of heavy boots stormed the house.

It wasn't until Officer Ruth, with her kindly blue eyes and sweet-smelling perfume, took Tori's hand that her nightmare finally began to end. The terror continued to re-emerge for years afterward—but at least when it did, Tori awoke in her parents' or Melissa's embrace rather than Appleton's.

The heat of Tori's renewed anger reassured her as it melted the coldness from her bones and banished her hysteria.

Images flickered until she reached the earliest article. The photograph of her distraught parents appealing to the public outside their family home. Flames of anger licked at Tori's insides giving her strength and belief that either she or the police would find little Abby alive and unharmed.

Shutting down the machine, she rolled the chair in front of one of the computers. She brought up a search engine and typed in Abby's father's name, Simon Brady.

Leaning forward, Tori read the text and with each passing second, she found it a little harder to breathe, a little harder to maintain control. Lawyer. Affluent. Suburban. Stay-at-home wife with two daughters…

The similarities between Mr. and Mrs. Brady and her own parents struck Tori's chest.

Her father had been a lawyer her entire life, her mother, a stay-at-home presence that comforted and supported Tori and her sister into becoming the women they were today. Assured and affluent, her parents had been a comfortably well off, suburban family that one might see on a TV commercial promoting familial bliss. On paper, her mum and dad appeared to be what ideal parents should be—kind, comforting, fair and always there when their children needed them.

The possibility Tori was supposed to see Abby taken gathered strength inside her. Was it her fault Abby was no longer safe in her parents' arms?

Sickness gripped Tori's stomach.

Could Brian Appleton have been preying on little girls for the last twelve years since his release?

No, she couldn't go there.

Snatching her purse from the desk, she hitched the strap onto her shoulder and marched toward the stairs.

She hurried through the library's automatic doors.

Once outside, she bent at the waist, her fingers digging into her thighs. She breathed deep. In and out. In and out. Just like her therapist had taught her.

When her heart rate slowed, inner strength glided over her shoulders like plated armour. She would go to see Sergeant Jansen and if he didn't listen to her, refused to see the similarities between her case and Abby's, she would find another officer who would.

Her phone vibrated inside her purse and she drew it out, looked at the display.

Mark Bolton.

He'd called her several times, leaving his number and a message asking her to call him back.

She pressed the reject call button, dropped the phone into her bag and strode along the street toward her parked car. He would only serve as a distraction she didn't need right now. Yet, temptation taunted her. Mindless, no strings attached sex had served her well in the past and provided a way of making her feel desirable, wanted and sexy. Virtues so much better than the vices of aversion, rejection or apathy.

She couldn't go there with Mark Bolton. She already sensed through the intelligent gaze of his brilliant blue eyes that he saw far too much when he looked at her.

He was a potential threat to her tried and tested existence and she would endeavour to protect it. Always.

Sliding into the driver's seat, she turned the ignition and joined the high street toward Barlington Police Station trying and failing, to shove Mark from her thoughts.

That was the fourth time he'd called that morning.

Tori gripped the steering wheel, her stomach knotting with an unfamiliar sensation. The guy unnerved her. Worse, he unnerved her in a pleasant rather than terrifying way. Talking to him would serve no purpose for either of them. She didn't need his concern—and he didn't need her crazy.

*Yeah? So why did you save his number in your contacts?*

Cursing, she forced her concentration on the road.

Mark Bolton had pushed himself forward when he could have walked away and she was woman enough to respect him for that. On the other hand, she wasn't foolish enough to think she could take on a predator like Brian Appleton alone—and her gut told her if she was forced to clasp a helping hand for the first time in forever, it might not necessarily be a bad thing if that hand belonged to Mark.

She tilted her chin.

For now though, she would go along well enough without him.

\*\*\*\*

Mark smoothed his hand over the sanded oak of Principal White's bureau and waited for the usual pride he felt in his work to materialize. But all that swept through him was barely controlled frustration, the one picture he'd seen of Abby Brady, concern for Olivia and thoughts of Tori Peterson.

He glanced at his watch. One-thirty. He had to leave to pick up Olivia from school in an hour. Time passed so slowly. The end of the school day might as well have been a lifetime away. He didn't doubt every parent with a child at Barlington County Primary was experiencing the exact same fear and apprehension.

Putting put the sander down on the bureau, he walked to the open door of his workshop and gripped the top of the door frame with both hands. His workshop was attached to the side of his three-bedroom house and the view ahead consisted of little more than the road at the end of his driveway and a row of three houses opposite. A nice street, a good neighborhood— and one that didn't seem quite as safe as it had yesterday.

With Tori refusing to pick up his calls, an alien helplessness badgered him. No matter how much he tried to leave the police to do their job, his need to scratch beneath the surface of their endeavors refused to abate. Tori had stood in front of him and blatantly admitted she was going to do all she could to find Abby Brady. Now that he knew Tori's history, protectiveness for her and what she intended to embark upon burned deep inside him.

He didn't doubt for one minute she'd reject his concern and offer to help, but he fully intended to ask her anyway.

Pushing away from the doorway, Mark strode into the workshop for his phone. He picked it up and scrolled through the previously dialed numbers.

He stared at Tori's sister's number. If Tori wouldn't speak to him, maybe Melissa would. What could he actually say to her? That he knew what had happened to Tori when she was a child and didn't want her running headlong into something likely to break her? How arrogant was he to even presume Abby's abduction would break Tori? He had no idea what the woman was made of.

She'd made it out alive after enduring God only

knew what at Appleton's hands. Who was to say she wouldn't face off Abby's abductor too? Yet, the thought of her doing so sent an icy chill through his gut.

Clutching the phone, Mark paced.

The fire raging in Tori's eyes told him all too clearly that her understandable fury had been ignited. Her anger was palpable—and he worried that what she'd suffered would turn her investigations into vengeance. Abby's abduction would have undoubtedly sparked something inside Tori that Mark could never begin to understand—all he understood was that the scum who'd taken Abby, could strike again…anywhere and at any time.

Next time, it could be Olivia.

Or another little girl at Barlington County.

He dialed Melissa's number.

"Hello?"

"Melissa, this is Mark Bolton."

"Who?"

He closed his eyes, feeling more like Tori's stalker than a father concerned for his daughter's safety. "Mark Bolton from the school. I was the one who called you yesterday and asked you to come and collect Georgia."

"Oh, right. Sorry. How can I help you? Have you heard something about Abby?"

"Afraid not." He opened his eyes and stared at the half-finished bureau. "I'm calling because Tori isn't answering her phone. Is she…" He shoved his hand into his hair. "How is she?"

"If she isn't answering your calls, it might be best for you to leave my sister alone. If she wants to speak to you, she will. Look, I mean this is the best possible way, but Tori's not the type of woman you want to hassle. No matter how good your intentions. You'll come off a darn sight worse than she will if you annoy her enough, believe me."

Mark strolled toward the open workshop door. "I appreciate the warning. The last thing I want to do is annoy her, but there was something in her eyes yesterday—"

"That told you she would go after the bastard who took Abby? If I were you I'd concentrate on your own child and leave Tori to do what she thinks best. There's no stopping her when she puts her mind to something and this…" She inhaled. "This is eating her up from the inside out. If she wants to speak to you, she'll call. Unless you want to become number two on her hit list, I wouldn't call her again."

"The last thing I want is to hassle her. I—"

"My sister isn't about to lean on you, me, or anyone else. Tori is a woman who likes to work and live alone. Just leave her be, okay?"

Before Mark had a chance to respond, the line went dead.

He ended the call and gripped the phone, his adrenaline pumping.

Frustration and the need to do something whispered through him. It was pointless even attempting to concentrate on work until he'd collected Olivia and knew her to be safe.

Grabbing his keys from the top of the bureau, he walked outside and pulled down the workshop door, bolted the padlock.

Marching to his car, he got inside and gunned the engine before heading for the school.

When he pulled up outside Barlington County

fifteen minutes later, the row after row of parked cars echoed his panic and concern. A rainbow trail of sedans, hatchbacks and sports cars were parked bumper to bumper—even though there was still a good half an hour before the kids were due to finish for the day.

The press was there too.

Turning off the engine, he glared at the assembled men, women and cameras.

Tori was a journalist. She had asked Sergeant Jansen to let her help with publicity and he'd refused. What was stopping her from turning up at the school today and speaking to some of the other parents? Maybe even a few of the kids. He didn't doubt she'd be doing something just as he sat here doing nothing.

He picked up his phone from the passenger seat and dialed Tori's number for the fifth time that day. When she picked up, surprise lurched his stomach. He opened his mouth to speak, but she got there first.

"What do you want, Mark? I'm kind of busy right now."

The curt, snappish tone of her voice screamed of her being with someone…someone clearly annoying her. He frowned. "I wanted to check how you're doing."

"I'm fine."

"No, you're not." Mark stared ahead, determination to get something out of the conversation, pushing the words from his mouth before he could consider the consequences. "Could we meet later?"

"Why?"

He cleared his throat. "You said you're going after whoever took Abby, I want to help."

"No."

"Why not? If your motivation for trying to help Abby is the right one, you'd welcome all the help you can get. If not—"

"I don't want you involved because I've no idea where this might lead. You're better off being nowhere near me right now."

"Thanks for the warning, but I can look after myself. My daughter has a singing lesson later. I'll meet you across the street from her tutor's house. Do you know the Flowers Pub?"

"Yes, but—"

"Great. I'll see you in the bar about six-thirty." He ended the call before she could answer and tossed the phone onto the passenger seat.

Swiping his hand over his face, Mark blew out a breath and debated whether he had entirely lost his mind by pushing further into Tori's life. Not that he had a choice. He couldn't walk away. Whether irrational or not, Abby's abduction now meant a very real risk to Olivia. Either he worked with Tori, or worked alone. For the moment, working with Tori seemed the wiser option.

Yanking on the door handle, he got out of the car and strode toward the school gates.

There was a reason Tori Peterson had come into his life—even if the circumstances were more evil than either of them could have imagined.

Her motivation for finding Abby was undoubtedly coated in vengeance; his reasons were steeped in the need to keep a potential threat from coming near his daughter.

Sooner or later, he and Tori would join forces. It was just a case of making her understand he was a father. A father who'd lost his wife and would protect his daughter from any and every visiting evil.

Chapter Five

*He hung up on me. Who does this guy think he is?*
*Meet him in The Flowers?*

Tori gripped her phone in her lap and lifted her gaze to her editor.

Neil Rose, wily, astute, and heartbreaker extraordinaire stared back, his gray eyes hard. "Who was that?"

"No one."

"You get that look on your face from no one?"

Tori held his stare.

He tossed his pen onto the notepad in front of him and lifted his hands to the back of his head. "So what are you going to do about the unique situation you have going on here? You saw whoever took Abby Brady. We can't just ignore that."

"I did, but if you think I'm going to use my *unique situation* to burrow into her family's life, you can think again."

"So what are you going to do? Run for the Tory government? Change school policy? Jesus, Tori, you were the first at the front line. You need to get yourself around to the parents' house and form a relationship with them."

"Their house will be crawling with police. There is no way I'll get within an inch of the Bradys."

"I want you to try. We can help. You just have to

convince Mr. and Mrs. Brady we're on their side."

Skepticism churned inside her and she raised her eyebrows. "The only reason you want me to visit them is to tell them we're on their side?"

"Yes." He dropped his hands and laid them on the desk. "What other reason could there be?"

Tori studied him. Neil ran his paper like a finely honed machine…a machine whose mechanisms were getting a little too small, a little too repetitive, for a man who had made his career aspirations clear to every single one of his staff after a pint or four on a Friday night after work.

"It's no secret how ambitious you are, Neil. You want a first interview with the parents, whereas I want to find Abby."

"And you think I don't? Do you really think so little of me? Look, I've got no idea why you're the way you are, Tori, but you need to get rid of that damn chip on your shoulder and start believing not everyone is out to get someone else. Trust me, if we can get inside the Bradys' house, Abby's parents will welcome our help, any help. Now, do you want in on this or shall I get another reporter on it?"

Tori slumped back into her seat and closed her eyes. "I want in."

"Good. You know as well as I do that eighty percent of child abduction cases are preplanned. The family is the key to this thing."

She snapped her eyes open. "This *thing*? This is a little girl's life we're talking about. Consider me on the case." She stood and hitched the strap of her purse onto her shoulder. "And, for the record, I'll be reporting in the best way I think might help in getting Abby home.

Nothing else. The public doesn't need to know the family's business, or that I was there when Abby was taken." *Nor does Brian Appleton.* "Let me do this my way. I know what I'm doing."

Neil raised his hands. "Fine. Get yourself to the police press conference this afternoon and have something to me by the end of the day for tomorrow's run. Whether you like it or not, you were the last one to see that girl and that matters."

Annoyance mixed with a horrible sense of responsibility. "And that's why I'll be doing everything I can to get her home." She turned but when she reached the door, she faced Neil again. "I need to work on this full time so I'd appreciate it if you didn't send me any crappy assignments in the meantime."

"I'll give you any assignment I please, but, for now, get out of here and do your job."

Tossing him a parting glare, Tori yanked open the office door and stormed through the newspaper office. The ride in the lift to the lobby took forever until, at last, she burst through the outer door and into the afternoon's hazy sunshine.

She breathed deep and planted her hands on her hips. Neil calling her into the office had superseded her intended visit to the police station, but now it was time to see Sergeant Jansen.

*Before* the press conference.

Visiting the station was routine in her line of work, but there would be nothing routine about her visit today. This would be all too reminiscent of the hours she'd spent in a different station, in a different town.

Memories burned.

Her mother's cold hands grasping Tori's as she

told and retold the police what had happened to her from the moment she'd gotten into Appleton's car, until the moment the police had crashed into his house. The gray police station walls, punctuated with postered warnings about theft, burglary, sexual assault and fliers for missing children had closed in on her, initiating her claustrophobia and underlining her new belief that adults couldn't be trusted.

The musty smell of the station wrapped her in the same fear as the horrible, gaudy interior of Brian Appleton's house.

There had been no escape. It didn't matter she had been found. Years later, she was still unable to fully trust anyone.

Tori opened her eyes.

There could be no faltering or weakness. She would find Abby and whoever had dared to take her would pay.

She strode across the parking lot to her car and slipped into the driver's seat. When she dumped her bag on the passenger seat, she stared at her phone.

No part of her wanted to meet Mark Bolton at The Flowers Pub, but she'd be there whether she wanted to or not. Even if only to tell him to back off.

Tossing the phone alongside her bag, Tori started her car and cursed the self-loathing that swirled inside her. Mark's soft, caring gaze and mile-wide shoulders had somehow mixed in her consciousness, right along with Abby's abduction. What sort of person noticed a guy, became attracted to a guy, while dealing with such evil?

She drove through the streets toward the police station, trying her hardest to fight the urge to seduce

Mark just for the hell of it.

Dating had always been on her terms. She liked sex…but called the end to any kind of relationship whenever the thrill lost its luster. Which is why she hated the niggling feeling Mark Bolton would never lose his luster as far as she was concerned.

She gripped the steering wheel. She shouldn't be thinking of his dark brown hair, olive skin or bright, sexy blue eyes. She should be thinking of a missing little girl and her terrified family, yet Tori had reluctantly taken to Mark from the moment he'd defended her against Susan Brady's slap. Tori inhaled. God help her, she'd even taken to that fiery daughter of his too.

Forcing her concentration on Barlington High Street as it heaved with the usual post-school traffic, Tori couldn't help but surmise the deluge of cars carrying kids meant Abby Brady had now been missing for twenty-four hours. It seemed patently obvious the fear of another kidnapping was rife in the minds of every parent in town.

She'd wasted enough time. She needed to get to the station and see Jansen. Even if it was entirely unfounded, her suspicion she was more involved in Abby's abduction than just witnessing it refused to disappear.

Everything she'd learned at the library could be deemed as circumstantial, and from her dealings with lawyers in the past, she was all too aware of how much they liked to spew that particular obstacle in a reporter's face.

Housed in a listed nineteenth century building, Barlington Police Station was conveniently located opposite the town's largest, and most frequented public park. It stood tall, proud and darkly intimidating, a solid reminder that the long-reaching arm of the law was in touching distance to the youths and vagrants who used the park for more than recreational play.

Tori pulled into a vacant spot outside the station and cut the engine. Dropping her phone into her bag, she checked for her notepad and pen and got out of the car. She walked into the station and stood in front of the reception desk.

The duty sergeant raised his head from the papers in front of him. He flashed a smile. "Tori. Fancy seeing you here."

"Irony was never your strong point, Sergeant Collins. I'd like a word with Sergeant Jansen, if possible."

"He's not here. Maybe I can help?"

"Who's in charge of the Abby Brady case?"

He frowned. "Why? Do you have some information?"

"Maybe."

"Come on, Tori. Don't you think we've already had several reporters in here today trying for something exclusive?" He turned back to his papers. "There's a press conference in the community center at six o'clock." He lifted his gaze to hers. "I suggest you're there along with everyone else."

Frustration wound through her. She had information that could be helpful…albeit that information was about her rather than Abby.

"Who's the detective inspector in charge of the case? You can tell me that, can't you?"

"DCI Thornhill."

Tori nodded as relief lowered her shoulders. "Can't think of a better person to be in charge. Can you ask him if he'll see me? Ten minutes. That's all I need. Trust me, he'll want to hear what I have to say."

Collins slowly laid down his pen on the pad, his stern gaze still on Tori's. "Give me a minute."

He picked up the phone and Tori glanced around the gray, nondescript lobby. Moving away from the desk, she ran over in her mind what she would say to the inspector. Her goal was to work side by side with the police, rather than against them. From the little her parents had told her about the police's involvement in her kidnapping, they'd done everything possible to help find Tori and comfort her parents.

Even if that were true, they wouldn't have her personal experience to add to the table—and to her mind, they wouldn't be doing their job if they ignored what she had to say, what she'd endured and how it had changed her. If Appleton was in any way involved in Abby's abduction, there was minute details only Tori could provide.

The sergeant put down the phone. "Okay, Tori, you can go on through. Second door on the left."

He pressed a concealed button beneath the counter and a door to her side buzzed. She pushed it open and entered a small hallway. The station had once been a residence, complete with staircase leading to upstairs rooms and the musty smell of age and untold stories. She reached the second door and knocked.

"Come in."

Taking a deep breath, she pushed open the door.

"Miss Peterson, nice to see you again." DCI Thornhill rose from behind his walnut desk and offered his hand, his gaze calmly assessing.

Tori confidently shook his hand. "You too."

"Take a seat." He waved her toward one of the two visitors' chairs in front of his desk and sat. "I believe you want to talk to me about Abby Brady?"

Tori sat. "Have you any new leads?"

"There will be a press conference this evening if we are no further forward. I assumed you had information for *me*, not the other way around."

Tori shifted back in her seat, the words and story she was about to share sticking in her throat. Her family's move to Barlington, away from where they'd lived when Tori was taken, had meant relative anonymity for almost sixteen years. Inspector Thornhill was about to learn something about her that very few people knew.

"Miss Peterson?" Thornhill raised an eyebrow. "Do you have anything for me?"

Tori exhaled a slow breath. "I think Abby's abduction might have something to do with a man by the name of Brian Appleton."

The inspector frowned. "Who is he and why would he have a hand in this?"

She clasped her hands tightly together in her lap. "Almost sixteen years ago, I was abducted from outside a school in Littledale."

A spark of surprise flashed in the inspector's eyes before it was replaced with sympathetic interest. "I'm sorry to hear that. I had no idea."

"I think there might be some link between my kidnapping and Abby's. I not only witnessed her abduction, I think I was *meant* to see it. The man who took her looked at me as though checking I watched him."

"Did you recognize anything about him?"

"Nothing, but Abby doesn't look entirely dissimilar to me at the same age…and I've looked into her family status which is also similar to mine. Her parents are affluent. Her father has a good job and her mother stays at home to look after Abby and her older sister."

Tori fought against the horrible sensation that her thoughts were slightly insane. The flimsy, coincidental details losing their depth now she sat in front of DCI Thornhill.

He cleared his throat and leaned back in his chair. "I sympathize with what happened to you, Miss Peterson, but what you're saying is not enough for me to pursue this Brian Appleton. Does he live in Barlington now? Is that what has you concerned?"

"I have no idea. The last my family or I heard, he was living abroad. I think you should check that's still the case. If he's here, he could be playing some kind of sick game and using Abby to get to me." Dread for Abby and what she might be enduring if Appleton held her, swept over Tori, hitching her agitation sky high. "The man is dangerous, Inspector. He is mentally unstable, despite being sent to regular prison and being out again before I hit my thirteenth birthday. You have to follow this up for Abby's sake."

He regarded her through narrowed eyes and shifted forward, pulling a notepad and pen toward him. "What else can you tell me about Appleton? Are you willing to talk about what happened to you? If I can build up a picture, it might highlight further similarities in what we know about Abby's abduction."

Nausea rose bitter in her throat. What else had she

expected to happen? The police were hardly going to go all guns blazing after Brian Appleton on her say-so. She briefly closed her eyes before opening them and holding the inspector's gaze. "I understand."

He nodded.

Tori took a strengthening breath. "I was lured into his car by his puppy. His name was Oreo…" She gave a wry smile. "And he disappeared as soon as Appleton shut the front door of his house behind me. For years, I blamed myself for what happened to me. It was my fault because just that one time, I ignored my parents' endless warnings about strangers and was tempted by a monster claiming to be my father's work friend. Brian Appleton was a kindly, smiling man who'd cradled the most adorable fluffy black spaniel. I trusted him." Anger swirled in her stomach. "But Abby didn't trust her abductor, Inspector. She fought back. She fought and she struggled. God knows, she would've probably screamed if the man forcing her into that car didn't have his hand over her mouth."

"If you believed the man you saw take Abby was Appleton, why didn't you tell Sergeant Jansen that at the school?"

"It definitely wasn't him who took her. That is one face I am never likely to forget. But that doesn't mean he's not involved. He'll be older now, people would be suspicious of a man in his late forties hanging around outside a primary school." She inhaled and tried to regain control of the flurry of anger and trepidation rolling around inside her. "The similarities might not seem much, but if Appleton has Abby…what he does…" A tear rolled down her cheek and she angrily swiped at it. "He dressed me up, Inspector. Dressed me up in pretty dresses, ribbons and bows. He sang and made me dance in his arms. He laid next to me in bed and he touched me."

Thornhill's jaw tightened and his cheeks darkened. "I see." He scribbled something on his notepad before lifting his eyes to hers. "I'll look into it. You have my word, but I'm not holding out much hope Appleton is involved. Abby looking a little like you and having the same family circumstances isn't a solid line of enquiry. Pedophiles tend to reoffend whether we like it or not. Children are their sexuality, like us being homo-or heterosexual. Some believe pedophilia is curable with the right rehabilitation or drugs." His dark blue gaze hardened. "Others don't. I'm not dismissing what you've told me, but if Appleton doesn't come up on any database as having reoffended these past years, the chances are slim Abby's case has anything to do with him."

"But you'll know where he should be, right? You can check databases internationally?"

"Yes."

Tori released a relieved breath. "Good. Then that's all I ask. And you'll let me know if he's back in the country?"

Thornhill nodded. "I will."

"Thank you."

"If what you've told me turns out to be a justifiable lead, it will be me thanking you."

"Could I ask another question?"

He nodded.

"Can you not make my name public knowledge for as long as possible?"

"We do our utmost not to reveal witness names,

Miss Peterson. You know that."

"I just needed to be sure." Pushing to her feet, she shook the inspector's offered hand before picking up her bag. "Is it okay if I use the bathroom before I leave?"

"Of course." He stood and came around the desk, walking ahead of her to open the door.

Tori followed him back along the short hallway to the bottom of the stairs.

He gestured toward the upper floor. "Door in front of you at the top."

"Thank you."

With another brief smile, the inspector turned and disappeared into his office, closing the door behind him. Taking a deep breath, Tori walked upstairs to the single bathroom, entered and locked the door behind her.

She strained her ears to any noise outside the closed door.

When she was certain no one would hear her, Tori dropped her bag from her shoulder, crumpled to her knees and lifted the toilet seat. Gripping its porcelain sides, she leaned over and threw up her lunch...and possibly her meager breakfast too.

Chapter Six

*Oh, Tori, my love…*

*Today I get to see you work.*

*I am holding these letters until the time is right to send them to you.*

*When you are mine, you will have no need to pursue your stories or right the wrongs that seem to drive your every wish and desire. I will be here to do that for you. All you'll need to do, day and night, is be a good wife to me. You will spend your hours making our home bright and beautiful, filled with love and perfection.*

*I've bought you a shiny new oven and shelves filled with pots, bottles and all manner of feminine things. You will dress in the prettiest dresses and wear your hair as I like it. I will make it so that I am your only wish and desire. Nothing or no one else will fill your mind and heart but me, my love.*

*The girl I borrowed from the school has stopped crying for her mummy already. See? I am a loving parent. Someone who wants to show you just how kind and caring I am.*

*Of course, once I have you I won't need her anymore. You and I will live without anyone else interfering. I will make love to you every moment I can. I will touch you, kiss you, stroke you until I have had enough, and then you will satisfy me, over and*

*over…until I tell you to stop and rest.*
*I look forward to seeing you today…I love you.*
\*\*\*\*

The police had chosen Barlington's community center to hold the press conference. The fact the center was in the very heart of the small town and close to the school would undoubtedly bring the reality of Abby's abduction to everyone's hearts and minds. Tori prayed the evocative location would prompt the public's support.

Taking a seat at the front of the room, she pulled her notepad and pen from her bag. Cally sat beside her, her eyes wide and her back ramrod straight.

Tori turned to look at the rows of journalists behind her, either talking to one another or into their phones. She doubted any of them had the same motivation as her for wanting whatever pieces of information DCI Thornhill was able—or willing—to offer the media that evening. She faced front.

Usually, the police tried to hold the press back, at least for a minimal time, because once news of a child kidnapping is made public there's an influx of sightings. Most of which lead to nothing and take officers away from urgent enquiries.

So tonight's conference was a clear call for help.

She shifted back in her seat and glanced at Cally. "I wouldn't have thought the parents will make a plea today. I can only assume the two empty chairs at the front are for the investigating officers Thornhill's working with."

Cally frowned. "Were you hoping to hear from the parents?"

Tori exhaled as further stories her mother had

shared with her resurfaced. "In a way, yes, in another, no. In child abduction cases, the parents are often kept high on the suspect list until the police have absolute certainty they aren't involved. I can't imagine how it feels to be under police scrutiny when you have a missing child and are entirely innocent of any wrongdoing." She glanced toward the door where Thornhill and his colleagues were due to emerge from at any moment. "On the other hand, it would be remiss to rule out the Bradys' guilt without having substantiated proof of their innocence."

Before Cally could respond, the door opened and DCI Thornhill entered the room, followed by Sergeant Jansen and another officer, both in full, and very official, uniform. All three men sat behind the table, a microphone in front of them, with Thornhill seated in the center.

He scanned the bank of journalists. When he met Tori's eyes, he paused, his concerned gaze lingering on hers before it moved along the remaining reporters in the row. Tori pulled back her shoulders and tried to shrug off her discomfort. The inspector's clear hesitation when he'd looked at her illustrated the shift, the sympathy, the fact he would never quite look at her the same way again now that he knew her history.

Self-loathing rippled through her, and Tori forced her mind to Mark. *He* hadn't looked at her differently. Her stomach dipped with unexpected hope. *He'd* looked at her like he wanted to kiss her. Which was why she had to be wary of the man, had to keep a tight leash on her attraction toward him. Things could get very messy, very quickly, if she allowed the cracks surrounding her heart and her deep sense of distrust to weaken.

"Ladies and gentlemen…"

Tori blinked at the deep timbre of Thornhill's voice, and she turned her full attention to the inspector.

He cleared his throat. "This is an information only conference. I will not be taking questions at this time. Abby Brady has now been missing for just over twenty-seven hours. This means we are rapidly approaching the time we wished to avoid. When a child has been missing for forty-eight hours, the hope of finding them unharmed begins to diminish, the worst case scenarios start to come into people's minds."

He cast his steely gaze around the room. "Let's stay focused on a positive outcome. I do not want public fears perpetuated by press reports. I have every hope we will find Abby alive and well. We are working with Mr. and Mrs. Brady to track down family members and friends who might provide vital information that could lead us to Abby's whereabouts."

Tori's impatience grew. The inspector's words were nothing more than the usual spiel the police gave to the press every time they either had nothing to go on—or else pursued a line of enquiry they didn't want made public. If Thornhill intended playing his cards this closely to his chest, he'd only increase her determination to pursue her own investigations.

"So far…" Thornhill continued. "We have witness statements to the following effect. Abby was seen being forced into a dark Ford Focus. The number plate, whether intentionally or not, was obscured. We have also spoken to many of the parents who were in the school playground at the time, and none of them remember seeing Abby leave. She was dressed in

Barlington's school uniform, which consists of a navy skirt, white blouse and navy v-neck jumper bearing the school's badge. She was also carrying a red book bag like this one."

Tori scribbled down the description of the uniform even though she'd seen her niece dressed in the exact same one a hundred times. She looked up at the book bag one of Thornhill's officers held aloft.

Her stomach tightened, and she thrust her hand in the air. "Inspector?"

He snapped his gaze to hers. "I said no questions, Miss Peterson."

"I know and I apologize, but can I just ask who saw Abby carrying her book bag?"

Thornhill held her gaze and leaned his forearms on the desk, clasping his fingers tightly together. "The school principal."

"I see." Tori nodded and pretended to make a note on her pad. "Yet, you said nobody saw Abby leave the school building." *And I know Abby was not carrying a bag.*

"And I stand by that. The principal spoke to Abby just before she left the school building. She was holding the bag then."

Tori's mind scrambled. Abby hadn't emerged until after the school bell rang…or had she? *I was too damn busy thinking about Halloween invitations to notice if she'd been outside before.* Guilt clawed at Tori's conscience.

The inspector ran his gaze over the assembled press. "We have yet to find a witness who can confirm whether Abby left the school alone. We do know there was no one else with her when she was on the street and taken, but that doesn't one hundred percent confirm she left the building alone. Our main objective is to be absolutely certain no one saw her leave." He scanned the bank of journalists. "Principal White was in Abby's classroom as the children were gathering their things to leave for the day. She then left and was in conversation with a teacher when the bell rang and the children headed for the doors.

"The bag has not been found in the school or on the grounds. We have scoured the area spanning from the school exit to where Abby was taken. As far as we are aware, the bag was with her when she climbed into that car."

Tori shifted in her seat. She didn't mention any bag in her statement to Jansen or since. So why was Thornhill talking about Abby's school bag?

Was he not taking anything she'd said to him seriously? Was he even going forward with her theory that Brian Appleton could be involved? The principal's observations about Abby were flimsy at best. If Principal White and Abby's teacher were the last people to see Abby before she left the school building, surely the principal would have felt compelled to say something to that effect to Mrs. Brady when the distraught woman had been shaking in Mark's arms.

"At this moment, we are asking the press to help us substantiate, one way or the other, those last vital minutes before Abby was taken." Thornhill scanned the gathered press once more. "Someone, somewhere, knows more than they have said or realized. No parent or teacher remembers seeing Abby leave, why? If she left alone, why? For a child of Abby's age to do so isn't usual practice. If she left with another pupil or pupils, how did she come to be alone long enough that her abductor managed to get her into that car without raising the alarm?"

*Exactly.* Tori stabbed her pen on her pad and nudged Cally. "I'm going straight from here to see someone. Could you go back to the office and see if you can find a list of the students in Abby's class? I need you to look on the school website for names or pictures of all the kids in her year."

Cally frowned. "What are you thinking?"

"I'll tell you more tomorrow."

Cally nodded.

Thornhill stood. "Once again, I ask that you keep your reports short and to the facts. We know Abby was taken at just past three o'clock and the abductor's vehicle was a dark Ford focus. If I think it necessary, there will be another press conference in a few days. Good evening, ladies and gentlemen."

The other officers rose and DCI Thornhill led the way from the room. As soon as the door closed behind them, the room erupted into a barrage of chattering and beeping phones as the journalists made their way toward the exit.

Tori's sudden need to see Mark Bolton and ask him what he knew about Principal White gathered strength. Cally's insistent chatter as they left the community center faded into the background. By the time Tori slid into the front seat of her car, she had no idea when Cally had left her side for her own car.

Tori pulled out of the parking lot and onto the road. As she made her way toward The Flowers Pub, her palms turned clammy on the wheel at the prospect of seeing Mark again. Regardless of the horrific circumstances under which they met, it was useless denying the frisson of attraction that simmered between them.

Then again, the guy had been single a long time. His wife had died horribly over five years before. The lingering looks he'd given Tori might have held zero significance. Maybe Mark Bolton looked at every woman the same way with those gorgeous blue eyes and sexy half smile. There was every possibility the guy viewed her as little more than a way in to the investigation. A way to serve his perpetual—and understandable—need to save the world after the loss of his wife.

Either way, Tori kind of liked him.

\*\*\*\*

Mark took another sip of his pint and looked toward the pub door for the tenth time in as many minutes. Tori was late. Twenty minutes late. He bounced his foot on The Flowers' dark floor tiles and thumbed blindly through the emails on his phone, guilt about the research he'd done on Tori niggling at his conscience.

He'd mentally rehearsed countless times what he would say to her if she did show. None of those times had his reasons painted him in a good light.

There was every chance, if her fiery temper was anything to go by, his half-drank pint could end up on his head.

Yet, still he contemplated looking her up on Facebook. He smiled wryly. Tori Peterson did *not* strike him as the Facebook type—at all.

A waft of musky, sexy perfume drifted under his nostrils and Mark lifted his head. His heart lurched.

"You're here."

"I am." Tori gave a half-smile. "Sorry I'm late."

He stood and waved her toward the velvet window seat beside him. "Take a seat. Drink?"

"A glass of Merlot would be great." Her careful gaze studied his. "Thanks."

"Coming right up." He walked to the bar. The woman was ridiculously attractive. All red hair, green eyes and fantastic figure. Yet, his awareness of her mixed sickeningly with the awareness the only thing they currently had in common was missing Abby Brady.

He glanced along the bar. At least three guys at the bar openly stared in Tori's direction.

"What can I get you?" The young barmaid stopped in front of him, her spiked hair and numerous tattoos a complete contrast to her soft gray eyes and lightly painted lips.

"A glass of Merlot, please."

"Sure."

While she poured the drink, Mark snuck another look at the men along the bar. Each continued to sporadically glance Tori's way and Mark turned. She was oblivious to their attention. Her head turned toward the pool table and her wide eyes glazed in thought.

"That'll be three pounds twenty, please."

Concern ran through him to see Tori's brow furrowed with obvious worry as he held out a five-pound note. "Keep the change."

"Thanks."

He picked up Tori's wine and rejoined her. As Tori was the first woman he'd felt attracted to in a long while, he chose to sit on a stool rather than on the long seat beside her. Enforced space between them suddenly felt imperative to his focus. "Here you go. One glass of Merlot."

She turned, her smile instant and far too wide. "Cheers." She took a sip and returned her glass to the table. Her eyes met his. "So, I'm here on your rather abrupt demand. What did you want to talk to me about?"

He lowered his glass beside hers and ran his gaze over her face before meeting her eyes. "I want to help you find Abby Brady."

She shook her head. "No."

He lifted an eyebrow. "No? That's it?"

"That's it." She took another sip of her wine. "Anything else?"

Mark stared, he couldn't allow her to just dismiss him. She had to know how seriously he wanted to help her, even if he couldn't tell her how he now felt duty bound to protect her. He cleared his throat. "I know what happened to you."

She stiffened and her cheeks darkened. "What?"

He leaned his elbows on the table, closing the space between them. Her eyes had turned icy cold and he lowered his voice. "Look, I'm sorry, okay? But I can no more leave Abby's disappearance to the police than you can."

"What does that have to do with you poking around in my business?" She took gulp of her wine and put it down with enough force splashes of red wine hit the table. "We're done here." She snatched up her bag and stood. Her gaze was angry as she leaned close to his face. "You had no right to nose around in my personal life."

Annoyance simmered inside him and Mark glared. "Sit down, Tori." The weight of the guys' stares from the bar bore into his temple and he tilted his head toward her vacated spot on the seat. "Let me explain. Please."

Her eyes were like a mirror into her thoughts. He watched in fascination as they flickered with annoyance, consideration and then surrender. "Fine." She tossed her bag onto the seat and plonked her butt down beside it, crossing her arms. "You've got five minutes."

Mark slowly pushed his pint to the side. "If you were hoping I'd stay out of this investigation, then I'm probably the worst person who could've helped you in the playground yesterday. I can't turn away from this. I have Olivia."

She frowned. "Your daughter?"

"Yes."

"Okay, but what does she have to do with Abby being taken?"

His gut knotted. "All Olivia and I have is each other."

She stared at him before her gaze softened. "I see."

"So you understand what I'm saying?"

"Yes. You're afraid she could be next. That whoever has Abby could take your daughter too." She took a sip of her wine. "As much as I understand that, I still don't understand what gave you the right to go snooping into my background." Her green eyes filled with irritation once more. "What happened to me is my business, no one else's unless I choose differently. You had no right."

Remorse rolled like a craggy boulder through his

chest. "I know and I'm sorry. My only excuse…" He shook his head. "My only *reason,* on top of protecting my daughter, is I think, between us, we could do some good toward finding Abby. The fact she was snatched from outside her school, where she should have been safe, terrifies me."

He curled his hand into a fist on the table. "Every parent in Barlington should be doing what I want to do. Find Abby alive and well. We all know there's only so much the police can do. I *have* to help. I can't sit around, going about my daily business, when God only knows what is happening to that little girl. Now I know what happened to you…" He stared into her eyes, willing her to trust him. "Let me help, Tori. You shouldn't be doing this alone."

Tears glazed her eyes before she blinked and they disappeared. "You don't get to be the hero every day, you know. Trying to stay by my side, I don't know, protect me or whatever you think you can do to fix me, won't work."

"That's not why I'm asking to help you. I told you, Olivia—"

"Is all you've got. I get it." She took a deep breath, her gaze concerned. "What happened to your wife?"

Surprise jolted through him and Mark picked up his glass, draining it. He put it back on the table and exhaled. "She died. Freak walking accident. Apparently, there was nothing I could've done. How the cops and bloody paramedics told me that when I wasn't even there to do anything that might have saved her makes their assurances nothing more than bullshit, but there you go." He held her gaze. "I will never again be in a position where someone can say to me there was nothing I could have done."

Her green eyes, wide and considering, searched his before she nodded. "Okay. Fine."

He frowned. "Fine?"

"You're on my team…for now."

He arched his eyebrow, satisfaction burning inside. "For now?"

"Yes. I don't trust people easily." She inhaled. "For obvious reasons. So, if it comes to me kicking you to the curb, dismissing what you're saying or telling you to leave me alone, that's exactly what you'll do. Until then, we'll see how we go along working with one another. Agreed?"

He should've been pissed off at her attitude; asked where she got off on talking to him that way, but the fierce gleam in her eyes and the way she leaned closer rather than away from him, only made him more determined than ever to help her.

"Agreed. I feel like I'm losing Olivia through my constant fear something will happen to her. That didn't start with Abby being taken, it started when Lauren died and if helping you now means I can give Olivia some space, all the better for our relationship."

"Lauren's your wife?"

He nodded. "I need to do something that will give me your strength of character to not let one event in my life dictate the rest of it." He gave a wry smile. "And I need you to kick my ass whenever my superhero tendencies show up at the wrong time." Her smile was like the damn sun coming out on a cloudy day. "Is that okay?"

She dropped her gaze to his mouth for a moment before meeting his eyes once more. "You've got yourself a deal." She tilted her head toward the bar. "Why don't you get me another glass of Merlot and we'll talk some more."

Chapter Seven

Tori left the pub and kept walking.

Mark's gaze burned into her back as she tried to stop smiling. The man's piercing blue eyes, his deep, calm voice and care for his daughter had drawn something out of her she hadn't known existed.

Need.

God-awful, unwanted, deeply feared need for someone to care for her. For so long, Tori had kept Melissa and their parents at arm's length to prove to them, and herself, that what Brian Appleton did to her hadn't defined her.

Yet, in the pub with Mark, something had momentarily shifted, scaring her so much, she'd quickly slammed in place an attitude of being in charge. When in truth, it had been Mark in the driving seat from the moment he'd confessed his love and fears for Olivia.

She risked a look behind her. He'd gone.

She released a shaky breath. Whether Mark Bolton realized it or not, she'd not only agreed to him helping her with the investigation, he had slipped a little way under her personal defenses too. Time and again during the hour they'd been in the pub, she had waited for an annoying comment to come out of his mouth. Waited for him to make a move or say something disparaging about the case or even about something she said.

Anything to put her off him, to give her reason to kick him to the curb as she'd warned she would.

Nothing. Nada.

The man was nice. Really nice.

She glanced at her watch. It neared eight. She turned the corner toward her office anyway. She'd left her car there earlier, assuming she'd not even make it through one drink. Instead, she got through two and would have easily stayed for number three if Mark hadn't needed to leave to pick up Olivia. So while she waited for the wine to leave her system, she might as well attempt some work.

In amongst the subdued undercurrent of some mild flirtation, she and Mark had talked about Abby and the similarities between her abduction and Tori's. Mark agreed there was something in Tori's suspicions to pursue—unlike DCI Thornhill who'd seemed skeptical about everything she'd told him.

She had to find more, another link or reason, to convince the inspector she wasn't clutching at straws or acting out of fear. Not that she wasn't scared, but her adrenaline didn't work that way. Every time she considered Abby's home life and her own, the way the abductor had looked straight at her and her similar looks to Abby, it was too much to ignore.

Taking her keys from her bag, Tori let herself into the newspaper office. Surprised the alarm had already been deactivated, tension snaked through her body. She locked the door behind her and slowly walked to the elevator. Once she was in the paper's office, she glanced toward Neil's glassed corner office.

Empty.

The rapid tip-tap of a keyboard floated across the

otherwise silent space.

Tori spotted Cally at her desk and released her held breath. "Cally? What are you doing here so late?"

Cally snapped her gaze from her computer screen. "Hi, Tori." She pushed her glasses on top of her dark-blonde head, her pretty face lighting with a smile. "I'm just catching up with some fillers for the next couple of editions. Neil isn't too happy that I've slipped behind."

"If you've slipped behind, it's because of the work you've been helping me with. I'll talk to him."

"Oh, no, I didn't mean for you—"

"It's fine. You're doing great and Neil needs to see that."

Cally blushed. "Thank you."

Tori hung her bag over the back of her chair and sat behind the desk facing Cally's. "So, any new views or ideas on the Abby Brady case?"

"Me?" Cally's brown eyes widened. "No, not really."

Tori frowned. The junior journalist showed real promise but Cally's self-confidence constantly faltered. The only person in the office whose attention she seemed to flower under was the photographer's. Admittedly, Greg Falmer looked great…if you went for that long-haired, stubbled jaw, kind of lanky type. Tori was beginning to suspect he was exactly Cally's type.

She wheeled closer and leaned her forearms on the desk. "You must think or feel something about Abby's case. This is the first child abduction to ever occur in Barlington. If you want to be a certified journalist someday, you're going to have to push yourself forward, share with others what you feel in your gut. Now, hit me with it. What's ran through your mind since Abby was taken?"

Cally slowly drew her gaze over Tori's face whilst chewing her bottom lip. "Okay." She blew out a slow breath. "I think that maybe she didn't have a lot of friends, kept to herself a bit, most likely a little neglected by her parents. Don't pedophiles tend to target kids they've followed around for a while? I don't think this was a random snatching. I think her kidnapper either knew her or knew of her."

"Okay, good. So, say you were in charge of reporting on Abby's kidnapping, what would you do next given your theories?"

Cally's gaze frantically sought Tori's as though seeking her approval. Her shoulders slumped. "I don't know."

Tori leaned back in her seat, giving the girl some space. "What we do next is pursue your theory and mine."

"What's yours?"

Tori caught herself. Having DCI Thornhill and Mark Bolton knowing her business was enough people for one day…even one lifetime. "I'll be sharing my theories on a need to know basis." She opened her laptop and met Cally's eager gaze. "I agree that whoever took Abby has most likely been watching her for some time. Your theory about the neglectful parents, not so sure, but it's something we should investigate. The problem is what we do next and how to do it. The cops have had people, dogs and God knows what else looking for Abby for the last twenty-four hours. The police and the media either work together or against each other. In Abby's case, I want to make sure it's the former."

"How?"

"By finding something significant enough to convince the police we are here to help, not hinder." Tori brought up a search engine. She typed in Susan Brady's name. "If my theory's right, Mrs. Brady is a good, loving, and, undoubtedly hysterical, mother right now. She will have a constant police liaison with her and could even be medically sedated. I have zero intention of causing the poor woman any more distress." She scanned the screen. "There's very little online about her. She worked as a receptionist in a veterinary surgery until she had her first daughter, Sally, and, since then, has stayed at home to raise her and Abby. So, we'll take a look at the husband."

"Can I ask you something?"

"Sure." Tori leaned forward and squinted at the screen. "Successful lawyer, now barrister." She sucked in a breath. "I bet the man is already planning the abductor's demise. What did you want to ask?"

"What if, rather than the family, the link lies with someone at the school?"

Tori stopped reading and looked at Cally. "Go on."

"Abby was taken in full view of the school, even though anyone could've intercepted the abduction."

*Yeah, someone like me.*

"So maybe the kidnapper knew Abby would come out of the school alone because someone in the school knew, or arranged it that way. Didn't you say in hindsight Abby must have been the first kid out of the school gates?"

"She was. I'm sure of it." Tori tapped her nails on the desk, her mind racing as it replayed the image through the back window of her car just before Abby was forced into her abductor's vehicle. "Why she left alone is something we really need to get to the bottom of."

"Yay me."

Resisting the urge to shake her head at Cally's continuous bouts of girlie immaturity, Tori looked to the screen. "I'll think some more about the circumstances leading up to Abby leaving the school. If I think it is a viable lead, I know just the man who can help find out more from the principal and her staff."

"Who?"

"A friend."

Tori typed in Mark's name on the search engine. Mark was a carpenter. A carpenter currently working on a bureau for the head teacher at Abby's school. The man wanted to help and, sooner rather than later, she might just have his first investigative role.

\*\*\*\*

Mark glided the sander over the top of the bureau, the easy back and forth motion going some way to soothing his thoughts and fears to a more manageable level. He hadn't heard from Tori since yesterday evening and, despite wanting to, he hadn't called her. The hours passed with no further updates on Abby's disappearance during the news bulletins blasting every half an hour from the digital radio sitting on a shelf behind him.

The sun beat in through his open garage door as he worked, sweat running down his bare back and his temples. Every moment he wasn't looking after Olivia or working, his thoughts raced and scrambled with images of Abby or Tori.

He had to do something to restore his belief that it

wasn't possible Olivia could one day be snatched too.

The purr of an engine grounded to a halt in the distance, but at the confident click of stiletto heels against stone, he stilled.

Tori.

The soft scent of her musky perfume drifted into his nostrils as she entered the garage.

His heart picked up speed as he forced himself to straighten up slowly, as though having her turn up at his home was no big deal.

He turned.

She held out a can of soda so cold, condensation trickled over its sides. Mark licked his lips and she lifted an eyebrow. "I see I was right to think you might be thirsty."

He switched off the sander, put it on the bureau and walked toward her, enjoying the way her eyes widened as they briefly flitted over his bare chest before meeting his eyes. As he took the can from her, their fingers brushed. "Thanks."

"You're welcome." She cleared her throat and snuck past him to the bureau, her cheeks flushed.

Mark snapped open the can and drank while appreciating the shape of her behind beneath a tight-fitting black skirt. He lowered the can, walked to the bureau and locked his gaze on hers. "What are you doing here?"

She flicked her focus over his chest before snapping her gaze toward the open workshop door. "I spent most of last night thinking about one aspect of Abby's kidnapping."

His libido instantly cooled. "And?"

"And, as far as I'm concerned, DCI Thornhill's

lack of information at the conference yesterday has given us the green light to pursue our own lines of enquiry."

He took another drink and moved around the bureau. "Okay. Good."

She instantly moved farther the other way.

Sensing her discomfort, he stopped and leaned against the bureau. God, did he frighten her? Surely not, or she wouldn't be here. Or did she sense his attraction toward her and would do all she could to deflect it? He didn't doubt for one minute his eyes gave away his appreciation whenever he looked at her.

He lifted the can to his lips. "So, what have you been thinking about?"

She tapped a peach-painted nail on the bureau. "This."

"The bureau?"

"*Principal White's* bureau."

He frowned. "How did you know it was hers?"

"She mentioned you were working on a bureau for her when I was in the school office. I assumed this is it."

"It is."

"Good, because that makes it all the easier for me to give you your first assignment."

"You want me to talk to her."

She smiled, took a few tentative steps closer to him. "Got it in one, Watson."

He smiled, pleased to see genuine mischief shining in her eyes. "I'm Watson?"

"Yep."

"So that makes you Holmes. Not sure I like being anyone's sidekick."

Another couple of steps closer until no more than a couple of feet separated them. She met his eyes and his heart kicked. Her V-neck shirt was just the right side of professional. Yet, the way it revealed her collarbones and hugged her full breasts made him want to reach out and pull her into his arms, kiss her, taste her…

"You're staring, Watson."

He blinked and snapped his gaze from her breasts, rare heat hitting his face. "Sorry. You look nice."

"Thanks." She raised her eyebrows and nodded toward his chest. "So do you."

He smiled. "Why don't we go inside? It's way too hot out here."

He led her through the back door of his workshop, into his small garden and the back of the house. He pushed open the door and took her through the conservatory into the kitchen. Grateful he'd cleared up after dropping Olivia at school, he walked to the sink and put his drink can down on the drainer to wash his hands. It suddenly mattered to him that Tori didn't think him a slob. The few times he'd seen her, she'd been immaculately dressed, classy and wearing, what looked to be, very expensive heels. Her gorgeous hair was always just right too, not a strand out of place.

He couldn't imagine a woman like her would be interested in a guy who lived like a tramp—and he wanted her interested.

He glanced over his shoulder. She looked around the room, her intelligent green eyes taking everything in at lightning speed. He turned back to the sink. The last woman he'd brought inside his house had been his last date…over a year before. With that date, he hadn't been overly concerned whether or not she liked his house, but with Tori, it unexpectedly mattered.

He wanted her to feel safe here. Protected.

Yanking a towel from the hook beside him, Mark coughed. "Do you want a coffee or anything?"

"No, I'm good." She met his gaze. "You have a nice kitchen."

"Thanks." He rehung the towel and nodded toward the living room. "Let's take a seat in there and you can tell me our plan of action."

She walked ahead of him into the living room and once again, Mark became entirely aware of his surroundings. He cast his gaze over the framed photos above the fireplace, on the walls and shelves. Lauren with her arm around Olivia, Lauren, and him snapped mid-kiss, Lauren, him, and Olivia on holiday…

When Tori walked to the fireplace and picked up a picture of him, Lauren and Olivia sitting outside a country pub the summer Lauren had died, he stiffened. Tori turned and smiled softly. "Is this your wife?"

Mark nodded, protectiveness seeping through him that a female other than Olivia touched one of his treasured photos. "Yes."

"She's beautiful."

"Thank you." Mark walked to the couch and sat. "Do you want sit down?"

"Sure." She replaced the photo and took the armchair beside him, crossing her bare legs. "Do you miss her? Your wife?"

"Every day."

She nodded and stared toward the picture.

Mark studied her profile, suddenly wanting to know what she thought and felt about his admission. Did it matter to her that he missed Lauren?

She faced him. "I did some research on you."

He leaned back. "Guess I deserve it after looking into your history."

"After the way your wife died, it's no wonder you're having such a hard time loosening up with Olivia. You're scared of losing your daughter too, aren't you?"

"Yes." He swiped his hand over his face. "She's growing up fast. I should be proud of her need for independence. Should like that she wants to do her own thing and make her own friends, but…"

She uncrossed her legs to lean closer. She reached for his hand where it lay on the arm of the sofa. "But what?"

His heart stumbled from the first skin-to-skin contact with her. He looked into her beautiful green eyes. "But I'm not. I want to know where Olivia is and who she's with twenty-four-seven. What kind of loving father does that?"

She gave a wry smile. "Most, in my experience." She squeezed his fingers before releasing his hand and shifting back into the armchair. "There's nothing wrong with wanting to protect her. After I was taken, my dad turned into a one-man army. He wanted to know who I was with and where I was going until I moved out of home at the grand old age of twenty-two."

He smiled. "I bet you loved his attention. Not."

She laughed softly. "I always knew his heart was in the right place, but I think his fears for me perpetuated mine instead of allaying them." Her smile dissolved and she looked deep into his eyes. "She's only eleven, but Olivia will grow up. You need to tread carefully with her or she'll rebel against that big ole heart of yours."

He clenched his jaw. "I'm trying but now…with Abby gone…it's made my need to keep Olivia safe stronger than ever. Until Abby's found, until she's back with her parents where she belongs…until the bastard who took her is behind bars, I can't relax. I have to have a part in finding her."

"You already have." She placed her forearms on her thighs, her fingers clasped tightly together. "When I saw Abby get into that car she was alone. No one else was around. What I can't figure out, in hindsight, was why? Was she let out a minute or two earlier than the rest of the kids? Did someone escort her to the gate and tell her to approach the man who took her? Plus…" Anger glittered in her gaze. "Principal White told the police the last time she saw Abby she was getting her things together in the classroom, ready to leave for the day. It's impossible that nobody saw her between then and when I saw her shoved into that car."

"You think the principal is lying? That she saw Abby leave the school?"

"I don't know and that's what I want you to find out. If she's telling the truth, something must have happened between the time Abby left the classroom to when she left the school building." Her eyes widened with certainty. "I swear to you, Abby was entirely alone when she was taken. Not a single parent or child was beside, behind or in front of her. No one. The police also seem to think she was carrying a book bag, which I know she wasn't. It doesn't make sense."

"I agree. I'll call the principal and ask if I can come to speak to her about the bureau."

"So you trust what I'm saying? You believe Abby was completely alone? That she didn't have a bag?"

"Of course. Why wouldn't I?"

She sighed and pushed some fallen hair from her eyes. "Because all night I've been asking myself if I was mistaken. What if I saw or missed something important, but I'm sure there was no one else around. I'm sure of it."

This time *he* took her hand and looked deep into her eyes, needing to take the fear and vulnerability from her gaze. "There was no one else there and she didn't have a bag. I've barely known you five minutes, but what I do know about you is enough to convince me you look at the world a whole lot deeper and more intensely than the rest of us. Trust what you saw. I do."

Her gaze dropped to his mouth before she lifted her eyes to his. "Thank you."

The temptation to kiss her whispered through his mind and Mark slipped his hand from hers, leaning back in his seat before he made a really bad error of judgment and did something that would send her running for the door.

He inhaled. "So, I guess I'll speak to Principal White asap."

She nodded. "One way or the other she knows more than she realizes or otherwise, what she does know she's keeping quiet about."

The funky, tinny beat of a Bruno Mars track burst from inside Tori's purse and she pulled out her phone. Pressing talk, she held the phone to her ear. "DCI Thornhill, how can I help you?" She closed her eyes and stood, fisting her hand on her hip. "No, go ahead. I can talk."

Mark ran his gaze over Tori's turned back, lower over the curve of her backside to her long, shapely calves, slim ankles and feet encased in black and white stilettos. His attraction soared and he snapped his gaze to Lauren's picture on top of the TV.

He held his wife's gaze as she grinned back at him. For the first time since she died, he could've sworn Lauren laughed at him the way she did whenever she knew what he was thinking. He waited for the shame at being busted...and ended up smiling instead.

"He's in Menorca? Are you sure?"

Mark flicked his gaze to Tori as she turned around and locked her angry gaze on him. His smile vanished.

"Yes, Inspector. No, of course not. Yes, I understand. Thank you." She jabbed the end call button and pushed the fallen hair from her brow. "Damn it."

Mark frowned. "Who's in Menorca?"

Her eyes glistened with unshed tears. "Brian Appleton. He's exactly where he should be."

Standing, he closed the space between them. "Well, that's good, isn't it?"

"Yes. No. I don't know." A tear rolled over her cheek, and she angrily swiped at it. "I could've sworn... I was sure..." She met his eyes. "I thought he was back. I thought he was back and hoped it was me he really wanted and not Abby. But now..."

"Hey, it's all right." He pulled her into his arms, relieved when she didn't pull away. He rested his chin on her head. "It's going to be all right."

"You don't know that. Nobody does."

Mark pulled his lips tightly together. She was right. Nobody knew what would happen next or if the faceless monster would strike again soon. The only thing Mark knew for sure is the abductor wouldn't get Olivia and he wouldn't get Tori.

Not on his watch.

His tightened his hold around Tori and slowly, tentatively, she circled his waist with her arms and held tight too.

Chapter Eight

Tori tossed her purse onto her desk and sat, drawing her wheeled chair forward to her laptop. She typed in Brian Appleton's name and scrolled through his past, desperate to learn something about his present.

Biting her bottom lip, she scanned the data but found nothing to indicate where he was now. Thornhill had confirmed Appleton was in Menorca, but she knew with as much certainty as any other journalist that, on any given day, there were over a hundred or more offenders lost to the authorities.

Staring blindly ahead, Tori leaned back in her chair and gripped the edge of her desk.

Abby's abduction couldn't have been opportunistic. A pedophile attempting a random snatching would not do so outside a school's gates. The chances of him or her being seen and apprehended were too high. Which further proved Abby's kidnapper must have been certain she would come out of those school gates alone.

Tori glanced at the onscreen clock on her computer.

Ten past three.

Abby had now been missing for forty-eight hours. She hoped Mark had called Principal White and managed to arrange a meeting with her later today.

Time slipped by too quickly—not that Abby would

be feeling that way.

Nausea coated Tori's throat and she pushed up from her chair. She stalked across the office toward the staff kitchen. It was time to dig deeper. She walked into the kitchen to find Cally and staff photographer, Greg Falmer, huddled closely together by the coffee machine.

She cleared her throat. "Mind if I get myself some coffee?"

They leapt apart and Tori resisted the urge to smile.

Cally smiled, her brown eyes wide with innocence. "We were just talking."

"Uh-huh." Tori grabbed a cup, jabbed her fingers over the buttons of the coffee machine and waited for her latte. "So, as you two seem to be getting along better and better these days, how about joining forces with me on something?"

Greg leaned against the opposite counter, his tall, lean frame topping Tori's five feet six inches by good half a foot. "What's up?"

She pulled her coffee from the machine and picked up a packet of sugar, flicking it back and forth with her finger. "What's up is I am getting nowhere on the Abby Brady story. I want you two to look into something for me." She ripped open the sugar and emptied it into her cup. Leaning across the counter, she grabbed a wooden stirrer. When she turned, Cally watched her with puppy-like eagerness, whereas Greg looked his usual skeptical self. "Well?" Tori arched her eyebrow. "Will you help me?"

Cally nodded, her eyes bright. "Of course. What do you want us to do?"

"You do know I'm a photographer, not a journalist,

right?" Greg crossed his arms. "Can't see how I can help with anything."

"I'm just asking for an extra pair of eyes and ears here, Greg."

He shrugged. "But—"

"Greg…" Cally laid her hand on his arm and looked adoringly into his eyes. "If you won't do as Tori asks, then will you consider doing it for me? Please?"

Tori fought a grimace as Greg turned to a lapdog in front of her eyes. His shoulders slumped and his gaze lingered hungrily on Cally's mouth. "Sure."

Cally turned to Tori and smiled. "We're all yours."

"Good." Tori stirred her coffee and sipped. "Did you find a list of Abby's classmates?"

"Yes. It's on my desk."

"Excellent. I want you to split the list and each take half. Call every parent. Introduce yourself. Say you're trying to piece together a picture of Abby's last movements. A few may slam the phone straight down, but hopefully, half a dozen or so will be willing to talk to you. I want you to ask them if their child saw Abby leave before the end of class, or if they left the school building with her."

"And that's relevant, why?" Greg dumped the remainder of his coffee in the sink.

"I'm not entirely sure, but I know it matters somehow. While you're chatting with the parents, I'm going to try and set up a meeting with Abby's mum and dad."

The brightness in Cally's eyes faded to concern. "Do you think they'll talk to you?"

"I don't know." Tori pushed away from the counter. "But I have to try."

"But…" Cally cast a worried look at Greg.

Tori frowned. "But what?"

"Shouldn't you be leaving the parents to the police? Why would you want them to pin their hopes on you finding Abby?"

"Why not? I *am* hoping to find her."

"But you're not the police, Tori." Her gaze turned somber. "This could be dangerous. Why would you want to get that involved?"

Irritation rippled through her and Tori gripped her coffee cup. "I saw her being taken, Cally. I was involved from the moment Abby was shoved inside a car right in front of us." Tori walked toward the open kitchen door and turned back. "I'll find her and when I do, the bastard who took her will know it was me who put his slimy ass behind bars."

Tori stormed from the room, Cally and Greg's stares boring like bullet holes into her back. It was time for them to either be in the investigation or out. There could be no in between.

They didn't need to know about her past, to know how personal this case was to her, but they needed to do *something* to help.

She sat at her desk and pulled her phone from her bag. Mark had said he'd text her when he had secured a meeting with Principal White.

Her phone was void of any such text.

Mumbling a curse, Tori pulled up a search on Abby's parents. She located the street address and thumbed it into her phone. She didn't think for one minute Mr. and Mrs. Brady would be alone. At the very least they'd been accompanied by a police liaison officer—who would be within his or her rights to slam the door in Tori's face if she turned up at the Brady house unannounced.

Tori tapped her phone against her bottom lip and made a snap decision.

She dialed, shoving her uncertainty she was doing the right thing into submission.

"Barlington Police Station. Sergeant Collins speaking. How may I help you?"

Tori leaned her elbow on the desk, her gaze scanning back and forth over the Bradys' address. "Sergeant Collins, this is Tori Peterson. I wonder if I might have another word with Inspector Thornhill? It's regarding the Abby Brady case."

"I'll see if he can take your call."

Pleased the sergeant hadn't vetoed her request, Tori waited. Classical music filled her ear for a few moments before the phone clicked.

"Miss Peterson, DCI Thornhill. How can I help?"

Tori took a deep breath and pushed forward with her request. "As you've confirmed Brian Appleton is still out of the country, I feel reassured he has nothing to do with Abby's disappearance, but I wonder if you might give me authority to interview Mr. and Mrs. Brady?"

"Absolutely not."

She closed her eyes. "But I have a good idea of what they'll be going through right now and—"

"Then you know talking to a reporter is the last thing they'll want. If nothing else is uncovered in the coming hours, Mr. and Mrs. Brady will have the option of whether or not they wish to conduct a public appeal. You will hear what they have to say there and then, not before."

Tori opened her eyes. "Inspector—"

"The last thing I want is for the media to stir up an influx of calls giving false sightings which will take my officers away from acting on substantiated follow-ups."

"I understand, but if I share my story with them, they might be willing to talk to me. I might not want the public knowing I was the last person to see Abby, but I want her parents to know and have the opportunity to ask me anything they want. It's the least I can do."

"You have my every sympathy for what happened to you, and I understand how upsetting for you this kidnapping must be, but you're a journalist. A journalist who seems intent on drawing wasteful conclusions by clutching at straws to connect your experience to Abby's. I'm sorry, Miss Peterson, but so far anything you've told me hasn't helped. So unless you have anything concrete, I do not expect to hear from you again."

The line went dead.

"Damn it." Tori jabbed the end call button and tossed the phone onto her desk.

Thornhill was perfectly in his rights to lose his patience. She had no evidence she was meant to see Abby snatched; the similarities in their home lives and looks could be purely coincidental. Yet, those two things were enough to evoke a painful and gnawing dread in Tori's stomach and a terrifying fear in her heart.

If she was to blame for what had happened to Abby…

Tori closed her eyes. She'd never get over it.

Mark might not have dismissed her theories as crazy, but who was to say he hadn't placated her for his own irrational needs? His deep and protective love for his daughter was clear in his eyes and words. It was probably that adoration that drew Tori toward him. His over-protection of Olivia was no worse than Tori's ridiculousness that evil lingered behind the smile of practically every man she'd risked getting close to for the last sixteen years.

For better or worse, she couldn't help thinking hers and Mark's paths had crossed at the school for a reason. For the first time in a long time, the idea of getting to know a man better didn't fill her with the urge to run a hundred miles per hour in the opposite direction.

Opening her eyes, Tori stood and grabbed her phone and bag. As she passed Cally and Greg on her way from the office, Tori shook her head at the two of them huddled together in deep conversation. Neither looked in any kind of hurry to start on the task she'd given them.

If a girl wanted something done, she was better off doing it herself.

****

Mark accepted the glass of wine Principal White offered him and leaned further into one of the three overstuffed sofas in her sun-filled conservatory. She sat beside him and smiled. "Cheers."

"Cheers." They touched glasses and drank before Mark put his glass on the low table in front of them. "I'm sorry to disturb your evening to talk about a bureau."

She smiled, her brown eyes watching him over the rim of her glass as she took another sip. "Not at all. It was nice to hear from you. I can't wait to see it."

"It's going well. I just wanted to ask if you wanted

110

it stained? If you do, I have some sample shades, colors, etc. Like I said, we could've discussed this over the phone—"

"Not at all. I wanted to see you." She put her glass next to his on the table. "We haven't seen each other since poor Abby was taken. Such a sad, sad time for the entire school. Have you seen Miss Peterson since it happened?"

Mark frowned. "I've seen her once or twice. Why?"

Her cheeks darkened and she huffed a laugh. "I detected a little *frisson* between you and I've only ever seen you alone since your wife's tragic passing. I didn't think you were dating, that's all."

The glint of flirtation in her eyes would've been visible from Mars, but he would take his pain for Abby. He smiled. "I started dipping my toe in the dating pool about a year ago. I must admit the dates have been few and far between, but at least my eyes are open to possibility again."

"And Miss Peterson has opened them wider still?"

"She's…interesting. Yes."

"Have you asked her out?"

"Not yet."

"But you will?"

Mark shrugged. "Maybe."

Her smile strained. "Well, that *is* good news."

She lifted her glass and the liquid trembled as she raised it to her lips.

Mark shifted in his seat, slightly uncomfortable with her line of questioning. Was the principal interested in him romantically? That was the last thing he expected, but if he had to keep her onside for any chance of extracting information about Abby, so be it.

Mark picked up his wine and lifted his ankle to the opposite knee. "As for Abby Brady, and considering the lack of information the police have provided so far, I can't help thinking all of us who were there that day should be doing more."

She took another sip of her wine and returned it to the table. "I agree. If there was anything else I could tell the police, I would."

"Where did you last see Abby?"

She sighed. "In her classroom. She was gathering her things, getting ready to leave. If only I had seen her leave, escorted her onto the playground…" She shook her head. "It's all so impossible."

Mark searched her face and eyes, but he didn't detect even a whisper of deceit. He frowned. "I've been picking Olivia up from the school for years now, Principal Whi—"

"Karen, please." She smiled. "We're out of the school playground now. It's adults-only time."

The meteor-sized glint flashed in her gaze again and Mark stifled a grimace. "In that case, call me Mark. 'Mr. Bolton' always makes me feel as though I'm in trouble."

She grinned. "I can imagine you could be very troublesome to a few women, Mark."

He smiled and picked up his wine. "As I was saying, I pick Olivia up from school most days and you're usually in the playground. You weren't the day Abby was taken. I had to send another dad into the school to find you."

"Unfortunately, I was delayed by another teacher."

"I can imagine your absence that afternoon plays

on your mind. I know everything about that day plays on mine."

"It does. I got caught up in conversation with the vice principal. In fact, I was talking to him when Mr. Williams, the man you sent into the school, found me. Of course, I raced outside as soon as he told me Abby was missing. I didn't think for one moment she'd been abducted. Who has ever heard of such a thing happening in Barlington?"

"It's a first." Mark scrambled for another question; something else to say to find out if the principal saw Abby leave alone as Tori suspected. "I can't help thinking Abby was targeted by the kidnapper. This wasn't a random snatching."

"What makes you think so?"

"I'm not sure. Is she quiet? Unassuming? What are her friends like?"

"That's a lot of questions." She laughed and drained her glass. "Would you like a top up?"

He put his hand over his glass. "Driving, unfortunately."

"That is unfortunate. Maybe we'll find the time to finish a whole bottle together some day."

He forced a smile. "Maybe we will. So Abby's friends—"

"Do we really have to talk about this? My nerves have barely recovered from the shock of it all. Abby is a nice girl, a trusting, happy girl. She's known for her red hair, of course." She scowled. "Children can be so cruel. Yet, with Abby, I feel it enhances her looks rather than diminishing them."

Suspicion skittered over the surface of his skin at the principal's surprised tone and derogatory observation. "I can't see how having red hair could ever diminish a child's looks."

"Well, we all have our preferences of hair color, don't we?" She ran her gaze over his hair. "I prefer dark. Considering your interest in Miss Peterson, I can only assume red is a favorite of yours."

"Maybe it is."

"Then I apologize if you felt I was disparaging to poor Abby…or Miss Peterson. I was merely responding to your questions and I assumed the scale of Abby's popularity came into your ponderings too. She was teased somewhat about her hair but otherwise, a perfectly happy child from a perfectly happy home."

Mark finished his wine. "Well, good. Let's hope she's found and back in that home sooner rather than later." He stood. "I'd better go."

"Oh, but you haven't shown me your color samples." She stood. "You have them with you, don't you?" Distrust darkened her gaze before she blinked and it was replaced with the glint once more. "Unless you had another motivation for coming here this evening?"

"No, just the samples." Mark lifted his jacket from the arm of the sofa and reached into the inside pocket. "Here you go."

She hesitated before taking the array of cards. "Thank you. I'll have a look at these and let you know. Maybe…" She blushed. "We could discuss them over a meal sometime?"

"Maybe we could." His cheeks ached with strain of his smile. "But right now, I have to go. I don't want to be late picking up Olivia from her friend's house."

"Of course."

She brushed past him, and Mark exhaled as he followed her through the house to the front door. She opened it and gazed up at him. "Goodnight, Mark."

He nodded. "Good night, Princ...Karen."

She laughed and Mark turned to make a quick exit. He tried hard to casually open his car door and not bash the lock into place once he'd slid into the seat.

He turned the ignition, gave the principal a departing wave and sent up silent gratitude that he'd got out of her house with his jeans still on.

Chapter Nine

The ringing of her doorbell the following morning jolted Tori out of her stunned stupor. She dropped the letter that had arrived moments before onto the kitchen table, her hands shaking. Forcing one foot in front of the other, she walked through the house to the front door and checked through the peephole.

Mark.

She pulled the door open. No matter her relief it was him, she could neither smile nor speak.

He frowned as he stepped forward, concern darkening his gaze. "What is it? What's happened?"

She crossed her arms around her shaking body and turned away from him to return to the kitchen. Vaguely aware of the front door closing behind her, Tori forced her feet forward until she sat at the kitchen table. She inched away from the letter as though it was contaminated.

Mark entered the room, hesitated on the threshold. "Tori? What's going on?"

She lifted her gaze. Despite, or maybe because of her current state of vulnerability, she indulged in a gentle perusal of his handsome face. The guy had a certain something that made her insides soft as though she were in the throes of a teenage crush, rather than being a grown and necessarily hardened woman. His bright, blue eyes could darken in anger or glint with laughter. His lips and strong jaw…

*Don't do this. Don't use sex to mask the pain.*

She snapped her gaze to his. "Brian Appleton is back."

"What?"

Tears blurred her vision. "He's haunting me, tormenting me. Maybe he brought you into my life to give me hope of something more than just working day in, day out. Maybe he won't ever let me be happy."

"What are you talking about?" Mark came closer and dropped to his haunches beside her. He laid his hand on her thigh. "What's happened?"

"He wrote to me." She tilted her head toward the table and Mark followed her gaze.

His hand slid from her thigh and he reached for the letter, but the heat of his touch remained on her skin like an invisible comfort. He stood and Tori stared at her hands, clasped tightly together in her lap.

"When did you get this?" Mark demanded. "Did he come here? Have you seen him?"

"It was amongst the mail." She lifted her head. "There's no stamp, no postmark."

He looked at the letter again. "What is this? He talks about you being his wife. Dressing you, touching you. This is sick. Have you called the police?"

"No. Not yet."

"Why not?"

"I don't know what I'm supposed to do with it. Is it him? Is he back? Thornhill was adamant Brian Appleton was in Menorca. What if someone else sent it? What if they know about my history?"

His eyes blazed with anger. "You can't think like that."

"How can I not?" Hysteria threatened and Tori closed her eyes, her body strangely numb. "He's back and he's taken Abby because of me." She opened her eyes. "I knew it all along and the police didn't believe me."

He tossed the letter onto the table. "Come here."

She stared at his open arms.

The need to be held by this strong, capable and loving man was too strong to resist. Tori stood and, for the first time in years, allowed someone else to hold her together. To comfort her. Her body trembled and her heart pounded. The memories, the long ago smells and sights that had enveloped her for the previous minutes vanished.

Mark pressed a lingering kiss to the top of her head and Tori closed her eyes. She inhaled the masculine, heady scent of him and slowly relaxed.

"We need to take the letter to the inspector." His lips brushed her hair again. "We have to let him read it and then maybe he'll listen to you. God damn it, I'll make him listen."

Panic for Mark's safety swelled inside her, and Tori pulled from his arms. She looked deep into his eyes, willing him to listen. "I don't want you involved in this. Not anymore. You have Olivia to think about. Whether this is Appleton, a copycat or whoever, you can't expose yourself or your daughter to whatever might happen next. It's too dangerous."

"Listen to me." He gripped her hands. "I'm going nowhere until we catch this bastard and bring Abby back to her parents. Don't push me away, Tori. Please. I like you. I think you like me. When this is all over—"

"When this is all over?" She snatched her hands

from his and pushed her fingers into her hair. "When this is all over, who knows what kind of state Abby, her parents, even we will be in? We have absolutely no idea what Appleton has planned. What if someone gets killed…"

"If, Tori, *if* this is Appleton."

Tears burned behind her eyes. If she lost Mark's belief now after she'd seen understanding and respect in his eyes, it would send her full throttle back to the shell she'd lived in alone for what seemed like forever. She never should have opened up to him, should not have allowed even the tiniest part of her armored guard down. This was what happened. Trusting and losing focus only exposed a person to deeper and deeper pain.

She dropped her hands and stepped back. "You should go."

"No. You're not shutting me out. It's too late for that. I want to be here. I want to be with you and I want to find Abby."

He came toward her, his gaze soft and resting on her mouth. Tori's heart thundered with fear, yet her blood heated with a need so raw, so intense, she couldn't stem her desire to be up close and personal with him.

She had no idea who reached for whom, but then she was in his arms, one hand gripping the hardened ridge of his shoulder, the other tangled in the slightly too-long hair at the nape of his neck. His lips were firm against hers, his tongue demanding and hot in her mouth. He pulled her tight against the wall of his chest, her breasts pushing almost painfully against solid muscle.

The hard, long length of him pressed deliciously

against her abdomen, and she trembled with the desperate need to have him inside her. Hot, hungry and hers for a single moment in time, with the rest of the world and all its terrifying evil far, far away.

His lips pressed into her neck and Tori tipped her head back, holding him there as he nipped and groaned against her skin. She fumbled her fingers over the buttons on his shirt, desperate for the feel of his skin beneath her palms. Adrenaline pumped and determination roared, joining them in a frenzied bout of need that was as dangerous as it was sexy.

She stepped back. What were they doing? This could end in disaster, yet there was nothing she wanted more in that moment than Mark.

He stared deep into his eyes. The temptation to stop this from happening edged into her mind and, before it could take hold, Tori gripped the hem of her shirt and yanked it from her skirt. Pulling it over her head, she dropped it to the floor. His gaze slid hungrily over her satin-covered breasts before he snapped open the remaining buttons on his shirt and tore it from his shoulders.

She pulled on the tie holding her wrap skirt in place and it fell to her feet. "If you want to be with me through this, I want you to make love to me. Now."

His jaw clenched as indecision warred in his eyes.

Frustration rippled over her skin and insecurity into her heart. She flicked her gaze over his magnificent chest and up to his eyes, walked closer until his breath teased her lashes. "Are you worried that taking me here, like this, is the right thing to do to someone who has gone through what I have? If you are, please, don't think."

Challenge and determination burned in his gaze. "I'm not thinking that. I'm thinking if I make love to her now, will she let me touch her again? Or will the act make her think of the intimacy and how it's too much, too soon, sending her running a million miles in the other direction?"

Tori swallowed. How could he know so much about her so soon?

"Will you run, Tori?"

Her heart beat fast. Would she? Could she stay with this man...even for a little while? He'd come into her life under the worst circumstances possible, yet there was something about him that pulled at her.

She shook her head. "I won't run. At least, not yet."

He ran a finger down her cheek, his eyes full of admiration and desire, lower over her jaw to her collarbone and the deep crevice between her breasts. Tori trembled. "Mark…"

She gasped when he gripped her waist and lifted her off her feet into his arms. She locked her ankles at the base of his spine as he covered her mouth with his, his deliciously demanding tongue warring with hers.

He lifted her onto the kitchen counter before discarding his shoes and socks and pulling his wallet from the back pocket of his jeans. With his gaze on hers, he extracted a condom packet. He held it between his teeth and pulled off his boxers. With their gazes locked, he ripped open the packet and sheathed himself.

Stepping close, he stood between her open legs. He kissed her as he snapped the strings on either side of her panties. His fingers roughly circled her clitoris, causing sensation after sensation to rip through her body. She dropped her mouth open and dug her nails into his shoulders, holding on as the tremors whispered and grew.

She looked into his eyes and her heart kicked with longing to trust this man…to be with him with every part of her.

He briefly smiled before his eyes grew dark with hunger. Slipping his hands behind her knees, he yanked her forward, caressed her, teased her and as she readied, he thrust deep inside her.

"Oh, God." Tori squeezed her eyes shut as he filled every part of her.

She clung to him as they moved faster, harder, over and over until her orgasm crashed through her and Tori gratefully rode wave after fantastic wave.

His body stiffened and his teeth clenched as he shuddered his release and closed his eyes.

Slowly, softly, Tori gained her equilibrium as his eyes flickered open.

She reached up and trailed her hand over his shoulder, lower to test the span of his biceps. Her stomach knotting, she smiled. "I knew there was something special about you, Mark Bolton."

His answering laugh was all she needed to hear.

****

Mark waited in his car as Tori locked her front door. He cast a slow study over her turned back, lower to her butt, and down over her shapely calves. His cock stirred awake once more and he snatched his eyes front. What was happening to him? His libido had been buried under five years of memories and impossibilities all wrapped up in a Lauren-shaped box. But now? He turned as Tori approached the car, her sexy green gaze on his.

Now, he wanted to forget Thornhill for a little longer, grab hold of Tori and carry her upstairs to her bedroom. This time, make love to her as she deserved. Slowly awakening every inch of her.

She opened the door and slid into the passenger seat. "I'm still not sure you coming with me to the station is a good idea."

Forcing the erotic thoughts and wants into submission, he turned the ignition. "If Thornhill sends me away, I'll come back later and pick you up. I'm not coming with you to cause you hassle. I'm coming to help."

She looked to the window beside her, her silence revealing her uncertainty.

After their impromptu lovemaking, he'd made them coffee while Tori disappeared upstairs. She'd return to the kitchen with her long, red hair neatly brushed into a ponytail, make-up freshened and smelling sexy as hell under a mist of resprayed perfume. Mark had thought about touching her again, but one look at her concentrated gaze told him the fun and games were over and her head was back in full mission mode of finding Abby.

The guilt he'd felt had been humbling…and focusing.

He gripped the steering wheel. "What do you think Thornhill's going to say about the letter?"

She sighed. "I've no idea, but he can't dismiss it. There can't be any more doubt that my abduction and Abby's is connected. I asked him to give me permission to speak to her parents and he refused. I hope this letter will let me do that, at least."

"And if he refuses again?"

"I'll go anyway."

He glanced at her. She stared through the windshield, her body tense. The temptation to touch her, to reassure her, was too much and he covered her clenched hands with one of his.

She faced him. "What?"

"I just wanted to hold your hand. Is that okay?"

She nodded, her shoulders ever so slightly relaxing as she curled her fingers around his. Relief unfurled inside him. "So, do we have a plan of action with the good inspector or do we just storm the station?"

"We storm the station. I think the desk sergeant might have a soft spot for me. Getting past him should be easy. Getting Thornhill to listen to me is another matter entirely." She exhaled. "How did it go with Principal White?"

He glanced at her. "Not as I expected."

"Meaning?"

"Meaning I think the woman would've stripped me naked and rode me to America and back given half the chance."

She laughed. "Think a lot of yourself, don't you?"

He lifted an eyebrow at her. "Says Miss Prim over there."

She blushed. "She must've said something interesting throughout her seduction?"

"All I really got out of her was that she didn't see Abby leave the school. Oh, and she prefers dark hair over red."

"She said that?"

He shrugged. "She's kind of, I don't know, intense. Yet seemingly great with kids. I've never had a problem with her when I've seen her with Olivia. Plus, I'm making her a bureau. If I thought she had me pegged as her next mission, or couldn't be trusted, I wouldn't have accepted work from her."

"Believe me, more often than not, it's the people in positions of authority we need to watch."

"And being a journalist, you've come across your fair share of abuses of power?"

"Yes, and it doesn't paint the world as a very nice or trustworthy place. Principal White knows more than she's saying. I'm sure of it."

Mark nodded. "I think you're right."

They travelled the rest of the distance to the station in silence, Mark pleased their hands only separated when driving the car made it necessary. As fearful as he was of the emotions tumbling through him, he wanted to at least try to see how Tori fit into his life. How she fit with Olivia. It was a huge step after feeling a loving, committed relationship would forever be out of his reach since Lauren. A huge, invisible barrier had stood between him and anything romantic, but he could definitely imagine spending more time getting to know Tori.

He pulled the car into the Barlington Police Station car park and killed the engine. Before he'd even taken the keys from the ignition, Tori grabbed her bag from the footwell and got out of the car. She stood outside and waited for him.

Mark got out of the car and their eyes briefly met before she headed up the station's front steps ahead of him. Trepidation tensed his muscles. He might be skidding along a probable Tori path of emotional destruction, but finding Abby came first above everything he might or might not be feeling.

He had to find Abby and the scum currently terrorizing the town before he had hell's chance of touching Olivia…or coming after Tori.

Chapter Ten

Tori had never been so aware of a man's proximity than she was of Mark's as she pushed open the station's doors and he walked inside behind her. Their impromptu sex lingered on her body and mind, making her wonder what had just happened. Had it meant anything to him? Had it meant anything to her? Uncertainty and insecurity pulsed through her. She had been fine on her own for so long. Surely they'd just reached for something tangible amidst an event that had roused their deepest fears?

She approached Sergeant Collins at the duty desk. All she knew for sure was that as warranted as Mark's fear was of anything happening to his daughter, his tender care of Olivia and his passion to help find Abby, made Tori's fear of evil lurking behind every male smile falter.

"Miss Peterson, you can't seem to stay away from here."

Tori blinked and gave a wry smile. "Believe me, Sergeant, I wish the circumstances were different and I had no reason to be here. It would fill my heart with joy to know Abby Brady is alive and well and moaning to her parents how she doesn't want to go to school today."

He flicked his gaze behind her. "And I see you've brought company."

Tori turned. Mark stared at the sergeant, his face impassive, if it weren't for the bright glint of determination in his eyes. She faced Sergeant Collins. "This is a friend of mine, Mark Bolton." She drew the letter she'd received that morning from her inside pocket. "I have something to show Inspector Thornhill. Is he here?"

Collins glanced at the letter. "Is he expecting you?"

"No, but this is important. I believe this letter is connected to Abby's case. It was delivered to my house this morning."

He held her gaze and lifted the phone beside him. He pressed a couple of buttons. "Inspector Thornhill, sir, I have Tori Peterson here to see you. She claims to have a letter connected to the Abby Brady case. Yes, sir. She has a Mr. Bolton with her." He looked at Mark. "And your connection, sir? Other than being a friend of Miss Peterson's?"

Mark stepped up beside her. "I was the first person to help Miss Peterson when she ran onto the school playground after Abby was taken. Miss Peterson asked me to accompany her here."

Collins turned back to the phone. "He says he was the first person to approach Miss Peterson when she called in the abduction, sir. Yes, sir." He put down the phone and faced at Tori. "You can go on through." He looked to Mark. "But the inspector has asked you stay here."

"As you wish." He faced Tori. "Do you want me to wait?"

Unexpected sympathy for Mark twisted inside her. This case was significant to him. Maybe not to the depth it was to her, but significant all the same. She'd have the same pissed expression as Mark if she were so blatantly dismissed. "Why don't you go? As soon as I know more, I'll call you. I can just as easily walk to my office when I'm done."

"You'll be okay?"

She nodded. "I'll be okay."

He tossed Collins a glare before he faced her again. "Speak to you later then."

Mark pushed open the station doors and Tori waited for him to turn, wave, wink…anything to give her some indication he understood her asking him to leave was to save him from sitting around doing nothing and not misinterpret it as her rejecting his help.

But he only kept walking.

Turning around, Tori nodded to the sergeant, and he buzzed open the door leading deeper into the station. Alone once more, she walked along the dark hallway until she reached Inspector Thornhill's closed office door. Taking a deep breath, she knocked.

"Come in."

Tori entered the room. "Good morning, Inspector."

"Miss Peterson." He rose from his chair, his hand outstretched. "How are you today?"

She shook his hand. "As well as can be unexpected under the circumstances."

He waved her toward one of the visitors' chairs and resumed his seat behind his desk. The increased creases around his eyes illustrated all too clearly the level of his stress and lack of sleep. "I'm afraid nothing of use has come to light. I'll shortly be visiting the Bradys to see if they'll agree to a televised appeal later today. There have been no public sightings of Abby or further information."

Tori handed him the letter, fighting the reemergence of fear she'd felt when she'd first read it. "This might help. It arrived at my house this morning. No stamp or postmark. Whoever wrote this must have delivered it personally."

Frowning, the inspector took the letter and unfolded it. As he read the typed script, despite her efforts to remain calm, Tori's hands trembled. If he dismissed the letter out of hand, what then? For all her bravado when she'd been in the car with Mark, she had no idea of her next step if she had to continue this investigation alone.

"You do accept this letter can't be from Brian Appleton?" Thornhill lifted his gaze to hers. "He's definitely out of the country. I want you to be reassured of that." He looked to the letter again. "Are you the only person who's touched this?"

"Me and Mark Bolton."

"Your friend?"

She nodded.

"Right, well, in that case we'll need both yours and Mr. Bolton's fingerprints for elimination." He frowned. "It looks to be typed and printed on any standard home computer, but I'll send it to be analyzed to make sure the source can't be narrowed down."

"Why do you continue to dismiss Brian Appleton so easily as a suspect, Inspector? I don't understand." Frustrated, she shook her head. "Even if I was convinced he's where he's supposed to be, which I'm not, it states pretty clearly in that letter I was meant to see Abby taken. It proves her disappearance has something to do with me."

He carefully laid the letter on the desk and laced

his fingers, his gaze intense on hers. "How many people in Barlington know what happened to you?"

Tori's throat dried. Hadn't she subconsciously hoped the inspector said something to alleviate her fears that Brian Appleton could be back as irrational? "Unless anyone else has researched me, it's just you and Mark."

"You've known Mr. Bolton a long time?"

"Not at all. He found out about my past through his own endeavors. I didn't tell him."

The inspector arched an eyebrow. "What does *through his own endeavors* mean, exactly?"

Battling her embarrassment over how Mark had not only researched her, but she'd then gone on to have sex with him in her kitchen, Tori coughed and shifted further back in her seat. She forced her gaze on the inspector's. "He researched me. When I saw Abby taken, it brought everything back and that fear must have shown on my face when I ran shouting onto the playground about Abby. Mark is a very astute man. He worked out for himself that something else was going on with me."

"I see. And it's his astuteness that made you bring him with you today? That made you share the contents of this letter with him?"

"Yes."

"Why would you do that when you think you are somehow involved in this case? How well do you actually know Mr. Bolton?"

Her annoyance grew as Thornhill's clear accusation of her recklessness stabbed a little too close to being accurate. She lifted her chin and held his questioning gaze. "Mark is one of the good guys. You only have to see him with his daughter to know that he would never do anything to harm a child."

"You've known this man for less than a week, yet you trust him enough to allow him to follow you into a police station and learn more about you than anyone else? That seems pretty unorthodox to me considering your fears over Brian Appleton."

Her cheeks turned hot. Three days and she trusted Mark enough to have sex with him. It was a phenomenon to her, let alone DCI Thornhill.

She lifted her shoulders in feigned nonchalance. "I'm not here to talk about Mark Bolton. I'm here to talk about that letter and what it means. I hope it will be enough for you to at least accept you need me on this investigation. I could come with you when you speak to Mr. and Mrs. Brady. Help answer their questions. Convince them a public appeal is worth trying. Whoever wrote that letter, whether or not it was Brian Appleton—"

"It's not Appleton, Miss Peterson. He's in Menorca."

The inspector's warning tone poked at Tori's nerves. "Maybe he is, but in the letter he says, *you will understand why it had to be you who discovered the coincidences. I don't want anyone else involved, but you and me.* That, in itself, should be enough for you to see I need to be involved."

He stared, his dark gray eyes assessing.

Tori resisted the urge to fidget, to snap, yell, anything to make him listen. She curled her hands tightly together in her lap.

"Okay, here's what we're going to do." He stood and came around the desk, leaning against it in front of her. "You're going to tell me, all over again, everything you remember about Abby's abduction, and every similarity between her case and yours. Everything you know, sense or think. That done, I'll decide whether or not you get to talk to the Bradys. If, and it's a big if, you were meant to witness the abduction, how did the kidnapper know you would be there?"

"I don't know."

"Do you collect your niece regularly?"

"Once, maybe twice, a month."

He nodded. "Which means someone had to have known you would be picking her up that day. Who would've known that?"

"My sister and her husband. A couple of my colleagues, Georgia's teacher…" Dread struck deep in Tori's stomach and she inhaled. "Do you think this could be someone who knows me now? Not someone from back then, when what happened to me, happened."

"It's something we should consider."

Tori closed her eyes. "I really don't want to have to do that. My trust in people is already paper thin."

An hour later, Tori stood beside Inspector Thornhill outside the Bradys' beautiful four-bedroom detached house, its latticed windows glinting beneath the midday sun and its dark red front door gleaming. She pressed her hand to the butterflies in her stomach. For all her insistence she speak to Mr. and Mrs. Brady, now she was here, standing on the edge of the gray paved pathway leading to their front door, nerves leapt in her stomach, making her underlying nausea worse.

Thornhill stared toward the house, his jaw tight. "I'll lead the questioning. You do not, under any circumstances, bombard the parents with your ordeal when they are slap-bang in the middle of their own. We need to approach this professionally and with the sole purpose of getting Abby safely home." He looked at her. "Okay?"

Annoyance simmered in a ball of heat in Tori's stomach as she held his stare. Did he think her callous or just plain stupid? "Of course."

He brushed past her toward the door, leaving Tori to follow on behind.

Even though she'd seen photographs of Mr. Brady, the man who opened the door and looked directly into Inspector Thornhill's face was an almost macabre version of who Michael Brady had been before his daughter was kidnapped. He was ashen, his hair seemingly grayer, dirtier and more unkempt than the previously highly groomed, impeccably turned out lawyer smiling widely in his website picture.

Thornhill held out his hand. "Mr. Brady, might we come in?"

Proffered hand ignored, Mr. Brady stared hard at the inspector. "Do you have news? Have you found her?"

Tori closed her eyes and dropped her chin. Did she really have the right to be here? Would her words do anything to help this man? His wife? God only knew if their little girl would ever come home again. Would it really mean anything to Mr. and Mrs. Brady that Tori had once been taken? How would they react when they learned her abduction could be connected to Abby's?

She forced herself to meet Mr. Brady's stare.

Mr. and Mrs. Brady could blame her for Abby's disappearance and she would shoulder their condemnation. They could tell her to fix this, to bring Abby home and she'd promise them she would do everything in her power to do just that...because she wouldn't rest until she damn well had.

"We have no further news as yet, sir." Thornhill's voice cut through her thoughts. "Might we come in?"

Mr. Brady stood back, pulling the door wide, his previously tall frame seeming to shrink. Swallowing hard, Tori followed the inspector inside.

When she was face to face with Mr. Brady, she touched his arm. "I am so sorry you are having to go through this, Mr. Brady. Really, so very sorry."

He merely nodded, not asking her who she was or why she was there.

Helplessness washed over her and Tori slipped her hand from his arm before following the inspector into a large living room. Sat on the black leather settee, Mrs. Brady looked like a tiny mouse perched, tense and wary.

She lifted her gaze to Tori's and her heart jerked as though a grief-filled bullet shot straight through flesh and bone. Mrs. Brady's gaze was desolate, empty and dark with such a heavy, eerie, paralysis that Tori struggled not to look to the carpet.

The soft murmurings of DCI Thornhill and Mr. Brady drifted through the room as Tori approached Mrs. Brady and slowly sat down beside her. "Mrs. Brady? I'm Tori Peterson. Do you remember me from the school?"

Susan Brady turned. "Who?"

"Tori Peterson." Had this poor woman blocked out everything that had happened the day Abby was taken? If she couldn't remember Tori, she wouldn't remember the slap or Mark gently cradling in her arms. Maybe it was better that way. Who was to say Tori's mother hadn't done the same thing sixteen years before?

Resisting the urge to take the other woman's hand, entirely unconvinced the gesture would be in any way welcomed, Tori cleared her throat. "I asked Inspector Thornhill if I could accompany him here this afternoon. I hope to be able to do something to help find Abby."

Mrs. Brady stared into Tori's eyes. "You're a police officer?"

"A journalist." Tori waited for the fall out, but nothing came from Susan Brady but her continued chilling, sedated staring. Tori took a deep breath. "I want to assure you I'm not here to bother you, Mrs. Brady."

"Everything has already been said. Over and over and over. Nothing changes. Abby still doesn't come home." She turned away. "Could you please leave?"

Tori looked at this mother's profile. The luminous beauty and pride that had shone from the pictures Tori had seen of Susan Brady with her children had faded into obscurity. Why couldn't she be here to tell this mother Abby had been found unharmed, or that she'd been taken by a mother bereft of her own child? A desperate woman who had taken Abby and gently cared for her before coming to her senses? Wasn't that the best scenario any parent could hope for under these terrifying circumstances?

Tori hesitated as the need to embark on the tentative retelling of her own ordeal in the hope her survival might give these horrified parents hope, surged to the surface. The inspector had asked her not to tell Mr. and Mrs. Brady anything without his say-so—Tori was here as a witness only as far as he was concerned. Tori swallowed. She had no idea what she'd come as…

Thornhill and Mr. Brady each took an armchair positioned on either side of the settee. She had no choice but to let the inspector lead this difficult conversation. He was the professional. She was the witness, the survivor.

Mr. Brady reached across and clasped his wife's rigid hand. "There's no more news, sweetheart. DCI Thornhill has asked Miss Peterson here to see if she can help us."

"She's a journalist."

"I know, darling, but—"

"Mrs. Brady?" Tori inched forward on the settee and stared into Mrs. Brady's eyes praying she trusted her, saw something in her gaze that might give this mother the courage to listen, even if she didn't want, or care to know, what Tori had to say. "I was taken many years ago by a man called Brian Appleton. He spoke to me outside my primary school, lured me into his car and took me to his house. He held me there for six days before the police came. A neighbor…" Her eyes stung with her tears as the weight of Thornhill's glare bore into her temple. "A neighbor reported something suspicious and the police came, Mrs. Brady. They came and I went home to my parents."

The silence was sudden and heavy.

"I'm sorry that happened to you, Miss Peterson." Susan Brady looked deep into Tori's eyes, a tear slipping seemingly unnoticed over her cheek. "Are you telling me you know Abby will be missing for four more days and then the police will find her? That they will bring her home?" She looked to her husband. "Is that what she's saying?"

"Mrs. Brady." The inspector cleared his throat and tossed Tori a cold look before his gaze softened and he looked at Susan Brady. "Miss Peterson hoped by sharing her own story, it might go some way to giving you hope we will get Abby home safely." He leaned forward, his elbows on his knees as he turned his hat between white-knuckled fingers. "I want to ask you a few more questions. You might say or remember something that could trigger a moment or memory in Miss Peterson's mind about her experience. Something that could be imperative to us finding Abby."

"But I…we've…told you everything." Susan faced her husband. "What else is there, Simon? What haven't we told them?" She slowly turned to look at Tori. "Did he hurt you? The man who took you?"

Tori's stomach clenched, denial screaming in her head. The words to comfort this woman—to lie to her—nipped and bit at her tongue. "He tried to. He tried really hard, but I could withstand a lot more than I ever thought possible. Abby will too. She's a strong girl, isn't she? Strong like her mum and dad." Tori gripped Mrs. Brady's hand. "My parents were like you both. Good, hard-working people, raising their daughters the best way they knew how. Caring for us, loving us and teaching us right from wrong. When I was taken, I knew I had to stay strong, no matter what. If I didn't, the man who took me would win. I think Abby will know that too."

The tiniest flicker of hope lit in Susan Brady's eyes. "She is strong. Really strong." She glanced at her husband. "She's more like Simon than me." Mr. Brady winked, the gesture twisting Tori's heart. "She'll know she needs to be strong."

Tori smiled and squeezed her hand. "Of course, she will."

The inspector shifted in his seat. "I want to ask you both if you can think of any person, no matter how little you know them, who might have caused you concern in the past. A person who maybe befriended you, rather than Abby. A colleague who asked just a little too often about your home life? Often these things give us little concern at the time but, in hindsight, our intuition tells us there was something in that person's manner, look or questions, that just didn't seem appropriate or wasn't entirely welcome."

Mr. Brady shook his head. "I can't think of anyone with an over-interest in my family or me. I've told you and I've told your colleagues, it can't be someone we know who has taken our daughter…it can't be."

Tori carefully watched Susan Brady. Her cheeks had changed from deathly pale to bright red, the skin at her neck shifting as she swallowed over and over. *She knows something. Talk to us. Talk to me.*

"There is someone." Mrs. Brady stared hard at Thornhill, her hands clasping and unclasping in her lap. "But I'm sure it's nothing."

The inspector stared. "Tell me."

"There's a father at Abby's dance class. He's…" She glanced at her husband, who watched her intently. "He's quite the bully. He considers his daughter the best at everything. He accuses other parents, including me, of not doing enough to move our children on in their practice."

Thornhill frowned. "Has he singled Abby out amongst the other children? Said more to you than he has other parents?"

Susan Brady shook her head. "I don't think so. He's equally as horrid to everyone."

Tori cast her mind back to how it came to light that Brian Appleton had befriended her father while they attended the same gym three times a week. The police finally managed to learn from Appleton that his obsession with Tori had begun when her father had taken her swimming one evening, sacrificing his usual gym session to spend time with his youngest daughter. The revelation had made her father irrationally shoulder the blame for Tori's kidnapping for a long time afterward.

"Would you consider him threatening?" Tori murmured the question aloud and the Bradys turned to look at her. "Do all the parents have the same reservations about him?"

"I think so, yes." Susan Brady glanced at her husband. "Simon hasn't met him. It's only me who takes Abby to dance class. Huw Valentine is strange. I suppose that's how I'd describe him. He's not strange looking or anything. Just an average looking man, but his manner, his choice of words are, I don't know…strange."

"Do you have any idea where Mr. Valentine lives, Mrs. Brady?" DCI Thornhill drew a notepad and pen from his breast pocket. "We will want to speak to him. Eliminate him from our enquiries."

"I'm certain he hasn't nothing to do with Abby being taken. I wouldn't want him to think I named him—"

"He won't. My officers will ensure it."

"I'm not sure which number house is Huw's, but I

know he lives on Starling Drive. I assume he'll be at work at this time of day."

Thornhill nodded. "Do you know where he works?"

"No."

As Mrs. Brady and the inspector continued to talk, Tori stood and wandered toward the window, slowly pulling her phone from her purse. With her back turned to conceal her texting, she quickly typed a message to Mark.

*Pick me up from 134 Gladstone Road. Urgent. Possible lead. Say Neil, my editor, sent you here to collect me.*

Chapter Eleven

Outside a house that belonged to God only knew who, Mark stared at the uniformed cop standing sentry next to a black Mercedes. Whose car was it and why had Tori summoned him here? He'd come from the station after Collins called him back asking for his fingerprints to eliminate him as the author of the letter Tori had received. Now this…what was she up to?

He got out of his car and studied the large, detached house ahead of him. Was this the Bradys' house? Brian Appleton's? It couldn't be the latter. Tori had said she'd moved to Barlington from somewhere else—away from her terrible memories.

The officer approached. "Can I help you, sir?"

Mark pulled back his shoulders and endeavored to give the impression he had every right to be there. "I have an urgent message for Tori Peterson, officer."

"And you are?"

"A colleague."

The officer narrowed his eyes and seemed to assess Mark before tilting his head toward the house. "If you give me the message, I'll pass it on."

Mark held his gaze. "Can't do that, I'm afraid. It's of a personal nature."

"Is that right?"

"Yes."

The officer smirked, his gaze suspicious. "Then in

that case, I'll escort you the door but step back a little so you can have some privacy. How's that?"

Mark smiled. "Sounds fair to me."

The officer shook his head and brushed past Mark toward the house. He followed on behind, his mind scrambling with what he was supposed to say or do once he knocked on the door. There was only one way to find out.

After a few moments, Tori pulled it open. Her eyes were bright with determination as she widened them in warning. "Hey, the office rang ahead. Is everything all right?"

Mark nodded. "There's been a change of plan. You need to come back to the office. Neil wants to speak to you."

"Now? But…" She shook her head. "I don't believe this. Fine. Okay, okay. Just give me a second."

Mark opened his mouth to speak but her garbled words were shot at him so succinctly, he didn't have the chance. She disappeared into a room to the left of the hallway, leaving him standing on the step.

He turned and nodded at the officer standing behind him, his arms crossed and his gaze full of mistrust.

Tori reappeared and shot Mark another warning look before brushing past him and heading for his car. Having no choice but to trust whatever she was up to was something good, he tipped another nod to the officer and followed her along the path.

Mark got into the driver's seat of his car as Tori yanked on her seatbelt. "Drive. Quickly."

He turned the ignition, threw the car into first and pulled away. "Where are we going? And whose house is that?

"The Bradys'. We need to get out of here before Thornhill suspects my pretty flimsy excuse of an emergency at the paper."

Mark pressed on the gas and sped as fast as driving limits would allow from the Bradys' street. "Where are we going?"

"Starling Drive. I estimate we've got about ten, maybe fifteen minutes, head start on the police. Susan Brady has some concerns about a guy who lives there, Huw Valentine. I want to see if I can speak with him before the police."

"Is Thornhill still not letting you be a part of the investigation? Even after seeing the letter?"

"Yes and no. He allowed me to speak to the Bradys, but his skepticism about me being linked to Abby is still as obvious as it's always been. We have to do what we can without the police."

"I had a thought this afternoon." He glanced at her. "What do you think about hiring a private investigator?"

"It's an idea, but I don't think any investigator would be willing to get involved in a high profile, very much live case, whilst the police are all over it. We'll bide our time and involve as few people as possible. God knows how much trouble we'll be in if Thornhill finds out what we're up to now." Bruno Mars sang from her pocket and she pulled out her phone. "Starling Drive is about four streets away, keep taking the second left on each street." She pressed talk. "Hello? Neil?"

Mark concentrated on the road as Tori had a conversation with her boss. He clearly wasn't happy. Impatience to find out more about Huw Valentine tightened Mark's grip on the steering wheel.

"I'll have something for you in the next hour or so." Tori shoved her hand into her hair. "Yes. Just give me an hour and I'll email a report through. Although it might be better to wait and see if the Bradys give an appeal later. Thornhill told me an appeal will be the next step if nothing comes through about Abby's whereabouts in the next few hours. What? Oh, Neil, come on. I asked for no additional assignments. Vandalism at the local church? Are you serious? Send Cally. Fine. Okay. Bye." She ended the call. "Damn it."

Mark glanced at her. "What's going on?"

"Next left." She sighed. "That was my editor. I've been sending him the odd report about Abby but, as I've got so little to say or add, he's sending me out to report on some petty vandalism at St. John's. The guy can be a complete ass sometimes."

"Who's Cally?"

"My trainee. No, my shadow."

Mark smiled. "You don't like her?"

"I do, she's just a little wet behind the ears. Neil wants me to get back to the office and take her with me rather than letting her go it alone. The fact he doesn't trust the girl to report on petty vandalism solo says just how wet her ears are. God, I'm so bloody frustrated. Abby's still missing and, because I was the one who saw her taken, Neil thinks I should know more than any other reporter."

"And you wish you did."

She met his eyes. "I do. So much."

Mark reached across and squeezed her fingers, wishing he could do something to bring Abby home and make the Bradys' living nightmare come to an end.

He put his hand back on the steering wheel. He wished he could do something to take the haunting look in Tori's eyes away too. He glanced at her. "Who is this Huw Valentine?"

"A dad from a dance class Abby goes to. Susan Brady said he always made her uneasy, but she wasn't exactly willing to throw his name out there. The police will be right behind us. Most likely Thornhill himself. I just want to catch the guy unaware first."

"Won't that just piss him off?"

"Who? Valentine? I couldn't care—"

"Thornhill." Mark glanced at her. "We both want Abby home, but the last thing we want to do is aggravate the inspector in charge of the case. What's stopping him from having us arrested for interfering in police business? I'm pretty sure he won't, but I need to keep in mind what my actions could mean for Olivia."

"Of course. Sorry. Sometimes I get a bit carried away because, more often than not, I fly solo."

Hating the thought of Tori being alone, Mark cleared his throat. "I suggest we leave the police to deal with Valentine and concentrate on you and what you already know. If you're linked to Abby's disappearance—"

"I am."

He looked at her. Her eyes were dark with defensiveness, her cheeks flushed. It was this underlying anger, this risk of recklessness, which motivated his words. Tori was a woman on the edge. An edge Mark would do everything in his power to pull her back from before she disappeared from his life and he hadn't had the chance to express his increasing like of her.

He stared ahead. "And I believe you are too. I also think the main priority is for you to identify every link possible. It's those links that will pull everything together to find Abby. I'm sure of it."

The weight of her stare bored into his temple, but Mark kept his eyes on the road. He'd had sex with this woman. Great sex. He'd let down his guard and allowed the possibility of her becoming a part of his and Olivia's life. Yet, none of that would matter if Abby Brady wasn't brought home safe and well. If she was hurt, or worse, it would destroy the Bradys, Tori and him.

She sighed. "You're right. I'm sorry for snapping."

He fought to hide his surprise. For all his determination, he'd been braced for a much harder and more arduous fight.

She slumped back in her seat. "The truth is, I'm a journalist, not a cop. I don't want to get this wrong and ruin any chance of Abby coming home safely."

"Well, I'm here to help as much as I can for the next couple of hours before I collect Olivia from school." He grimaced. "I just hope she's talking to me when I get there."

"You two had a fight?"

"She wanted to go to a sleepover at a friend's and I refused."

"Why?"

He shrugged.

"Mark?"

"What?"

"You have to let her breathe."

"I am." Now it was his turn for defense, to have the burn at his cheeks. "This whole thing with Abby going missing—"

"You let Olivia have a little fun before that happened?"

"Of course."

"You sure about that?"

"Fine. Maybe I'm kind of hard on her, but when we lost Lauren…" He shook his head. "You wouldn't understand."

"Hey, if I lost the love of my life the way you lost your wife, I can't say I wouldn't protect the essence of that relationship for the rest of my life either, but you can't lock Olivia in a cage. It's not fair and, ultimately, you'll lose her or at least frighten her."

His defenses rose and slotted into place like the planks of wood he worked with every day. Tori had unwittingly overstepped his boundaries and his annoyance soared. How could she understand what any of this was like for him? She didn't have children. She didn't know what it was like to live in fear of losing your child every single day.

He clenched his jaw. He needed some space. "Maybe it would be best to leave Valentine to the police for now and I'll drop you back at the office."

Silence.

He glanced at her.

Her angry green gaze bored into his. "Fine, but drop me at my place rather than the office. I need to pick up my car."

"No problem." He faced the road, trying to believe the tension pressing down on his chest and filling the interior of the car was Tori's fault and not his. He was a father doing his best. Tori was a victim of a horrendous crime and she was doing hers. They were angry, vengeful and most likely far too poisonous for one another.

Yet, the simmering attraction between them was intoxicating rather than toxic. Whichever way he looked at it, they understood each far too well.

**\*\*\*\***

Tori stalked into the newspaper office, her temper strained and her feelings hurt. Mark's clear drawing of the line as far as her opinions were concerned had made her realize just how stupid she'd been to have sex with him. Tensions ran high and she was old enough to know sex fueled, rather than doused, a fire—of every kind. Good or bad.

Well, they would go their separate ways. And he could take his damn possession/daughter issues with him. Not her problem. Not her concern. Her only concern was Abby.

"Tori? Can I have a minute?"

Rolling her eyes, she turned on her heel and marched toward Neil where he stood at his open office door, hands fisted on his hips and his lips pursed.

Avoiding his gaze, she walked past him and sat in one of the chairs in front of his desk. The door closed behind her.

He came around his desk and glared at her. "What the hell's going on with you?"

Irritation rippled through her. "I'm trying to work on the Abby Brady case and I get called back in to report on some petty vandalism, that's what."

"The reason I called you in was because I had a call from Thornhill asking if you were here. Now why would an inspector who's up to his eyeballs searching for a missing kid take the time to find out if you were at the office or not? What have you been up to?"

She crossed her arms, returned his glare. "Nothing."

"Nothing?"

"Nothing."

"So Thornhill just called asking after you for no good reason? He suggested it might be necessary for me to assign someone else to report on Abby. Why would he do that? You need to level with me, Tori, or you'll give me no choice but to take you off this story."

"This is more than a story." She practically spat the words through her gritted teeth. "You'll be making a huge mistake if you take me off this one. I'm doing my job. I'm giving you all the updates I have and more."

"More?" His eyes widened with incredulity. "What *more*? The piece you sent me last night was nothing but a bloody filler. That little girl is out there somewhere. You were the last to see her. We need to go public with that."

"*We* need to go public? You mean *you* want to go public and treat me like some kind of exclusive ruse in the case." She stood, matching his domineering stance from where he loomed above her. "I don't want my name splashed across the papers along with Abby's. This is about her. Not me." He stared at her for so long, Tori dropped back in the chair as the exhaustive worry and need to find Abby took its toll on her body and mind. "I wish there was more I could give you but, right now, that's all I have."

Sighing, Neil sat behind his desk. "Look, I know there's more to Thornhill's call than you're telling me. If reporting on this is affecting you personally, then maybe Thornhill's right and I need to give it someone else."

Tori grappled to get a hold of the frustration and fear inching through her. Neil was her boss doing his job. His ignorance of her situation and her potential involvement made the secrecy that much harder. The more she became convinced Brian Appleton was back, the more her grip on her self-preservation and trust in others slipped. Suddenly, Neil was the enemy; someone else she could no longer trust to do right by her.

She needed to leave, put some space between them before she spewed her past across the desk and yet another person knew about her history. In just a few days, more people had learned what happened to her at Appleton's hands than anyone had in sixteen years.

She stood. "I'll take Cally and go to the church. See what's happened and what we can do to help, okay? Call me if the police notify you that the Bradys will be doing an appeal. I want to stay on this one, Neil. You can trust me to do this right, okay?"

He stared at her before he flicked his hand toward the door. "Go on, get on with it. I'll call you as soon as I hear anything."

"Thank you."

Leaving his office, Tori headed for her desk.

Cally stood as Tori approached. "Here." She thrust some papers across the space between them. "The names of the people I've managed to call from Abby's class list. No one saw her leave the school early."

Tori took the list and scanned Cally's notes. "And no one saw her leave alone either."

"It's weird, huh?"

"Definitely." Tori scanned the open plan office. "Where's Greg?"

"I think Neil asked him to go ahead to the church and take some photos. Do you want me to check his desk for his list? See if he's managed to get his half of the class done?"

"Would you mind?"

"Not at all."

As Cally practically skipped across the office, Tori sat and scanned through her emails and memos. Nothing of any importance. Nothing new about Abby. They were still at square one and too much time had passed. Now, more than ever before, the police relied on public eyes and ears. There was little to no evidence from the scene, or anywhere else. Someone needed to bring something new to the table.

"It looks as though Greg finished his too."

Cally's voice cut through Tori's contemplation and she shoved aside her building despair. "Let me see."

Tori read through Greg's messy scrawl and, from what she could decipher, the parents he'd spoken to had no more to add either. A complete waste of time.

"Okay." Tori tossed the list onto her desk and pushed to her feet. "Grab your bag and notebook. We've got some top-notch investigative journalism to do."

Cally's eyes brightened. "We do? Me and you? Wow."

Tori smiled. "That was me being ironic, Cally. Neil already told you about the vandalism at St. John's. He sent Greg there to take pictures, remember?"

"Oh, that." Cally laughed. "Sorry."

Shaking her head, Tori slipped the strap of her bag onto her shoulder and led the way out of the office.

St. John's church was located across Barlington

town center and out toward the neighboring town, but still made up part of Barlington's parish. Tori had called ahead, and when they arrived at the church, Reverend Raymond Dudley stood at the entrance as Tori and Cally walked along the ancient pathway toward him.

With white tufts of hair above his ears, the rest of his head smooth and bald enough that it shone under the day's sun, and his permanently rosy cheeks, the good reverend was an almost cartoon-like friend to everyone, young and old. As a fairly new Barlington resident and very rare church-goer, Tori had only met him a handful of times, but had taken to him immediately.

She smiled and put out her hand as she neared. He certainly didn't deserve to have his church desecrated and guilt about her early attitude with Neil niggled at her conscience. "Reverend Dudley, it's lovely to see you again."

He took her hand in his and warmly covered it with the other. "You too, Tori. You looked tired, child. I hope Neil hasn't been working you too hard."

"He has, but don't tell him I said so."

He released her hand to take Cally's. "I don't believe we've met. I'm Reverend Dudley. Welcome to St. John's."

"Thank you, Reverend. You have a very pretty church." Cally tipped her head back to stare at the stained glass window to her right. "That window is beautiful."

He sighed. "It is. I thank the Lord the vandals left the windows alone, at least. Why don't you ladies follow me and I'll show you what they've done."

Tori nudged Cally, who seemed more interested in

the building and the lych gate at the very end of the pathway than the vandalism. She jumped and mouthed 'sorry,' before following behind Tori and the reverend.

The defacing was awful.

Spray-painted obscenities and various crudely painted genitalia covered part of one wall. Gouges had been made in the ancient stonework and an array of junk food containers and beer bottles were strewn across the grass and amongst the gravestones.

"I am so sorry, Reverend." Tori shook her head. "I have no idea what goes on in the minds of people most of the time."

Reverend Dudley lifted his shoulders. "It's a lesson to the people involved and all of us. We must have faith that when bad things happen, they happen for a reason. Otherwise what is the point of it all? Only Jesus knows the truth and we must be strong in order to follow in his plan."

Tori's mind filled with the photograph Principal White had shown her of Abby. Innocent. Angelic. "Sometimes that's a tough ask, unfortunately."

"You must trust in God, Tori. Trust He is the truth."

Unable to answer or agree with him while Abby was yet to be found and quite possibly being subjected to all kinds of evil, Tori stepped closer to the graffiti. "The police have taken photographs? Spoken to you?"

"Yes. Your photographer was here a while ago too."

"Good. Well, all I can promise is a report in tomorrow's paper, Reverend. It may help identify whoever did this."

"I'm grateful. Thank you.

Tori stared at the desecrated wall. "Do you have anyone to help get that paint off?"

"Yes. One of the parishioners has some special substance that will limit the damage to the stonework. He'll be here first thing in the morning."

"Good." Tori exhaled and stepped back from the wall. "Cally, take a few notes. Anything you think will help in a report to catch whoever did this. I really hope it was someone out of town. The thought of a Barlington resident doing this to one of their churches sickens me."

Once Cally had taken her notes, she and Tori declined the reverend's offer of tea and walked back through the gate to Tori's car. Cally slid into the passenger seat.

As Tori walked around the front, her gaze fell to the scarf fluttering in the breeze from her wing mirror.

Her heart hammered as she looked left and right along the road. "No. No, no, no."

Cally opened the car door. "What is it?" She stepped onto the pavement. "What's that?"

Hands shaking, Tori stared at the scarf. "The scarf Abby Brady's kidnapper was wearing when he took her." Tori met Cally's wide-eyed stare before she pulled her phone from her jacket pocket. "I need to ring Thornhill."

With her fingers shaking, Tori dialed Barlington Station and fought the shameful need to cry, to slump to the floor and wrap her arms tightly around her knees just like she had in Brian Appleton's basement. Even if it came to be that Brian Appleton wasn't behind Abby's kidnapping, someone, somewhere, was using what he'd done to Tori to kick-start a whole new evil.

Chapter Twelve

Mark looked up from the bureau and slowly put down the sander, pulling his safety goggles down to hang around his neck. Through the view from his open workshop door, Principal White closed her car door. As she walked toward him, her expression was relaxed and her posture easy. His initial fear that something had happened to Olivia eased.

The principal waved and Mark waved back, wondering what she was doing at his house so near the end of the school day. He rubbed his hand along his jaw as she entered the workshop.

"Hi Mark, how are you?" She flicked her gaze over his chest in a way that was nowhere near as satisfying as it had been when Tori had done the same thing.

"So, so, considering." He grabbed his denim shirt from a workbench beside him and shoved his arms into the sleeves. "How come you're here, Princ…Karen? Is Olivia okay?"

"Oh, she's fine." She rifled in her bag and brought out the samples he'd given her a couple of nights before. "I've chosen the varnish I'd like and thought I'd drop it by on my way home."

He took the samples.

"I have mounds of work to get done for the board and sometimes home is just the change of scenery I need to get it done." She came closer and smoothed her hand over her bureau. "You've done an amazing job. It looks fantastic and it's not even finished yet."

Mark snapped the final buttons on his shirt and stuffed his hands into the front pockets of his jeans. The tension coming from the principal was palpable. "Is your bureau the only reason you're here?"

She met his gaze, her laugh a little too high and her smile a little too bright. "What do you mean?"

"I mean you look on edge."

Her eyes darkened with what he could only guess to be annoyance. She abruptly turned away and her high heels tip-tapped across the concrete floor as she walked around the bureau until she stood opposite him. "How do you think Olivia is coping with everything, Mark?"

Discomfort rippled through him and he stood a little taller. "What do you mean?"

"She's a kind girl, an intelligent girl…" She smiled softly. "A girl who loves her daddy very much."

"I'm glad you think so."

"Oh, I know so. It's written all over her face every time she looks at you. Yet, I can see how unhappy she is too." The principal tapped the bureau a couple of times with her fingernail. "I think Abby's abduction has shaken Olivia to her core. Shaken her more than some of the other children."

Tension snaked across his shoulders and Mark curled his hands into fists inside his pockets. "What makes you think that?" His mind filled with the numerous conversations he'd shared with Olivia since Abby's disappearance. What if he'd taken Olivia's assurance she was okay too easily? Maybe Tori was right and in his bid to keep Olivia safe, he was actually frightening her. "Has she said something to you?"

"Not in so many words. Yet, she doesn't seem the same girl she was before. I wonder if there is something more upsetting her? Something at home maybe?"

He clenched his jaw as he fought the guilt he was failing to be the father Olivia needed since they'd lost Lauren. "We're fine."

"Oh, I'm sure you are." The intensity in her eyes softened and the principal smiled. "You know, I've always wanted a little girl of my own." She glanced toward the open workshop door. "Yet, each year I get older and the fantasy seems more and more out of reach." She met his gaze. "Even the idea of being mum to another man's child doesn't bother me. I just want to mother, you know? Maybe sooner or later, a divorced man with a brood of little girls will take pity on me."

Mark put the samples on the bureau and moved to the sink, suddenly concerned the principal might be suggesting *she* mother Olivia. "I'll talk to Olivia when I pick her up, but I'm sure she's fine." He turned on the tap and squirted some soap onto his hands.

"I didn't mean to upset you, Mark."

"You haven't."

"Good, because I care about Olivia. I care about all the children. It's my job as their principal to inform parents of any concerns I have. To make sure I do all I can to help if they are having problems at home. I wondered if your new, and sudden, relationship with Miss Peter—"

"There's no relationship with Miss Peterson." He swiveled around, irritation pulsing inside him as he snatched some paper towel from the wall dispenser. "We've spent a little time together. That's it."

Two spots of color darkened her cheeks. "I'm

sorry. I thought…" She briefly closed her eyes before opening them again. "It doesn't matter what I thought. As long as you're aware of my concern for Olivia and her feelings. That's all I came here to say. Oh, and to give you my varnish choice." She splayed the samples before selecting one and holding it out to him. "Here. This one."

"Thanks." Mark took the card and placed it on the drainer. "Well, I'd better think about collecting Olivia from school." He held the principal's gaze, hoping she got the message through his tone that she needed to butt out of his business. "I'll talk to her. Make sure everything's okay."

Her gaze lingered at his mouth for a moment before she met his eyes once more. "That's all I ask. She's a lovely girl. I just want her to be happy and for you to know I'm here if you need me. Any time."

"Thank you."

The seconds beat out like minutes, her chest rising and falling as though she debated saying more. At last, she cleared her throat. "You know, it did occur to me the other day that Mrs. Brady hadn't seemed herself for a while before Abby was taken. I hope there isn't something, no matter how small, that I might have done to prevent Abby's disappearance."

Mark stilled, suspicion whispering through him. "Like what?"

She shrugged. "We all hear of child abduction cases where the root lies within the family." She flicked some hair over her shoulder, her brow creased in apparent concern. "I hope it doesn't come to light that Susan or Simon are in some way involved."

Nausea clenched Mark's gut. If the parents were

involved, everything that was already terrifying about this case would grow ten-fold. He crossed his arms. "The police are still at their house. As far as I know they are speaking to them all day, every day. It's been three days. I would've thought if the Bradys were under suspicion, something would've come out about it by now."

"Hmm. Maybe." The principal sighed. "Abby was such a pretty little girl."

Mark glared. "Is."

"Sorry?"

"Abby *is* a pretty girl. You said 'was.'"

"Oh, Mark, for goodness sake. Don't look at me as though I'm the villain here. That was a slip of the tongue. You are looking at me as though I'm involved, not her parents."

"I don't want to think you, or they, are involved. What I *am* thinking is this conversation is making me uncomfortable."

She opened her mouth before snapping it closed. With a curt nod, she turned out of the workshop, her head held high.

Trembling with suppressed anger, Mark didn't release his held breath until Principal White had pulled away from his house.

Walking forward, he yanked the door closed before marching back through the workshop and into the house. Taking the stairs two at a time, he entered Olivia's bedroom and stared around the overly neat space. Ever since her mother died, Olivia had developed a deeper and deeper need for order. Whether that order was her bedroom, the house, or her and Mark's schedules. She had to know everything was in its place, and where they had to be and when. All things Lauren had taken care of before she died.

His haunting sense of failure gathered strength. Was he letting Olivia down? Letting Lauren down? Becoming a worse parent, rather than a better one?

Never before had he felt the need to snoop through Olivia's private space. Never before had he felt as though he'd missed something going on with her.

He slumped his shoulders and sat on Olivia's bed, drawing his gaze over her white bedside cabinet, her wardrobe and matching dressing table.

A horrible feeling of being out of his depth, of not being the father he thought he was, slid over him, heavy and unwelcome. He pushed his thumb and forefinger into his brow.

"Tell me what to do, Lauren. Tell me how to help her."

His words sliced the air as he waited for his dead wife's guidance.

Nothing but silence reigned.

His phone rang jolting him from his self-hatred. Cursing, he stood and pulled the phone from his back pocket, looked at the display.

Tori.

Indecision battled as he hovered his finger over the talk button, before making a snap decision and answering the call. "Tori."

"You've been bum calling me for the last five minutes. I'm guessing you don't want to talk to me?"

Lauren snuck into his mind. Was she trying to tell him to lean on Tori? He squeezed his eyes shut.

"Mark?"

The need to be somewhere else, anywhere else, but

alone in his big, empty house, gripped him. "Where are you?"

"St. John's church."

He walked from Olivia's bedroom, shutting the door firmly behind him. Today would not be the day he risked his daughter's trust. Hopefully, he'd never have to. "The vandalism. Right. I forgot."

"Whoever's playing with me, or maybe whoever has Abby, knew I'd be here. The abductor's scarf was tied to my wing mirror. The police are with me now."

"What?" He hurried downstairs and grabbed his keys from the hook by the front door. "Do you want me to come down there?"

"No."

Her tone was abrupt, thick with urgency and distance. Mark stilled, his hand on the front door. "Why not?"

"Because clearly the bastard who has Abby thinks this kind of game playing is funny. The trouble is, I can only think of a handful of people who could've possibly have known I'd be here."

He frowned. "And?"

"And one of them is you."

\*\*\*\*

Tori's first glass of wine had been glorious…the third like a liquid nail in the coffin currently boxing in her need to scream. Although giddy from too much alcohol and too little food, however ill she felt later or in the morning, she deserved it.

Mark had hung up on her and she didn't blame him. She didn't blame Susan Brady for breaking down at the televised appeal earlier either. Both incidents were Tori's fault and both incidents meant the people involved were justified in not wanting to see her face ever again.

Another day drew to a close and the police appeared to be no closer to finding Abby. With zero leads and Tori drawing a blank why some sick freak had chosen to resurrect Brian Appleton's torment, the night ahead felt cruel and threatening.

"I really think you should've taken the police up on their offer of protection, Tori." Cally's eyes were wide with concern. "Leaving that scarf for you to find like that—"

"Whoever started this with me can come and get me. I'm not going to hide behind the police."

"But aren't you even a little scared?" Cally took a sip of her Diet Coke and cast her gaze around the swanky, up-market wine bar, where the majority of Barlington's suits met and mingled after work. "I mean, what if he's watching you right now?"

"Don't be so melodramatic." Tori took a mouthful of wine in a valiant effort of nonchalance. "Whoever this person is, he's a coward. Someone willing to get up close and personal with me wouldn't play silly buggers and leave pieces of evidence lying around for me to find. If he wants me, he can have me. He'd just better give Abby Brady back first."

"I don't want to see you hurt."

"Who cares what happens to me?" Tori drank another mouthful of wine, impatience, anger and fear rolling around inside her. "I just want Abby home."

"But why you?" Greg leaned back in the booth, his arm along the back of the long seat. "That's what I want to know. You don't even look surprised by what's happening. Like you're, I don't know, prepared for it."

His slurred words hitched Tori's impatience. She was supposed to be getting drunk, not him. Why was he so bloody pissed off? It wasn't as though he was the key to saving Abby Brady from abuse…or worse.

Tori took a drink. "Isn't it time you were going, Greg?"

It wasn't the just the smell of fresh air and sandalwood that alerted Tori to the fact Mark had joined them. It was the way his shadow fell over her as though covering her body with his wide, deep and potentially dangerous protectiveness.

She didn't bother to look at him…even though Cally was seriously looking. Tori lifted her hand in a half-hearted wave. "Take a seat, superhero."

"I will." He sat beside her. "Thank you."

Every now and then, when she was alone at home, she'd picked up a book. And every now and then, she would toss the book across the room whenever she read the words, "The air crackled between them." Well, whatever instantly plagued the atmosphere between her and Mark as she forced her gaze to his, she was loath to call it crackling. Maybe humming…screaming…burning…but definitely not crackling.

She swallowed. "What are you doing here?"

"Olivia's staying at a friend's. I was at a loose end."

Despite her best efforts to fight her smile, it was ruthless and broke through her barriers like they were made of sugar paper. "Loose end, my ass. You were no doubt pacing around the house and doing everything you could not to get in the car and go get her."

He smiled and put a glass on the table. "Merlot, right?"

Dragging her gaze from the dark blue of his, Tori glanced at the glass of wine before she looked at Cally and Greg. Cally stared at Mark with a strange mix of interest and dislike, while Greg looked at Cally as though gauging whether Mark was a potential rival for her affections.

"Why don't you guys go home for the night?" Tori lifted her glass and drained it, before sliding the glass Mark had bought her closer. "Noble Mark will look after me."

"Are you sure?" Cally continued to stare at Mark, her gaze wandering slowly over his face and chest. "I'm happy to stay longer."

"Go. Honestly." Tori sipped her drink. "I'll be fine."

Greg slowly stood, unfolding his lanky frame from the seat. "Come on, Cally, let's get out of here."

"If you're sure, Tori?" Cally's eyes were wide with concern. "I'm worried about you after what happened at the church today."

"I'm fine." Tori smiled. "Mark's got me, okay?"

With another final look at Mark, Cally and Greg turned and walked through the crowded bar toward the exit. Once their retreating backs were blocked from view, Tori faced Mark. "So, you let Olivia go and have some fun, huh?"

"I did." He took a gulp from his beer glass, licked the froth from his upper lip. "She practically squeezed me to death during the process too."

Tori's stomach knotted to imagine the joy on Olivia's face over something as simple as a sleepover. "Good. Hopefully next time will be easier."

"Maybe."

His uncertainty was clear in his tone and the way he stared around the bar as though someone might sneak out to look for his daughter any minute.

"Hey." Tori covered his hand where it lay on the table, her heart softening toward this gorgeously tall, built and beautifully loving father. "She'll be fine. Letting her do this a good thing, I promise…even if, as you so subtly pointed out, I don't understand."

"I shouldn't have said that. I'm sorry."

She shrugged. "I don't have kids, most likely never will, but that doesn't mean I don't know what it's like to have an overprotective daddy. I still have one of those. Even now." She sighed. "Yep. It isn't just me Brian Appleton haunts. It's my entire family. Now either him, or someone who wants to be him, is doing their best to frighten the hell out me and do God knows what to Abby Brady." A sudden realization pulled her hand from his and she frowned. "How did you know I was here?"

"I was on my way back from the police station and dropped into your office. Your editor said—"

"Why were you at the station?"

"They had to retake my finger prints for some reason. They weren't clear the first time around or something."

She frowned. "Did you see Thornhill? Did he say anything else about the letter?"

"I only saw the officer who took my prints. It was all procedure. Look, I wanted to see you. Check you were okay. I went to your office and Neil said I'd most likely find you here if, by some miracle, you'd done as he asked and gone out for a drink." His brow furrowed. "Did you tell him about the scarf?"

"Yes, which is why he sent me to the pub. He said I needed a few hours down time. Not that alcohol is doing anything more than increase my paranoia." She sipped her wine before meeting his eyes. "The police offered me protection."

"Let me guess. You didn't take it?"

Annoyed at his accusatory tone, Tori glared. "Why would I when I want whoever left the scarf and sent me the letter to have access to me? I want to know what they want. Whatever it is they feel strongly enough about that they took an innocent child from her family. He's not going to approach me if I've got a random cop hanging around."

Anger blazed in his eyes before he squeezed them shut as though trying to gain some self-control.

Tori couldn't fail to notice the creases of fatigue and strain on his face that she swore hadn't been there when they'd first met. Empathy twisted her heart. She probably had more than a few new wrinkles herself.

He opened his eyes.

"I'm sorry about what I said to you earlier." She shook her head. "I know you have nothing to do with the scarf. I know you have nothing to do with any of this."

His gaze bored into hers, his jaw tight. "Do you honestly mean that? Because if there's even the smallest doubt in your mind—"

"There isn't. I was lashing out." She looked into the ruby red depths of her glass. "Thornhill called me earlier. He's spoken to Huw Valentine." She lifted her gaze. "Apparently Valentine is nothing more than a father who is a little overexcited about his young daughter's future in dance. Thornhill is adamant that

Valentine was forthcoming enough answering the police's questions. He admitted he'd had run-ins with other parents, but nothing that really bothered him."

Mark took another drink. "That doesn't mean it didn't bother the other parents. Who's to say whoever took Abby wasn't another dance parent? A friend working with Valentine? We have to keep our minds wide open. So should the police."

"Thornhill did say Valentine was a little evasive when it came to Abby and Susan Brady. I got the impression the police aren't entirely done with him and he'll remain a possible suspect." Tori sighed. "But, in the meantime, I have absolutely nothing else to go on."

"Principal White dropped by my house this afternoon. She claimed to be worried about Olivia…and then mentioned she wants a little girl of her own more than anything."

Tori frowned. "A hundred and one women feel that way, Mark. We can't use that as evidence to suspect the woman. That's what you're thinking, right?"

"Maybe, but also that she was the last one to see Abby leave the school. Where's Abby's missing school bag? Why does Principal White keep asking questions about you? I swear to God the woman had zero interest in my life or me before Abby was taken. So why now?"

Unease rippled through Tori. "Maybe I should pay her a visit tomorrow. Ask a few more questions about the last time she saw Abby."

"Maybe you should." He took a long drink and put down his glass. "But, before then, you can come and spend the night at mine."

"What?" Panic sped Tori's heart. Having sex in her kitchen was one thing, but spending the night with him?

That just smacked of intimacy, of a growing relationship. "I don't need you to look after me, Mark. I can do that myself."

"Listen to me." He took her hand, his gaze intense as he drew his thumb over her skin in slow circles. "Whoever abducted Abby knows where you are and what you're doing. Like you said, this could be someone who knows you. We have to put our heads together if we are going to help the police find Abby. They want you protected. Stay with me, Tori. Trust me."

Tori stared. *Trust me...*

She inhaled a long breath and slowly released it. "Okay."

Chapter Thirteen

*I see you with him, Tori.*

*I see you with him and it makes me so very mad.*

*He will never love you as I do…he will never touch and caress you as I will.*

*Why do you look at him that way? Why is it only him who makes your pretty cheeks pink, your eyes so succinctly and completely distracted from everything around you?*

*I hope the scarf didn't frighten you, my love. I wanted you to know I am close by; I am always watching you.*

*Abby has a friend of mine with her always. He took her for me and stays with her when I need to watch you. He doesn't hurt her…or I will hurt him. When I am with her, she is taken care of. I love her as if she were mine to love. As soon as I have you, I will set her free.*

*But you must stop looking at the carpenter that way!*

*I will hurt him. I will destroy him.*

*Do not love him, Tori. Do not touch him. Do not trust him.*

*I'll be watching you. Always, always, watching…*

\*\*\*\*

Mark opened his front door and gestured for Tori to enter the house ahead of him. During the drive there, she'd held her overnight bag on her lap, clutched to her stomach like a lifeline. Guilt poked at him. The thought she might have felt pressured to stay the night with him didn't feel good, but now the police had mentioned protection, there was no way Mark could've let her go back to her place alone.

It made sense she stayed over. Whoever had taken Abby knew where Tori lived and worked. God only knew if they were aware she was at his house tonight. Before he closed the door, Mark looked out into his dark front garden, glancing as far as he could see in each direction along the street and out toward the row of opposite houses.

Everything was different now. Nothing safe. Nothing untouched.

"You going to close that door?"

Tori's question came from behind him. He pushed the door shut and turned. Her dark, green eyes were nervous, no matter how hard she clearly tried to hide her unease with her overly-wide smile.

He nodded toward the living room. "Go on in and take a seat. I'll put some coffee on."

She held his gaze, before dropping her bag on the hardwood floor and walking into the living room. Mark exhaled and took a final peek outside through the window by the side of the front door.

Everything seemed as it always did…yet everything was entirely different.

As he walked past the open living room door, he glanced in at Tori. She sat straight-backed on the sofa, her hands screwed into the cushions either side of her and her glazed stare directed toward the window.

"Why don't I shut these curtains?" He strode into the room, purposefully keeping his tone light. "We can have a cup of coffee and chill out in front of the TV."

"Sounds good."

Her tone almost, but not quite, matched his. God only knew how he was supposed to relax her after that scarf turned up—not to mention the misplaced guilt he saw, time and again, in her eyes. With the curtains drawn, he flicked on a few lamps and left for the kitchen.

Once he'd made the coffee, he surreptitiously checked the back garden and locked the door. Shaking off his jumpiness, he headed into the living room, holding a tray containing two oversized mugs of coffee and some toast. He had a sneaking feeling Tori hadn't eaten anything with her several glasses of wine.

"Here you go. Supper a la Noble Mark." He winked at her and placed the tray on the low coffee table in front of the settee. "I have jam, marmalade and chocolate spread. Anything savory on toast is not allowed in this house."

She smiled. "As it should be."

"Tuck in."

"Thanks." She reached for one of the mugs. "But I'm good with just coffee."

"Tori, you have to eat something. As much as I'd sometimes like it to be, wine and coffee isn't much of a diet."

She shrugged and leaned back into the sofa, slipping off her heels and drawing her legs beneath her. She blew across the top of her mug and Mark glued his gaze to her pursed lips. When he snapped his gaze back to hers, she smiled. "Don't even go there."

Rare heat pinched his face and he lifted the second mug from the tray, brought it to his mouth. "Nothing wrong with looking."

"So…"

"So…"

"As you pretty much know everything about me, tell me about you."

He shrugged. "Not much to tell."

"I don't believe you."

His knee-jerk need for privacy reared its ugly head and he cleared his throat. "You already know everything. I'm a widowed carpenter with one daughter I'm scared shitless I'm going to lose. I am currently fighting, what appears to be, the unwanted interest of a school principal. I'm involved in a child abduction case, and the first woman I've been truly attracted to in five years, is sitting on my sofa." He smiled. "That about covers it."

She smiled softly, her eyes shining. She looked beautiful.

She sipped her coffee. "Okay, so what about Olivia?"

He looked toward the blackened TV screen, his libido cooling. "What about her?"

"You've checked your phone about thirty times in the two hours we've been together. You've been good. You've resisted texting her, as far as I know. Somehow, even with Abby gone, progress, as far as your daughter's concerned, is being made. You should be very proud of yourself."

He faced her as fear for Olivia's safety while she was at a friend's once again edged in. "I never had any intention of contacting her, but that doesn't mean I hadn't hoped she'd contact me."

She smiled. "Why should she? She's safe. She's

having fun. Kids don't contact their parents unless there's something wrong. Even I know that much."

He blew out a breath. "Maybe you're right." Mark surrendered a little more of his apprehension and relaxed his shoulders. After putting his coffee on the table, he leaned back. "Lauren was the best mother Olivia could have hoped for." He exhaled. "She was the best wife."

"Then you have something pretty special to remember her by. Don't let your fears taint the amazing job you and your wife started with Olivia before Lauren died." She straightened and put her coffee next to his before taking his hand. "You still have Olivia, Mark. With God's grace, you always will."

His gut clenched. "Don't you think Simon Brady assumed the same about Abby?"

As soon as the words were out of his mouth, he wanted to retract them.

The atmosphere shifted and changed as she slipped her hand from his arm.

"Don't let whoever has Abby do this." Tori's eyes darkened with warning. "You'd be a fool to let him edge in, get anywhere close to ruining what you have with your daughter. To ruining the good, kind and honest man you are." She briefly closed her eyes before opening them again. "Before Brian Appleton took me, my dad looked out for me, cared for me, but I had a certain amount of freedom. Afterward, he watched me like a hawk. I don't doubt for one minute that would've gone on forever if I'd let it. That's why I moved away and purposely haven't lived near my parents for a really long time." Her eyes glinted with tears as she looked at him. "Don't force Olivia to do the same. It's a lonely way to live."

Sympathy for this beautiful woman gripped his heart. "But you have your sister. You have Melissa."

"Only because she followed me here." She looked deep into his eyes. "Who else, apart from you, does Olivia have to follow her?"

Her words struck like a knife through his heart, severing his defenses and unleashing his helplessness in one cruel slice. He pushed to his feet. "I'll grab some blankets and a pillow."

"Mark…"

He left the room and stormed up the stairs, taking them two at a time. Marching to a cupboard on the landing, he put his hands on two blankets, digging his fingers into the soft fleece. He hung his head and clenched his jaw. His ferocious protection over Olivia would only grow worse the older she became and the longer Abby Brady was God knew where.

Tori was right. The longer he carried on this way, the more likely he was to lose Olivia, like he'd lost Lauren and would undoubtedly lose Tori.

Pushing and pushing until he was all alone—the one thing he feared and the one place Tori seemed to know only too well.

Grabbing some blankets and a couple of pillows, he headed downstairs and into the living room. Tori stood in front of his bookshelf, her back turned and her shoulders high.

He coughed and headed to the sofa. "I'll sleep here tonight. You can take my bed."

She turned. "I'm good down here. Thanks."

He met her gaze. Her eyes were blank, her expression impassive, but her arms tightly crossed.

"Tori, look, I shouldn't have stormed out like that, but—"

"It doesn't matter, honestly." She dropped her arms and walked across the room toward her overnight bag. With her back turned, she unzipped it and pulled out a pair of satin pajamas. "I'm bushed. Why don't we just go to bed and start again tomorrow?"

"Okay. My bedroom is second on the left." He fought the urge to go to her, to run his hands over her tense shoulders, lower to rub the base of her spine.

She faced him. "I want to stay down here."

There was no room for argument in her tone or in her eyes. Mark exhaled and raised his hands in surrender. "There's a toilet downstairs, second door on the right and the kitchen's all yours. See you tomorrow."

She held his gaze. "Night."

Nodding, he left the room and walked into the kitchen. He pulled a glass from the cupboard and filled it with water at the sink. His throat dry and his chest aching, Mark drank deep before refilling the glass and heading back into the hallway.

The living room door was firmly shut.

He raised his knuckles to knock…then lowered them, turned and hauled his ass upstairs where he couldn't cause any more pain or hurt.

Self-disgust twisted inside him. He didn't deserve for Tori to wait for him to sort his crap out. His emotions, his messed-up feelings, were his problem, not hers. She deserved more; more than Mark suspected he would ever be capable of giving.

Tori Peterson was a woman whose past had shaped who she was today. Mark was a fixer—a problem solver. Yet, he had no clue if he possessed the right tools to put Tori back together again.

Considering how long he'd known her, the stench of impending failure rankled far more than it should. He had to get a grip; had to fight for a better life than the locked box he'd created for himself and Olivia.

His life was his own and, goddamn it, Olivia's was hers too.

****

The day had broken with a clear blue sky usually reserved for the height of summer, rather than the end of October. Yet, the sun did nothing to alleviate the thump of the previous night's over-indulgence currently having a full-on party in Tori's head. She'd left Mark's early and caught a cab home—mentally flicking the finger at whoever the hell tried to frighten her. The choice to risk her appearance to whomever chased her had been empowering rather than terrifying.

She would be a victim no more…sixteen years was long enough.

Squinting against the early afternoon sun, Tori walked through the gates of Barlington Primary and stopped. With all the kids and teachers inside, the space was eerily quiet. Unoccupied and entirely disconcerting. She glanced toward the scaffolding to her right where work had been going on and off at the school for what seemed like weeks. As no one was around, either the workmen had a day off or the work was complete.

She scanned the area around her. Every place she'd gone since Abby disappeared, Tori sensed she was being watched. Witnessing the abduction and the appearance of the kidnapper's scarf, proved she was the lynchpin in the case. Thornhill asking her to consider police protection confirmed he thought the same. He had phoned her first thing this morning. Courtesy, he'd said.

But it was Abby who mattered. Not her.

Slowly walking forward, Tori stared at the tall glass windows of the school's assembly hall at the front of the building. They provided a clear view of the parked staff vehicles outside and of the school gates. How could nobody have seen Abby leave? Someone could have walk through the hall at any time and looked out the window. Even now, the darkened silhouettes of adults and children were visible.

She looked behind her. The street outside the gates remained quiet. Much as it had been the day Abby was snatched.

Tori's mind turned to Mark. Maybe she shouldn't have said what she did about him, Olivia, and his wife. Yet, when they'd spoken last night, her feelings had bounced from angry, to sorry, to indignant and now, several hours later, they'd landed slap bang in regret. As much as she liked him, she couldn't afford to get involved with someone right now.

Finding Abby and whoever used Tori as a tool in their sick games was all she could—or would—care about.

She turned around and bypassed the circular shrubbery that acted as a roundabout at the school entrance and walked to the main doors. She pressed on the buzzer and peered through the glass.

A teacher sat with a child around the age of seven or eight in the waiting area. She looked up and her gaze met Tori's, before saying something to the little boy and then walking toward Tori with a tentative smile. She unlocked the door. "Hi, I'm Miss Lawrence. Can I help you?"

Tori smiled. "Hi. I was hoping to speak with Principal White."

"Do you have an appointment?"

"I don't, I'm afraid. What I have to say shouldn't take long. It's about Abby Brady."

"Oh, I see." Miss Lawrence cast a curious perusal over Tori's face before she stepped back and pulled the door wide. "I can direct you to the main office where her secretary will be able to tell whether the principal is free. Your name is…"

Tori stepped inside and held out her hand. "Tori Peterson."

Miss Lawrence shook Tori's hand. "The main office is just around the corner there. First door on the right."

"Great. Thank you."

Tori followed the directions to a small office along the corridor. A woman Tori guessed to be in her mid-forties sat typing at a computer. Tori stopped in front of the desk. "Hi. My name's Tori Peterson. Would it be possible to see if Principal White is free to speak with me? It concerns Abby Brady."

"Oh, of course. I'm her secretary, Mrs. Worrall." She rose from her desk and smiled. "The principal has asked to be interrupted if there is any news or enquiries regarding Abby so I'm sure she'd like to speak with you. If you'd like to follow me, Ms. Peterson. Principal White's office is right this way."

They walked a short distance along the corridor. Mrs. Worrall knocked softly on the principal's office door and gently pushed it open. She peered inside. "I'm sorry to interrupt, Principal but I have a Ms. Tori Peterson to see you. She says it's in connection to Abby Brady."

"Of course. Show her in, please."

Mrs. Worrall flashed Tori an encouraging smile and opened the door wider. Tori stepped inside and the door closed behind her.

Marginally brighter, due to the sunlight streaming through Principal White's open window, the office didn't feel quite as claustrophobic as it had the first time around. Or maybe it was that Tori could breathe a little easier than she could just after Abby's abduction.

"Principal White, thank you for seeing me."

"Not at all." She waved toward one of the visitors' chairs in front of her desk. "Please. Take a seat."

Now she was here, worry how best to approach the principal with her questions overrode the confidence Tori had felt last night and this morning. She wasn't a cop. She was a journalist at a local paper. The principal would be perfectly in her rights to throw Tori out anytime she felt like it.

Maybe small talk was the best way to open the conversation. She smiled. "I understand you've seen Mark Bolton a couple of times since Abby disappeared."

"I have." Principal White returned the smile, her eyes kind. "And I believe you have too."

Unsure how to answer when she'd seen a damn sight more of Mark Bolton—in more ways than one—than the principal had, Tori veered the subject away from Mark. Mentioning the man she and Principal White had in common, wasn't quite the strategic opener she'd hoped it would be.

The principal shuffled some papers on her desk. "Do you have some new information regarding Abby, Miss Peterson? The inspector called me yesterday and said there had been no further sightings or anything else of use. I really can't believe how long she's been missing."

"I'm afraid I don't. As far as I'm aware, the police are still following every avenue of enquiry." Tori swallowed the lie. She did know more. She knew about the scarf. She knew she was a link, but Thornhill had made it clear he did not want her to mention the scarf to anyone. The police would reveal its finding to the public later today, purposely leaving Tori's name out of the bulletin lest it placed her in further danger.

"Well, that is a shame. I assumed you had some news." Principal White frowned, her gaze turning ever so slightly suspicious. "I do hope you aren't here in a professional capacity. I am under strict police instructions not to speak to the press."

Tori inwardly grimaced. She'd wrongly assumed the principal would be forthcoming, considering her questions to Mark about her and Abby. "I'm here in a personal capacity, Principal. Everything we say will be off the record. As I was the last person to see Abby, my interest bypassed the purely professional the moment she was forced into that car."

The principal held Tori's gaze before she exhaled and her shoulders dropped. "I understand. You must feel an inordinate amount of responsibility."

Whether it was guilt, or the fact Principal White so succinctly twisted the knife of blame in Tori's heart, her careful control threatened to snap. "Maybe I do, but instead of wallowing in that sense of responsibility, I intend using it to bring Abby back home."

"Well, that's most admirable."

The principal's slow and condescending smile hitched Tori's stretched impatience tighter. She clenched her hands together in her lap. "So, on that basis, I'd appreciate it if you could clear up a couple of things for me. A couple of facts that don't add up about the time between Abby leaving class and me seeing her outside."

Color darkened Principal White's cheeks, and her gaze hardened. "I've told the police everything I know."

"I understand, only the police seem to believe Abby left the class the same way as everyone else. They're also adamant she was carrying her book bag. Neither scenario adds up. I saw Abby come out of the school alone and not carrying anything. I want to be sure of what happened during those last vital moments."

Tori's pulse counted the seconds. Abruptly, the principal stood and came around the desk. Tori slid back in her seat, allowing space for Principal White to lean against the desk in front of her.

"Her bag has been found."

"What?" Tori stilled. "When?"

"This morning." Principal White pushed some fallen hair from her brow. "Some children were playing in the shrubbery outside the school entrance and found it just lying there. I called Inspector Thornhill and an officer came to take it away."

"But didn't the police search every inch of the school the day Abby was taken?"

"I thought so, yes. As far as I'm concerned, it's a police failure of epic proportions that the bag wasn't found immediately. Which is why I'm telling you now. If the police are going to be so shoddy in their work on a case as important as this, they don't deserve my silence."

Hope rippled through Tori. The sincerity and vehemence in the principal's tone was clear. Maybe Tori had been wrong to judge the woman so harshly. She clearly had the same taste in men as Tori, although it wasn't rocket science that a thousand women would find Mark attractive, but maybe hers and Principal White's sense of duty and justice were in sync too.

Tori relaxed farther into her seat. "So the police now have Abby's bag, but that still leaves the question of why she came out of the school gates alone. What did her teacher have to say about it?"

"I don't know. Miss Chalfield spoke to the police alone." She shook her head. "The police insisted all staff be interviewed separately. Clearly, every single one of us was under suspicion."

"If you were, that equates to good police work, rather than bad."

"I know, but it's still insulting."

Tori turned toward the window, her mind scrambling for an efficient tactic to get some new information out of the principal. She faced her. "Do you think maybe I could speak to Miss Chalfield?"

"That wouldn't be a very good idea."

"Why not?"

"Miss Chalfield is on sick leave, Miss Peterson." Principal White moved away from the desk and sat in her chair. "If you feel to blame for Tori's disappearance, Miss Chalfield is struggling with her part too."

"What does she feel she's done wrong?"

The principal closed her eyes. "I really shouldn't be telling you this."

"Principal White…" Tori looked at the nameplate in front of her on the desk. "Karen…please. This is a little girl we're talking about. Help me to bring her home."

When the principal opened her eyes, they were glazed with tears. "Miss Chalfield told the police that Abby left through the back doors of the classroom, which open onto the playground. A few hours later, Miss Chalfield came to me in floods of tears."

Unease trickled through Tori and she leaned forward, her body rigid. "Why?"

"Because she'd lied to the police. She couldn't be sure she saw Abby leave."

"Why would she lie about that?"

"She said she feels irresponsible not knowing where all the children were. It's understandable now that one of them has gone missing."

"I suppose." Tori frowned. "Has Miss Chalfield told the police the truth now?"

"No, but I did this morning. I presume Inspector Thornhill will be paying Miss Chalfield a visit today. You were right in what you saw, Miss Peterson. Abby walked out alone through the gates and without her bag. The question is, where was she if she wasn't with the rest of the class…and what on earth could have made her leave alone?"

Tori's mind raced with possibilities as her heart picked up speed. "She must've known her abductor."

"You echo my own terrifying thoughts. But who do we look for? I feel so helpless."

Tori closed her eyes and the image of Abby and her kidnapper, just before they vanished out of sight into the car, appeared behind her closed lids. "She fought him. She really did." Tori snapped her eyes open. "Which means she knew he'd lied to her. She was a clever girl, Principal. I wouldn't be surprised if she threw that bag into the shrubbery on purpose."

Hope lit the principal's gaze. "I have thought the exact same thing. We were meant to find it."

Chapter Fourteen

Tori pulled into the police station parking lot and killed the engine.

Whoever had taken Abby must have been grooming her for months in order to gain her trust. What else, other than a tantalizing promise, would tempt a child to slip out of his or her classroom unnoticed? Yet, between leaving the school to reaching the car, something he said, or did, had alarmed Abby enough that she fought back...even if his gloved hand over her mouth had ultimately prevented her screams.

Grabbing her bag from the passenger seat, Tori got out of the car and marched toward the station's doors. As much as she wanted to believe the police were questioning every adult who had regular contact with Abby, she wanted to hear confirmation directly from DCI Thornhill. She came to an abrupt halt when he emerged through the station doors.

"Inspector Thornhill, might I have a word?"

He slowed to a stop in front of her, his gaze irritated. "Miss Peterson. I am just on my way to speak with Abby's parents. If this can wait, I'll call you—"

"It can't."

The irritation in his gaze escalated.

"It's about Abby." She glanced over his shoulder at the two waiting officers behind him before meeting Thornhill's gaze once more. "I think you need to revisit the security tapes taken from the school. She knew her abductor, I'm sure of it."

"Why?"

"I…" Tori inhaled. The last thing she wanted was get Principal White into trouble, but this was too important. "I've just been speaking with Principal White. I understand Abby's teacher has confessed to not being completely sure how, or when, Abby left the school premises. I think she had pre-arranged to go with whoever took her. She was being groomed, Inspector." Another glance at the officers. "She was being groomed as Brian Appleton groomed me. Whoever has Abby would've been seen with her before. If you look at those tapes, CCTV around her home address, the classes she attends, I'm sure you'll see—"

"Well, I thank you for your input, Miss. Peterson, but firstly, Principal White should not have spoken to you about this case, and second, I have trained officers viewing the tapes as we speak." He glared. "You need to trust we are doing all we can. For everybody concerned."

"But—"

"Good day, Miss Peterson."

The inspector and the officers brushed past her. Tori spun around and glared at their retreating backs. Her heart beat faster with the strength of Thornhill's dismissal. She had told him of her history; told him of her suspected connection to the case. How could he brush aside her thoughts as though they held no value? She lifted her chin and blinked back the burning in her eyes.

Fine. If that's the way he wanted to play it, if he didn't want to make use of what she'd been forced to learn, then to hell with him.

Tori marched back to her car and slid into the driver's seat, pulling her phone from her bag, her hands shaking. She dialed Cally's number. Enough was enough. If Thornhill wanted to treat her like an ignorant hack, she would be forced to prove to him just how much she knew and suspected.

"Cally, it's me." Tori stared through the windscreen. "Where are you?"

"At the supermarket."

"Supermarket? What are you doing there? Do you know what, never mind. I want you to get back to the office as soon as possible."

"Is something wrong?"

"I need you to find out everything you can about a Mr. Huw Valentine."

"Valentine?"

"Yes, Valentine, as in hearts and flowers. I'll be back at the office as soon as I can. Thanks."

Tori ended the call and tapped the phone against her bottom lip. Helplessness threatened and she fought it back—just as Abby had her kidnapper.

She could not give in to the buried memories, the guilt and weight of responsibility.

The too-loud, too-annoying, ringing of her phone snapped her from her self-pity and Tori looked at the display.

Mark.

She clutched the phone tighter. Why did he have to call when she felt so bloody alone? So freaking useless?

She pressed talk. "Mark?"

"Hi."

His soft, deep voice slid down the line and around

her heart. It squeezed hard, demonstrating her scared and weakened state. She slumped her shoulders. "Hi."

"Can I see you?"

The sudden need to see him and look into his eyes was all she needed to hitch her self-inflicted barriers higher. She couldn't get into this—into him—right now. She was vulnerable, prone to making a huge mistake. "It's not a good idea, Mark."

"What isn't? Seeing me?"

"Yes."

"Look, I don't mean to keep shutting you out where Olivia is concerned. She's just…everything to me. I like you, Tori. Do you think maybe you could cut me a little slack over my parental issues, considering what we're doing?"

"What we're doing?"

"Trying to find Abby."

Tori squeezed her eyes shut against the stupidity he referred to anything personal between them. "Right. Sorry. Well, sure. I'll cut you some slack, but the same goes for you. We're both pretty messed up and, until Abby's found, I can't see how either of us will get any better." She swallowed, her heart stumbling with the need, the challenge, of showing a little of herself to him. "I like you too, but that doesn't mean us being together is a good idea. Especially not now. Abby's consuming me. She's all I want to think about."

"I understand." He sighed. "I spoke to Olivia this morning."

Tori frowned at the sudden sadness in his tone. "Is she okay?"

"I'm not sure."

"What do you mean?"

"She didn't know Abby very well, but Olivia said something that made me stop and think. She said all parents love their kids. Probably too much."

Tori smiled softly. "Hmm, maybe she's on to you."

"Funny. Do you know what else my beautiful, intelligent and far too savvy daughter said?"

"What?"

"She said, she can't help wondering where Abby played."

"Where she played? What does that mean?"

"I asked her the same thing and she took me upstairs to my study. She pointed to my computer and I fired it up. She looked so guilty and scared, it frightened the hell out of me."

Tori swallowed as her trepidation gathered. "What did she want you to see on the computer?"

"She told me to click on the history."

"And?"

"And it came up with a hundred and one sites that show parents possible scenarios of how easy it is for their kids to be taken. Actors pretending to be pedophiles luring kids from parks. Actresses luring them into cars. It was insane. The footage scared Olivia, but she said she couldn't stop watching." He exhaled a shaky breath. "I had no idea whenever she disappeared upstairs since Abby went missing, she's been looking at this stuff."

"Mark, that isn't your fault. You can't watch her all the time."

"She made me watch a video where, over and over, an actor gets kids to leave the park with him while their parents watch the whole thing from a distance. It got me thinking along the same lines as Olivia. That we should go back to wherever Olivia played. Maybe someone saw something, or someone, watching her."

Tori squeezed her eyes shut. "How could I have not thought of that?"

"Neither of us did."

"No, you don't understand." She opened her eyes and fumbled her keys into the ignition. "That's where Brian Appleton watched me."

"What?"

"Where I played. His interest started when he saw me with my dad at the gym but, later, once he was arrested, he confessed his favorite place to watch me had been where I played. What if there's a clue in my childhood that could unlock this entire case? Something that triggered Abby's abduction? We need to go back to Littledale, back to where he took me from. I'm the key to finding her. I know I am. Where are you?"

"At home."

"Will you come with me? I used to play in a woodland not far from where I went to school. I have to go back, Mark." Her stomach knotted with sickening dread. "I have to go back to where it all started."

\*\*\*\*

Nicknamed "the hunting ground" by local kids, no one could've guessed just how painful, or poignant, the name they'd given the woods would become to Tori.

As she steered her car toward the street that led there, she took a deep breath to counteract the heavy pit in her stomach. "I'm going to pull over. I need a second."

She brought the car to a stop at the side of the road, just before the street began its steep, downward slope toward the small woods at its apex. Gilmore Rise was a picturesque cul-de-sac that housed the moneyed homes Tori and her friends had often pretended were their own. It looked to be the ultimate picture postcard of the suburban ideal.

Nothing could've been further from the truth.

Tori pressed her hand to the nausea that churned in her stomach.

Maybe the woods and its surrounding houses had been idealized perfection once upon a time—now though, Gilmore Rise would always be the place where Brian Appleton had watched and planned while Tori played, oblivious to her starring role in his sick, theatrical fantasy.

"You okay?"

She turned. Mark was a man she was inexplicably growing to trust. Someone who, through his actions and words, had chipped away a little of the cement holding the bricks of her self-protection in place. The wall was still there, but it loosened a little more each and every time she saw him.

She exhaled. "No. I'm far from okay, but we need to do this. We need to go into those woods and try to find something that might give us a clue to what started this. Why it's my fault Abby was taken." She gave a small smile. "I'm glad you're here."

He cupped his hand to her jaw and looked deep into her eyes. "I got you, okay? We can stay here for as long or as little as you want."

She nodded, her heart stumbling with a sensation she didn't want to explore, her body responding to his contact. "Okay."

Ashamed of her need for physical release whenever she felt cornered by her emotions over Brian Appleton,

Tori lifted her face from Mark's hand. What did it mean that she acted so vehemently whenever raw, painful and inescapable emotions tore at her? She'd had numerous lovers over the years. Temporary, disposal men who served a purpose and then she could easily let go.

If the ache in her heart was anything to go by, it was painfully clear Mark would not be counted among those men. He had somehow caught her, snared her in a trap that was hopeful, inspiring and exciting, rather than suffocating, terrifying and unwanted. The question remained of what she would do about the situation…about Mark.

"Okay, let's do this." She shifted in her seat and shoved the gear stick into first. "The sooner we see if there is anything to find, the sooner we can get back to Barlington."

She slowly rolled the car down the spiraling road toward the bend in the very center of the cul-de-sac. The woods were deeper and darker than Tori remembered. Its outer trees tall and stretching to the blue sky, whereas beyond, the foliage grew thicker, denser, darker. All the better to build forts and dens, play hide and seek and tag.

Swallowing as her throat clogged with trepidation, Tori drew the car to a stop and unbuckled her seat belt. She and Mark got out of the car. When he reached for her hand, Tori gratefully took it and intertwined her fingers in his, pulling him forward.

Memories crashed into her mind—laughing faces, screams of shock and surprise; the distant calls of mothers for their children and the swish of car tires over wet asphalt. It was a different time; a different life. Now, as they walked deeper into the woods, she gripped Mark's hand tighter as she was thrown back in time to when she had been happy and unaware of the dangers that threaten children every day. A time when she'd been open, responsive and kind.

Brian Appleton had destroyed so much.

She ground her teeth as her anger swelled and determination to overcome what had held her back for so long grew stronger. Another little girl would not grow up to be who Tori was today. She would find Abby and she would save her from living her terrified, untrusting life alone.

As much as she would give anything for Abby's kidnapping to have never happen, Tori would use her anger as the weapon she needed to fight her fears and face her debilitating history. She would bring Abby back to her parents where she belonged—and win back her own courage once and for all.

"What are you thinking?" Mark's voice sliced through her reverie.

"How happy I was before Brian Appleton stole that happiness." She met his eyes. "How I need to do everything I can to get back the person I was before. I can't allow the same horrible changes happen to Abby, Mark. No child should have something change who they are so horribly."

Concern clouded his gaze as he looked over her face, his study lingering at her mouth. "I worried coming back here was a bad idea." He lifted his eyes to hers. "I don't want you any more distressed than you already are." He tipped his head back to look at the canopy of trees above them. "But I could hardly have stopped you. I had no right."

She squeezed his fingers, her heart once more

pulling toward his gentleness. "I like that you care."

He dipped his head and brushed his lips over hers before pulling back. "I care. A lot."

The strength of him, the goodness in him, surrounded her and Tori breathed deep before dragging her gaze from his and focusing ahead. "Follow me."

She led him deeper inside the cavern of trees and shrubbery until they came to a clearing. She surveyed the area. Voices and laughter of her childhood friends resounded in her mind and bounced from the bark as Tori walked toward a sawn tree truck. She eased her hand from Mark's and sat. "This was our meeting place."

"It's pretty cool."

She smiled softly. "Yeah, it was."

"Until he changed that." Mark sat beside her and laid his hand on her thigh. "Abby is too young to come to a place like this. Whoever took her could've only watched her at a park, a club or class where other adults were around." He passed his gaze over the greenery around them, his jaw tight. "The longer she's missing, the more I realize no matter what my intentions to look after Olivia, to keep her safe, it's an impossible dream." He faced her. "Susan Brady must've been near Abby whenever her abductor was. She's too young to play outside alone."

Tori recognized the agonizing fear in Mark's eyes and covered his hand with hers, hoping to offer *him* some comfort this time. "Let's think. What made whoever has Abby take her? Is it about me? Or is it about Brian Appleton? Or am I wrong and everything is really about an obsession with Abby?"

She stood and paced in a circle. "He told the police

he watched me from the road, both where I parked the car and through there." She pointed behind them. "Back there is another housing estate where he would park up. He took pictures. He took notes and he planned...planned how it would happen." She stopped and fisted her hands on her hips. "When he showed me the puppy, I didn't realize it at the time, but the reason I wasn't scared was because Appleton was a familiar face. One I had seen time and again, but couldn't place where because I was having too much fun. He wasn't a threat to me because my mind associated him with good memories."

"Then the same is likely to be true of whoever took Abby."

"Exactly. We need to find the place she is happiest. Where she goes and is never sad or afraid. I think whoever has her, persuaded her to come with him for even more fun, more happiness. Which is why I've asked Cally to find out all she can about this Huw Valentine." She sat beside Mark, her adrenaline pumping. "Susan Brady told the police, and me, that dancing was Abby's joy, her thing. The same was true of me, Mark. I loved to dance too." She smiled wryly. "Not that you'd believe it these days. My dancing stopped the minute Brian Appleton grabbed me. Everything stopped."

"Tori..."

She raised her hand, halting his embrace. "It's fine. I needed to come back here. It's been good to remember my childhood wasn't entirely tainted by what happened to me. I was happy once and I will be again." She stared around the trees. "All I want is for Abby's happiness to be less damaged. For her to have less to conquer."

"Then we'll start with this Huw Valentine. We'll go speak to him ourselves."

Tori turned. "I want to see him alone."

His eyes darkened and his jaw tightened. "I thought we'd sorted out this pushing me away? I'm in this whether you like it or not."

"I know you are, but for entirely different reasons than me. Please, Mark, let me drop you at home. You should be with Olivia. As soon as I know anything, I'll call you." She took his hand and hesitated for a second before raising it to her lips. She pressed a kiss to his knuckles. "I won't be responsible for something happening to you or your daughter. I need to do this alone."

Chapter Fifteen

"Dad? Where are you?"

Mark sat back on his haunches and squinted at the new lock on the back door of his house. "Out the back, sweetheart."

He moved his head from side to side and the bunched muscles in his neck clicked and groaned their indignation. Olivia's footsteps sounded along the floor tiles in the kitchen until she emerged into the conservatory.

"What are you doing?"

"Upgrading the locks." Mark grimaced, knowing full well the simple answer would not be enough to satisfy his overly suspicious offspring. "How was soccer?"

"Fine. Why are you changing the locks?"

"Not changing. Upgrading." Mark picked up a screwdriver and drove the final screw into place. "Done."

Olivia's familiar scent enveloped Mark as his daughter hunkered down beside him. "Is this to protect us from whoever's taken Abby?"

Mark's gut wrenched, and he turned. Olivia stared at the lock, her pretty face unmoving in concentration, her gaze focused. All the fears and worry he wasn't being a good enough father to her, all the grief and loss of control he thought he had a handle on since Lauren died, surged to the surface. What did it say to Olivia that he was barricading them in and preventing his pre-teen daughter from living the life she deserved?

His steadfast respect and admiration for Tori's strength and fortitude to move forward after everything she'd been through knotted his chest. He released a breath. "One way or another, he'll be caught. You do know that, right?"

"Maybe."

Anger at Brian Appleton and whoever had Abby brought Mark to his feet. He leaned forward and smoothed his hand over Olivia's back. "Hey, come here."

Her muscles tensed beneath his palm, her spine stretching as she inhaled. "I'm okay."

"Stand. Now."

With a theatrical sigh only an eleven-year-old girl could pull off, Olivia pushed to her feet and faced him. Her blue eyes, so similar to his own, burned bright with tears, her cheeks flushed. "What?"

"I'm not upgrading the locks to protect us from whoever took Abby."

"Then why?"

"For Tori."

Her cheeks darkened and she glared. "Tori? Your new girlfriend? Great, well, at least we all know our place now."

She moved to stalk past him and Mark gripped her elbow. "Wait right there."

Guilt pulsed at his temples. He had no clue where his frustration began and his daughter's ended. He stared into her eyes, willing Olivia to understand what he was saying. "When Abby was taken from outside your school, everything changed. I love you, Olivia. I love you more than life itself, but someone came to your school and took a little girl in broad daylight. Your mother's gone, and I'm trying my best to teach you, love you, keep you safe, but God, every day I feel as though I'm failing you." His eyes burned as tears rolled over his precious baby's cheeks. "Do you think you could meet me halfway and let me explain why the locks are for Tori?"

She yanked her arm from his grasp and lifted her chin. "Not if meeting you halfway is calling Tori mum. Sorry, Dad, I won't do that."

"Olivia—"

"Leave me alone."

She ripped her soccer bag from her shoulder and dumped it at his feet before fleeing from the room. Mark cursed and shoved his hands into his hair, trying to hold his head and heart together.

For five long years, he'd done his best to be in control. To control everything around him from his work, to his life, to Olivia's life. Now, everything was changing and, day-by-day, he lost his grip on everything he'd thought he understood.

Olivia, Tori, even he, had undergone a metamorphosis and evolved into beings he presumed too much about. He knew no more about himself, than he did the females currently haunting his every thought and feeling. The one thing he did know, he would not lose Olivia amidst the mayhem.

"Olivia?" He strode through the conservatory, the kitchen and into the living room. "I wasn't done talking to you."

She sat slumped on the couch, her glare aimed at a

teenage soap on TV, her arms crossed and her face reminiscent of his wife's when Lauren was mad. Mark swallowed his loss and focused on the parenting job in hand.

Olivia had to understand—*he* had to understand— his entire life could not constantly revolve around his child, twenty-four-seven, for the rest of his life.

"There's nothing else to talk about, Dad. If you want to be boyfriend-girlfriend, with Tori, then do it. I don't care."

Mark swiped the remote control from the arm of the couch and turned off the TV. He faced Olivia. "You do care."

"Do not."

"Look at me."

She turned from the blackened TV screen and faced him.

Mark sat beside her, clasping his hands between his knees to stop from reaching for her. The last thing he could handle now was her physical rejection. "I like Tori, but my main priority is you. Will always be you. I want to keep you safe and upgrading the locks is all I have right now."

Indecision and honesty waged a war inside him. How much could his bright, beautiful eleven-year-old girl handle? *God, Lauren, help me.* He swallowed against the dryness in his throat. "We think…maybe…Tori is central to why Abby was taken. We took your idea about where Abby played and went to where Tori played as a child."

Olivia stared, her confusion showing in the furrow at her brow. "Why is Tori to blame for Abby being taken? What did she do?"

"She isn't to blame, hon."

"I don't understand. You said—"

"Something happened to her a long time ago and it seems connected to Abby disappearing. The police are looking into it and so is Tori. We'll find Abby, Liv. I know we will."

"But if you really think that then why are you changing the locks?"

Mark swiped his hand over his face, hoping Olivia understood his motivation was buried in his caring and didn't hate him for what he was about to propose. "Because I think Tori needs to stay here for a while. I *want* her to stay here."

She pressed her lips tightly together, her gaze wary.

Mark exhaled. "Tori and I are doing all we can to help the police find Abby. If I…*we*…can find her, it will go a long way toward making me believe I'm enough for you. Do you understand?"

His words reverberated in his head. I, I, I…was this all about him? And not everything to do with Abby, as it should be?

"Is he going to come here?"

Mark frowned. "Who?"

"Whoever has Abby." Olivia uncurled her legs from underneath her, her eyes wide. "Isn't that the real reason you're changing the locks?"

Guilt slithered through him. Instead of making his daughter feel safer in her own home, all he'd done was scare her more. "Of course he isn't. Come here." He opened his arms and Olivia shimmied across the couch to snuggle beside him. He wrapped his arms around her and squeezed, pressing a kiss to the soft silk of her hair and hoped to God everything came to a successful end sooner rather than later.

Olivia eased from his arms. "You're right, Dad. Nothing will happen to Tori if you're here. She should stay with us…at least for a while."

Mark released his held breath, smiled, and pressed another kiss to his baby's head.

\*\*\*\*

Tori sat back in her seat at the paper, her phone clutched to her ear. "Thank you for agreeing to talk to me, Mrs. Brady. I know every hour that goes by with Abby missing must feel like a week."

"It does. Every *minute* feels that way. How can I help you, Miss Peterson?"

"Tori, please. I wonder if you would be willing to tell me where Abby danced and which days of the week?"

"Where she danced?"

Tori closed her eyes and sent up a silent prayer that Mrs. Brady wouldn't cut her off, that she understood everything Tori was doing was in an effort to find Susan's daughter. "I want to speak with Huw Valentine."

"DCI Thornhill has already talked to me about Huw Valentine. He said he has an alibi. What are you trying to achieve? I don't want a man wrongly accused."

"That's the last thing I want, too." Tori opened her eyes and looked across her desk. Cally frowned as she watched her. Tori grimaced as a way of communicating to her trainee journalist that the conversation wasn't going quite as well as she'd anticipated. "I just want to speak to him for my own peace of mind. You know I have a more personal experience of abduction than most, Mrs. Brady. Please, let me help you."

Seconds passed before Mrs. Brady sighed. "Fine. Abby dances at the sport center every Saturday morning and on Wednesdays from five to six-thirty."

Tori quickly scribbled the information on the notepad in front of her. "So he should be there at five today?"

Mrs. Brady huffed a laugh. "Oh, he'll be there. He'll be there with bells on. The man's obsessed."

*Obsessed. Obsessed enough to take a little girl? A little girl who poses competition to his own child?* Tori frowned. "How does Abby compare to his daughter in terms of ability?"

"They're pretty much the same. Abby shows great talent." Pride rang in Susan Brady's voice. "She won a gold medal for her age group in the modern category only last month."

Tori smiled. "That's fantastic."

"Yes…it was."

The abrupt desolation in Susan Brady's tone squeezed Tori's heart. It was as though this agonized mother felt guilty for smiling even for the briefest moment. Tori took a deep breath. "I'll go and see Huw Valentine, and if I think there's more for the police to pursue with him, I'll be sure to call you. Okay?"

"Thank you. For everything you're trying to do. It might not feel like it but I'm grateful, Miss Peterson. Truly."

"We'll talk soon." Tori hit the end call button and tossed her phone onto her desk. "God, this is so bloody horrible."

"You're going to see Huw Valentine?" Cally's

frown deepened. "But I didn't find anything on him. Why do you think he has something to do with Abby?"

"I don't. Not really." Tori stood and shrugged into her jacket. "But at least by going to see him, I'm doing more than sitting here feeling helpless."

"What did you mean when you said to Mrs. Brady that you have a different experience of abduction than most?"

"You heard that?" Heat hit Tori's cheeks. "I just meant that, as a reporter, I generally have a better access to the public than the police. You know how some people can be with the police. I've got a sneaking suspicion Huw Valentine, because of his over-zealous enthusiasm in his child and other people's children, wasn't overly forthcoming with Thornhill."

"That's it?" Cally's eyes turned intense with concern. "Because if there's anything else bothering you, I'd like to think you'd turn to me if you needed to."

Even though Tori had been reluctant to lean on anybody for many years, she couldn't help but be touched by Cally's offer of friendship. "Thanks, but I'm fine. Just doing my job."

Cally studied her for a moment longer before she smiled, her eyes shining with their childlike glee once again. "Good. So, do you want me to come with you?"

"No, I'm okay doing this on my own." Tori lifted the strap of her purse onto her shoulder. "Anyway, didn't you say you were at the supermarket earlier? Seeing as you're on work time, I'm guessing you were there doing something on Neil's demand?"

"Oh, that." Cally rolled her eyes. "There's some dispute between the staff union and the management.

Something and nothing, but I suppose I'd better get what I have typed up."

"You do that. I'll see you later."

With a wave, Tori strode through the office and out onto the street. The day was chilly, but bright, and a walk would help rid her body of some of its unease. If she walked through town to the sports center, she'd have time to work out how she would play her upcoming interview with Huw Valentine.

She prayed the mental images she had of the man did not come to fruition in person. Brian Appleton was considered a good-looking man before he brought his obsessions into the public eye so she knew how easily people could be duped by a potential predator. Yet, that didn't stop her from pinning Valentine as a slimeball of a forty-something male who spent his days surrounded by young girls in leotards.

Barlington Sports Center was a mammoth glass and chrome building situated high above the town like a continuous reminder to its people that their lifestyle could always use some improvement.

Tori walked through the automatic sliding doors and approached the circular reception area. A thin, spray-tanned twenty-something year old woman greeted her. "Hi, can I help you?"

Tori forced a smile. "I wonder if you can point me in the direction of under elevens modern dance class?"

"Sure. It's down the stairs, second studio on your left. The spectators' area is just along the corridor to the right."

"Great, thanks." Tori walked toward the spectators' area, irritated that nothing was asked of who she was, or why she interested in the young girls dancing. Was it any wonder kids were targeted so often?

The spectator section was narrow and glass-walled with an unobstructed view into the two dance studios below. The two rows of seats were approximately half full, but only one man sat amongst the nine or ten women. Tori took a deep breath and slid into a seat two down from who she hoped was Huw Valentine.

She surreptitiously studied him from the corner of her eye. One thing she could be sure of, even if Huw Valentine was somehow involved in Abby's disappearance, this was not the man Tori had witnessed take her. Valentine's dark hair and slight build were the opposite of Abby's abductor. Not to mention the man appeared shorter than Tori as they sat a few feet away from each other.

Tori forced her gaze to the class below. "Great, aren't they?"

"Really great. My daughter takes my breath away every time I watch her."

She turned. The guy's cheeks were red and a film of perspiration glistened at his top lip and along his hairline. Maybe he wasn't that far off a pedophile's stereotype after all. Tori faced front. "Which one is yours?"

His gaze lit with pride and he smiled. "The one on the far left, light brown hair and as pretty as a picture."

"Ah, yes, I see her. She's beautiful."

"Thank you. Not to mention talented, gifted, ambitious and driven. Beauty is not enough to be the best in this business, Ms…" He held out his hand.

Tori took it and tried not to pull back when his clammy paw grasped hers. "Spring."

"Nice to meet you. I'm Huw Valentine and that's

my daughter, Catherine." His smile wavered. "I don't think I've seen you here before. Is one of the girls yours?"

"Oh, no. I have a niece interested in taking the class so I told her I'd come along to see what goes on."

His smile vanished. "Not just anyone can join a class of this caliber, Ms. Spring. This is the advanced class. Only the very special girls come here. Girls with the potential to be the very best. I do hope your niece has that kind of training behind her?"

"Oh, I didn't realize. She has only been dancing for a year or so."

He shook his head and tutted before casting his gaze over the dancers once more. "Then she wouldn't be suitable for this class. Not at all. Only the best of their age group here, I'm afraid."

Tori drew a long breath and prepared to ask her next question, fear Huw Valentine would call her out prevalent in her mind. "I only heard of this class after someone mentioned at my niece's school that Abby Brady comes here."

He snapped his head around. "That is really most distasteful. To show an interest in a class only after one of its students has been snatched from the street? You should be ashamed."

Tori cast her eyes downward.

"Do you know something?"

She met his irritated gaze. "What?"

"You are the second person who has spoken to me today about that little girl. The first being the police."

"The police?"

"Yes."

"What did they want to know?"

He bristled and shifted in his seat. "I really don't think that is any of your concern."

"I'm sorry, but I was there, you see, at the school when Abby was taken. I can't help thinking there must have been something I, or any of the adults present, could've done."

"There is nothing anyone could've done. These animals who prey on children are calculating and callous monsters. There is no knowing how or when they will strike."

Tori resisted the urge to slide farther back in her seat. The man's eyes positively bulged with the vehemence of his words, his bottom lip glistening with spittle.

"Surely the police don't think you have something to do with Abby's disappearance? That's slanderous."

"Oh, don't you worry. I put them straight soon enough. I've had words with Abby's parents in the past and the police deemed that enough to track me down for questioning, but I soon sent them on their way. I'm a lover of dance. A lover of doing all I can to forward my daughter's chances. Just because I have views on other children's performances does not make me a predator."

"Of course not."

"Only according to the police, it does. I will not stand for it. If they contact me again, I shall lodge a complaint."

"You should."

He turned to the class. "They had the audacity to ask me where I was at the time Abby was taken. I was working on an application for my daughter's upcoming county competition."

"You were alone?"

He snapped his angry gaze to hers. "Do you now suspect me of wrongdoing, Ms. Spring?"

"Of course not. I am merely imagining that was the police's next question. Forgive me. I watch far too many police programs on TV."

He held her gaze before turning his focus to his daughter. "I was alone and that will be the end of it, I'm sure. I want Abby Brady reunited with her poor parents as much as the next person. I cannot imagine how I would ever cope if Catherine was taken from me."

Tori stared ahead. Hadn't Susan Brady said Huw Valentine had provided the police with an alibi? Yet, he'd just stated he was alone at home. Something wasn't right, and the longer she stayed in the man's vicinity, the more she wanted to grab his sweaty neck and demand he take her to Abby…regardless of the probability that he had nothing at all to do with her disappearance.

Tori stood. "Well, I should go. Clearly, this class isn't the one for my niece."

Huw Valentine turned and offered her a small smile. "Don't be too disappointed, Ms. Spring. This class is very special even with a talented girl absent."

Tori stilled. "I'm sorry?"

"Well, Abby, I mean." His cheeks darkened. "I hope her absence is only temporary, you understand."

"Of course." Tori smiled before turning and heading out the door, the bitter taste of anger coating her throat.

The man clearly viewed Abby's disappearance as entirely beneficial as far as any competition to his daughter's chances was concerned. Tori strode past the reception area and outside into the bright autumnal light.

She breathed deep, praying for something, anything to cleanse the evil currently hovering over the town where she'd come to seek refuge years before. Suddenly, it wasn't just Brian Appleton she suspected of having something to do with Abby's abduction, but every man in Barlington.

Chapter Sixteen

At Barlington Police Station, Mark pulled his car into a vacant spot next to Tori's blue convertible. She had her back to him, her butt against the car's hood as she chatted into her phone. He waited for her to finish her call, taking the time to appreciate the view without her knowledge. Her dark red hair was caught up in a ponytail, tendrils escaping over her slender neck and shoulders. Days had passed since their impromptu sex in her kitchen and the need to touch her again simmered.

She ended her call and turned.

Her frown vanished to be replaced with an almost shy smile. A smile Mark hadn't seen before. His desire to recapture their intimacy grew as he slid the keys from the ignition before getting out of the car.

He came toward her. "I'm glad you called. You had another couple of hours and then I was coming to find you whether you liked it or not."

She laughed, the sound nervous. "Your need to be a superhero is running a little thin."

He lifted an eyebrow. "Yeah? Well, until you give me the respect I deserve as a superhero, I'll have to keep finding ways to prove to you that's what I am."

"Knock yourself out."

The urge to kiss her intensified. He stared at her mouth before inhaling and meeting her eyes. "So, did you speak with Valentine? I haven't heard from you since we drove back from Littledale. What about Thornhill? Any new developments? I haven't heard or seen anything on the news."

The soft flirtation in her gaze vanished and she closed her eyes.

Concern bolted through him like a shot arrow, piercing deep in his gut. "What's happened?"

She opened her eyes. "Nothing further from Thornhill, but I did speak with Valentine *and* I've received another letter." She slipped her hand inside her jacket and pulled out a folded sheet of paper. "Here."

Mark slowly took the single sheet of paper, his focus on her bowed head and his heart pumping with dangerous possession. He unfolded the letter and read.

Each word hit like a knife slash to his ability to keep her safe. He looked up and met her worried gaze. "You know this is bullshit, right? So what if he knows we're spending time together? He won't get to me, Tori. You do know that?"

"No, Mark." She squeezed his arm. "I don't know that and neither do you. Whoever's doing this either knows Appleton, or is using what he did to me to get inside my head and now wants to start messing with my future too. Maybe it's someone who spent time with Appleton in prison. I don't know, but whoever it is, they've taken over where Appleton left off. He's said about dressing Abby up, about me spending hours making our home bright and beautiful, like I'm his Stepford wife or something. Appleton's house could have been a set for the movie. This is all the same mindset as he had when I was in his house, Mark. They are either the same person or someone's copying him."

She pushed some hair back from her face, her hand trembling. Mark stepped forward and eased her head onto his shoulder, relieved that she didn't pull away. "We need to show this to Thornhill."

"I know." She pulled back from him and slid the letter from his fingers. "I've made some interesting discoveries since I last saw you. First of which is Huw Valentine either lied to the police or to me. Either way, it's enough to convince me we need to make the police question him again."

Irritation bloomed. Didn't she understand the danger she was in? "I really wish you'd let me come to see Valentine with you. The police wanted you under protection for a reason."

Defensiveness flashed in her eyes. "Don't you see? I want whoever's trying to get me to have access to me. If it's me he wants, he can have me and let Abby go. Protecting me isn't your responsibility, Mark."

He clenched his jaw, frustration burning hot inside him. Didn't she understand how much he was coming to care for her? He'd had sex with this woman, yet suddenly felt no closer to her than he would a stranger on the street. "If you don't trust me to be a part of this, I can't understand why you asked me here…unless, you want me to speak to Thornhill with you. You either want me in this or you don't."

"I *do* want you in this." Her eyes glinted with tears. "I want you with me, but that doesn't stop me feeling as though I don't know what the hell I'm doing."

"With the investigation?"

"And with you. Everything feels out of control and I hate it. After I was found, I vowed, even at that age, that I would always be in control of my destiny. Now

Abby's been taken and you…"

He took her hand. "And me what?"

"You are making me *feel*, Mark. Feel something for you."

He dipped his head, his heart full of relief as he softly brushed his lips across hers. "For the record, my feelings toward you are scaring the crap out of me too." He winked. "Superhero or no superhero."

She smiled and swiped her fingers under her eyes. "You're an idiot. An idiot I trust. Probably too much."

"Trusting someone is a good thing, Tori. I promise."

"There. That's what I'm afraid of."

He frowned. "What?"

"The promises, Mark. I don't want you to promise me anything. Not with us and not with Abby. Broken promises are what hurt people more than anything else."

Mark studied every inch of her beautiful face, from her gorgeous green eyes to her perfectly bowed lips. So much had happened to her. So much that should never happen to anyone. "Then let's focus on the investigation. As for everything else, we just let it play out, okay?"

She exhaled a shaky breath and stared toward the station. "I'm just not used to working with other people. I even try to do as much as I can without Cally hanging around me." She met his eyes. "But for some reason I can't understand, or I'm too scared to understand, I need you with me more and more."

He smiled. To admit she needed him must have been like someone pulling out one of her fingernails. "And I need you. Don't let what we have building

215

between us fall apart because of whoever it is tormenting you. You do that, he wins."

"I'm scared, Mark. Of everything."

"Me too, but I've a feeling we'll be stronger together than apart."

Her eyes flickered with what he assumed to be hesitation, before she blinked and turned away. "We need to get inside and see Thornhill."

She slipped her hand from his and Mark clenched his fingers into a fist as if he could trap the feel of her skin against his. "Is he expecting us?"

"Yes, he called saying he wants to talk to me about the first letter and the scarf."

Mark frowned. "Do you think they lifted some prints or something?"

"I don't know. He wouldn't tell me over the phone. I'm convinced Principal White knows more about the day Abby was taken than she's saying and I'm going to tell Thornhill so. I will also tell him that the statement Valentine gave the police differs from what he said to me."

"What did Valentine say exactly?"

"That he was alone when Abby was taken, but Susan Brady said he'd given the police a solid alibi."

Discomfort rippled through him. It made no sense for either of the people they were talking about to be involved. "Had you ever met the principal or Valentine before Abby was taken?"

"No. Why?"

"As much as I hate how you're at the center of all this, wouldn't whoever took Abby have to know you?"

The clear unease in her eyes squeezed at his heart. She frowned. "What are you saying?"

He took her hand again. "I can't see how Principal White or Valentine can be involved if they don't know you. Maybe we're wasting time focusing on the wrong people. Think about the letters. They wanted you to see Abby being taken. They want your attention now. This has to be someone you know."

The color faded from her face. "Maybe, or whoever took Abby is the paid help and the person in charge is yet to get his hands dirty." The skin at her neck moved as she swallowed. "This could still be Brian Appleton, Mark. In fact, it feels as though he's right behind me at every step, waiting to reach out and grab me when I least expect it." Her eyes darkened as she drew her hand from his and lifted her chin. "I'm not going to let that happen and I'm going to get Abby home. Come on. Let's do this."

She walked ahead of him toward the station doors and Mark inhaled a long breath. They had made tentative steps forward with the investigation and with each other. He prayed that both aspects continued in the same vein, because now he had Tori's trust, he didn't want to lose it.

He followed her toward the station doors.

\*\*\*\*

Tori's impatience thinned with each passing second. She shifted in her seat as Thornhill read the letter.

At last, he finished and lifted his gaze to hers. "We'll check yours and Mr. Bolton's fingerprints against this letter as we did the first, just in case something shows up on this one. From what I can tell, the same computer and printer has been used, but I'll have that verified too. Whoever's responsible for this letter, his obsession is escalating." Thornhill's jaw tightened. "Which means, inevitably, he's becoming more dangerous."

Tori sat forward. "Brian Appleton is involved, I'm sure of it. Could you have your officers look into his whereabouts again? His new family?"

"I have and I assure you Appleton is still out of the country. As for his family, there is nothing suspicious there either."

"What about the men he served time with?"

Thornhill frowned. "What about them?"

"Couldn't Brian Appleton have told them to come after me once they got out of prison? He was obsessed, Inspector. Who's to say he wouldn't send someone after me while he was incarcerated? What if that person became idolized with Appleton and his crimes?"

"He was released years ago, Miss Peterson. Don't you think something would have happened before now if the person responsible for Abby's kidnapping was someone Appleton's associated with?"

"I don't know and neither do you. I can't believe nothing was on the first letter or the scarf."

Thornhill shifted his gaze from her to Mark, who sat as stiff as an upright corpse beside her. The tension emanated from him and clouded the room with its heavy weight.

The inspector faced Tori and placed his forearms on his desk, his fingers locked. "Both the letter and the scarf are clean. No prints. Plus, the letter could've been typed on pretty much any computer and printed on any printer. Believe me, I'm as disappointed as you are that there was nothing to further our investigations."

"But you'll follow up on what I've told you about

Principal White and Huw Valentine?"

"We'll speak again with Mr. Valentine but, as far as Principal White is concerned, we have no valid reason to re-question her. She has helped us as much as humanly possible."

"And Abby's bag?" Tori's frustration mounted. "Surely, she threw it in the bushes so someone would find it."

"Even if your supposition is right, the bag and its contents have given us no new leads. The prints on there were Abby's, her mother's or teacher's. We've taken each of their prints and they have been eliminated. The discovery of the bag hasn't helped in any way. I have officers searching every remote spot in Barlington and the surrounding towns. I have officers making door to door enquiries." His jaw tightened. "Each day that goes by, the more I fear the worst. We have to stay focused."

"But—"

"Miss Peterson, please. There's every chance whoever took Abby will come after *you*. He or she has made contact by letter and left the scarf for you to find. They knew you'd be at the school *and* the church. Someone's following you or knows your diary. I want you to stay safe." His gaze hardened. "Which means you need to stay away from this investigation."

"How can you ask me to do that when—"

"In this second letter the writer clearly states he'll keep Abby until he has you."

"Then use me as bait to flush him out."

"Tori." Mark covered her hand with his. "The inspector's right. You're at risk every time you step out of your house. It's time to trust the police to do their job."

Hard determination gleamed in Mark's gaze and she snatched her hand from his, her heart twisting with disappointment that he would agree with the inspector rather than supporting her. "No."

He glared. "Please. For me. I don't want anything to happen to you."

Thornhill cleared his throat and Tori dragged her gaze from Mark to look at him.

"When I mentioned police protection before, you refused it. I really think it's something you need to reconsider."

She wanted to scream her frustration. She'd bet a hundred British pounds that the inspector's words were less about her protection, and more about keeping an eye on what she was up to. "I don't need police protection."

"I can't insist on it, but—"

"No." Tori shook her head. "I won't let this confine me anymore than it already has. You're forgetting I'm no longer a child. No one is going to pluck me off the street and force me into a car without a fight. It happened once. Over my dead body will it happen again."

"And is that what you want? To be dead?" Thornhill's cheeks darkened. "Because if you don't start behaving as though you could be killed, being dead is exactly what I fear for you."

Tori glared.

Mark leaned forward. "There's no need to scare her, Inspector. She'll stay at my place until Abby is found and whoever has her is behind bars."

"I also suggest Miss Peterson not work for the next

few days until we know it's safe for her to do so. This animal could be anywhere."

Tori looked from one man to the other, indignation burning like fire inside her. "Oh, don't mind me. I'll just sit here while the big, strong men sort out what is best for me."

Mark turned and the anger in his gaze made her shift a little way back in her chair. "We're trying to keep you alive. If you don't want to stay with me, stay with your sister, but there is no way you're staying anywhere alone. Now, which is it to be? Me or your sister?"

Frustration formed a ball in her throat preventing her from speaking.

He nodded. "Good. My house it is then."

Tori snapped her gaze to Thornhill, her disbelief Mark would push her around rendering her speechless.

Thornhill's attempt to hide his satisfied smile was futile as he trained his gaze on Mark. "As for you Mr. Bolton, it might be best if your daughter stayed away from your house while Tori is there. If she's being watched, it would be best for Olivia to be elsewhere."

"No, you can't do that." Tori snapped, knowing just how much Mark needed to know his daughter was alive and well at the best of times. "She'll think my being there has separated her from her father."

"Then you must stay somewhere else."

"I'm not going to my sister's either. She has my niece to worry about."

Mark touched her hand. "I could let Olivia stay at a friend's for a couple of nights. She'll undoubtedly grab the chance with both hands."

"Mark, no." Tori slumped her shoulders, sympathy

and appreciation mixing inside her. "I know you don't want her away from you, so don't do this. Not because of me."

He gripped her hand. "This is for me too. And Olivia."

Guilt washed over her. In a matter of days, her life had begun to affect everyone around her. It was as though she was the first human domino in a row of others and, one by one, they were all being knocked down in a bid to keep her safe.

She shook her head. "I don't want you to do anything you don't want to do. Not for me. You don't owe me anything."

"I owe you plenty." Mark faced the inspector, his hand still tightly around hers. "My daughter will go to a friend's and Miss Peterson will stay with me."

Thornhill nodded before facing Tori. "Are you in agreement?"

Tori looked from one man to the other, their gazes equally dark with intent. What choice did she have? If Appleton came for her again, this time he would kill her. Of that much she was certain. He either resented his incarceration, or the fact she got away from him.

She could only hope and pray he didn't hurt Abby in any way in the meantime.

"I'm in agreement." She exhaled in defeat. "I'll stay with Mark."

Chapter Seventeen

Tori left Neil's office and walked to her desk, her fear of the future making her steps uneven across the carpeted floor tiles. A small part of her had hoped he would tell her Thornhill's concern that her life was in danger was over-zealous. Instead, instantaneous concern had burst in her editor's eyes and stiffened Neil's usual nonchalance.

Tori lifted her bag onto her desk with a purposely-heavy thump and Cally looked up from her computer. She smiled widely. "You're back."

"I am." Tori pulled open her desk drawer and removed some of her personal belongings. "At least for the next five minutes or so anyway."

Concern immediately darkened Cally's pretty brown eyes. "You're going somewhere?"

"Yep. It seems the world and its uncle thinks I'm in danger."

"What? Why?"

"I can't go into it. Sorry." Tori gripped her small make-up bag and looked across the desk. Cally was fragile at the best of times and Tori imagined the separation from her mentor wasn't going to be helpful in her young protégée's career. "Look, you'll be fine." Tori gestured with her hand for Cally's. "You're doing great and my not being here won't affect that."

Cally clasped Tori's fingers. "What's happened?

Why is everyone so worried about you?"

Indecision battled. How much to tell Cally? How much could the young woman handle? Tori took a deep breath. "The police have reason to believe I might be involved in Abby Brady's disappearance."

"Involved? How?"

"Remember the scarf at the church?"

Cally nodded.

"I was meant to find it." Tori eased her hand from Cally's and dropped into her chair. "I was also meant to see Abby taken."

"I don't understand."

Reluctant to distress Cally any more than necessary, Tori bit back her growing need to share her story with someone who she felt no overt emotional connection with. Somewhere down the line, she'd become emotionally connected with Mark. More than that, her burgeoning relationship with him filled her with an overwhelming sense of joy and possibility. He knew her story and still looked at her as a woman rather than a victim—the same would not be true of Cally if she learned of Tori's abuse.

She swallowed. "I'm not comfortable discussing it right now. All you need to do for me is keep working hard and support whoever Neil wants to cover Abby's story. I don't want it to be shoved to the background, or considered as less of a priority the longer she's missing."

"Neil wouldn't do that." Her eyes widened with worry. "Would he?"

Tori shrugged and reached into her desk drawer to remove a book containing her most vital contacts in and around Barlington. "I hope not. He's told me it will remain front cover news until she's found, but I'd still feel happier knowing you are here to speak for me."

Cally's cheeks flushed. "Of course I will."

"Good." Tori smiled and stood, lifting her purse strap onto her shoulder. "I'll be in touch, okay? I'm staying at Mark's, but ring me any time—"

"Mark Bolton's? But you hardly know him. Don't you think you should stay with someone you know? Why not stay at my place?"

Tori shook her head, touched by the fear in Cally's innocent gaze. "He'll look after me. He's a superhero after all."

"No, he's not. He's just a carpenter. This isn't funny, Tori."

Annoyance prickled at Cally's snarky tone. "You're right, it isn't funny, but…" She took a deep breath, inhaling her words and their sentiment. "I trust him. So can you. I'd better go. He's dropping his daughter at a friend's and then coming by to pick me up."

"Won't you at least come to my party next weekend?"

"A party is the last thing I want to think about."

"Should I cancel it?" Cally's eyes shadowed with worry. "Do you think people will think badly of me under the circumstances?"

"You should do what you want. It's your life. The one thing I know for sure, is life is too short to not grab what you want, when you want it. If you want a party, have one."

"But you won't be there."

"I'm not in the mood for a party, Cally. I'm sorry."

Cally stared at her a moment longer before she

slumped her shoulders. "I'll walk you out."

"There's no ne—"

"I want to."

Her sharp retort clipped the air and guilt pressed on Tori that she might have frightened her young colleague. She touched Cally's arm. "Everything will work out, you know."

Cally nodded. "I know it will."

As Cally walked ahead toward the exit, Tori took a final look at her desk before following Cally through the office and downstairs to the lobby. Through the floor to ceiling glass doors, Mark's parked car glinted beneath the amber streetlights. Relief skittered across Tori's heart knowing he was there. The knowledge someone cared for her, wanted to look out for her, took on a whole new meaning. Having someone so interested in her life no longer scared her. With Mark, it pleased her.

She turned to Cally and smiled. "I'll be okay. Don't worry."

Her protégé immediately stepped forward and drew Tori into a hug. "Call me if you need anything."

Tori smiled. "I will."

Easing from Cally's arms, Tori walked from the newspaper office and prayed her ongoing torment came to a close the following day. That Abby was returned home and whoever wanted Tori was captured, never to see the light of day again.

\*\*\*\*

Mark opened the front door to his house and waved Tori inside ahead of him. A permanent scowl had etched her stunning features during the drive over, but as much as he hated having to override her wishes about choosing where to stay, he couldn't stand by and let her put her life at risk so offhandedly.

It was as though she thought her life insignificant—that it wasn't as important as Abby's, her niece's or Olivia's.

Mark gripped his keys. Her lack of self-worth most likely stemmed from Appleton's actions. The bastard continued to cast his dark shadow over Tori's life even now.

"Mark?"

He blinked and faced her.

She swept her concerned gaze over his face. "Are you sure you're all right with Olivia being at a friend's?"

"I'm fine." He put his keys on the radiator cover beside him and shrugged off his jacket. "She looked as though all her Christmases had come at once when I dropped her off." He hung his coat on the row of hooks by the door, shouldering the rebuff he'd felt to witness such unequivocal glee on Olivia's face at the prospect of freedom. "She deserves this." He faced Tori and winked. "Of course, it helps my worry that her friend's dad is a black belt in Karate and has two daughters of his own he'd kill for."

Tori smiled. "Ah, now I understand why you aren't entirely flipping out."

"Ways and means. At least it's a step in the right direction. I hope when Abby's found and whoever has her is under arrest, I'll accept I can't keep Olivia as close to me as I'd like."

"You're a good dad. Don't be so hard on yourself."

He held her gaze, the need to believe her clawing at his heart. "Thank you."

She nodded and walked into the living room. He followed her, trying his hardest to relax the worry that ached across his stiff shoulders and neck. Why did he have to meet Tori under such horrific circumstances? For the first time since Lauren died, he wanted to properly date and court another woman; wanted to see Tori smile and laugh.

Until Abby was found alive and well, the notion he and Tori might spend some happy time together was futile. There was too much tension, too much at stake for both of them. The liberty to fully enjoy each other's company would continue to be a stretch too far.

When he entered the living room, Tori stood staring through the window into the darkness beyond. After a few moments, she abruptly snapped the curtains closed and walked to the sofa. She sat, dropping her head back and closing her eyes. "Please tell me you have wine."

He smiled, despite the helplessness raging a war inside him. "I do. Red or white?"

"White." She opened her eyes. "Please."

"You okay?"

"As much as I can be knowing another night drawing in, is another night Abby is being subjected to God knows what."

"Hey…" Mark sat on the arm of the chair beside her. "Whoever has Abby said she's stopped crying, that he's being kind and loving. We have to pray he's treating her well. If we don't—"

"We'll go mad? Because that's what I think is happening to me. I've never allowed myself to imagine what Appleton did to me all those years ago would resurface this way. I can't stand it. Everyone I know is in danger."

"Not everyone."

"No? Melissa, my work colleagues, even you now that Thornhill's demanded I stay here like I'm under house arrest." She pushed up from the sofa and tossed her purse onto the opposite chair. "How long does he expect me to stay here?"

"I don't know, but *I* expect you to stay here for as long as it takes."

With no need to emphasize or explain what "it" was, Mark searched his mind and heart scrambling for a way to find Abby and alleviate the guilt Tori had taken upon herself. "It's true what Thornhill said, you know. This has to be someone you know."

"I can't think that way. If I start suspecting every person I've come in contact with these past years, it will tip me over the edge. Doing that will not help Abby."

"Every hour that ticks by he gets more frustrated and the more dangerous the situation becomes."

"You think I don't know that?"

He got up from the arm of the chair and sat next to her. "Hey, I'm on your side, remember? When we went back to Littledale you said you wanted to go there to figure out the kidnapper's mind. The letters have confirmed, at least for us, that Appleton has a part to play."

"Yet, Thornhill is adamant Appleton is in Menorca."

"What about his family? Friends?"

"I'm hoping the police are looking into it." She darted her anxious gaze over his face. "I don't know what else to do."

"Come here." He opened his arms and hesitation passed through her gaze before she leaned into him. He pressed a kiss to her hair. "Maybe not tonight, but soon, either us or the police will have a breakthrough."

"I hope so."

The desolation in her voice wrenched at his heart and Mark silently willed her to fight her fear of broken promises and fully trust him. His steadfast need to take care of people and situations lodged like a rock in his stomach. If he failed and anything happened to Olivia, Abby or Tori, he would never recover. Lauren's untimely death would always lie like a fresh bruise on his heart, but the death of another girl, or woman, in his life would be the knife stab that killed him.

Tori eased back and looked into his eyes. "Kiss me, Mark."

He released his held breath and leaned closer, covered her mouth with his. Her lips were soft, her fingers feather light at his jaw. She moved her hand from his face and pushed it under the neckband of his T-shirt to splay her fingers over the ridge of his shoulder. Her touch inflamed his desire for this beautiful, caring, terrified woman. He kissed her deeper, harder, trying his best to show her how wonderfully tenacious she was; how much she'd already influenced him to loosen the shackles he'd held Olivia in for far too long.

Her nails dug into his shoulder and he pretended she held onto him because she needed him, that he provided something, no matter how small, that she couldn't find within herself. She pulled back and their gazes locked. He recognized the yearning—the need for blessed escape—in her eyes, because time and again, the same need had ripped through his body since Abby's abduction.

He gently eased Tori back onto the sofa and brought his face to hers, closing his eyes as he kissed her. She eased her tongue into his mouth and he savored her taste, letting it drift through his body and into his heart, regardless of the repercussions once they hurtled back to the terrifying reality currently surrounding their every thought and action.

For now, they were alone, together, and closed off from the rest of the world.

He would ensure she enjoyed this time, remembered it, and came to believe she deserved a man's unending and reassuring adoration.

He kissed her jaw and neck as he flipped open her shirt buttons. She slid her hand over his waist and pulled his t-shirt from his jeans, gliding her hands across his back and raising the hairs on his body.

Her breast was full and heavy in his hand and he thumbed her nipple until it peaked. She trembled and a surge of possibility of what he could be with this amazing woman by his side urged his need for Tori's happiness higher. He trailed his fingers over her ribcage, to the slender dip of her waist as she lifted his shirt.

Straightening, he yanked the shirt over his head. "We'll get through this. We'll get through all of it."

He kissed her hungrily, willing her to believe in him as his trust in her threatened to burst his heart from his chest. Throughout the parting and meeting of their lips, they stripped off the rest of their clothes until they lay in their underwear, her on her back, him on his side, their harried breaths exposing their arousal and yearning for one another.

Gently, she pushed him away from her. "Take off your boxers and sit up."

Blatant control flashed sexily in her gaze. Slowly, he rose and pushed down his boxers before sitting on the sofa.

She stood before him, dressed in a red, satin bra and matching, barely there, panties. His heart thundered. He saw nothing but her. He thought of nothing but her, in the middle of his living room, looking like something sent to him from heaven with a little spiciness of hell thrown in.

With her gaze on his, she clasped one hand to his knee and shimmied out of her panties. Slowly, she straddled him, her wetness at his pelvis.

"Christ, Tori."

"Shhh…"

She reached behind her and unhooked her bra, letting it fall to the floor. Her pièce de résistance came when she whipped the band from her hair. For the first time since he'd met her, her glorious red mane was let loose, wild and free. She shook her head and the thick strands waved over her shoulders and breasts, her tight nipples peeking sexily through the miniscule gaps.

Unable to bear this power game a moment longer, he sat forward, delving his hands into her hair and holding them tight to the back of her head. He kissed her, pouring all his frustration and sexual want into his lips and tongue. She matched his kiss with equal intensity, a soft whimper escaping into his mouth and further fueling every damn thing he wanted to show and do to her.

Pulling back, he clasped her waist and pulled her

onto her knees, her core hovering just out of reach. A soft smile played at her lips, the trust and enjoyment in her eyes equally as intoxicating as her silky, soft skin beneath his fingers.

With her panties gone, he slid his finger over her wetness, softly easing two fingers deep inside. Her mouth dropped open and her eyes closed. He massaged and explored, watching the flitter of her eyes beneath her closed lids, testing and learning what she liked. Her body was hot to the touch, her slight movements and gyrations sending him almost to the brink.

Still, he held back.

Not until she'd enjoyed him, until she'd relaxed and savored these blessed moments of intimacy and escape.

Her eyes fluttered open and the yearning fire in her gaze turned them a bright, almost dazzling green. She was so bloody beautiful.

"I need my bag."

He stared, his cock straining with need. "What?"

She lifted an eyebrow. "Unless you keep a condom behind your ear? You know, being a superhero and all."

He laughed and fell a little further for this amazing woman. "Go get your bag."

She grinned and slid from his lap. Snatching up her purse, she fumbled inside, buck naked and beautiful. She pulled out a condom and ripped the packet open. She came back to him and slowly sheathed him.

He took her hand and guided her back to her previous position, but when he reached out to touch her again, she intertwined his fingers and held them aloft. Palm to palm, she hovered above his erection before guiding him inside her without as much as a finger touching his skin.

She was hot, tight and everything he could have hoped for.

She murmured and met his eyes before leaning back and grinding him deeper. Mark clenched his jaw, tightened his grip on her hands. Together, they moved. Instinctively knowing each other's rhythms.

The sensations built fast and hot. His need to love and protect this woman burned deep in his gut and wrenched through his chest.

The tremors of her oncoming orgasm tightened her hold on him. Their lips met and stayed together as her entire body convulsed, tightening and pulsing around him. He shifted and came undone. He gritted his teeth and relished the most powerful orgasm he'd had in years.

Second by second, the waves eased and he slowly opened his eyes.

She watched him, her gaze happy. "So, you are a superhero, after all."

He smiled. "Haven't I been telling you that all along?"

Chapter Eighteen

Tori woke the next day to the aroma of fresh coffee and what smelled suspiciously like something burning. Mark's ensuing curse drifted up the stairs and into the bedroom confirming it was the "Damn toast!" Smiling, she pushed back his bed covers and then stopped, her fist tightening around the sheets. For a few moments, she'd forgotten about Abby.

Now, reality hit harder and deeper than ever.

Tears burned her eyes as Tori whipped one of Mark's shirts from his wardrobe and walked into his en-suite bathroom, her steps uncertain as her lingering vulnerability resurfaced. She gripped the porcelain sink and stared at her reflection. She looked the same, albeit her hair was a mess of knots and tangles, and the remnants of her makeup stained like bruises under her eyes.

Yet, nothing about her was the same.

The fear and irrationality she tried so desperately to fight had been reawakened and made stronger by an invisible face. If she couldn't see who was traumatizing her and Abby, how the hell was she supposed to fight him?

Tears rolled over Tori's cheeks. Here, locked in and alone, she would cry. Once she opened the door and went downstairs for burnt toast and coffee, her eyes would be dry and her mind clear.

Today she would find Abby.

Today she would go back to Brian Appleton's previous address and face her memories.

Today she'd use them to bring a little girl home.

She used the toilet, washed her hands and face and re-entered the bedroom. She put on Mark's shirt, lifted her chin and walked downstairs. Her heart stuttered as she entered the kitchen.

Mark stood by the table where he used a spatula to spoon two hefty piles on scrambled eggs onto toast, deliciously bare-chested and casual in nothing but crumpled pajama bottoms.

She smiled. "Hi."

He looked up and his appreciative gaze wandered over her from head to toe. "Hi."

She lifted an eyebrow. "No amount of eggs will hide black toast, you know."

"The black stuff is in the bin. I was forced to make a fresh batch." He looked her over again. "From now on, you only wear my shirts."

She laughed and sat at the table, picking up one of two glasses of juice. She sipped, her smile dissolving. "I want to go back to Littledale."

His hand momentarily stilled before he lifted his gaze to hers, his eyes dark blue with concern. "Why?"

She put down her glass. "I want to go back to Brian Appleton's house."

He turned from her and placed the pan and spatula in the sink. Tori's heart beat faster, her hands tightly clenched in her lap as she braced for his attempt to stop her, or at least try to talk her out it.

He stared through the window. "And what do you hope to find there?"

"A clue."

He faced her. "What sort of clue?"

"Thornhill is adamant Abby's disappearance has nothing to do with Brian Appleton, whereas I believe it has everything to do with him. I want to go back to where it all started. I've been to the woods where he watched me and it gave me nothing, I want to be sure the same is true when I visit my old primary school and his house. Those three places all link him to me. There will be something there to tell us who has Abby, I'm sure of it."

"Eat your breakfast before it gets cold." He came to the table, sat and picked up his fork. "I'm not sure I agree, but if you want to go to Littledale, we will."

"You'll come with me?"

"Of course."

He leaned in for a mouthful of food and Tori stared at the top of his head. Not once since her enforced incarceration had she leaned on anyone like she now leaned on Mark. She wasn't certain this increased dependability was a good thing. If the feelings between them deepened, grew stronger, and then something happened to her, Mark would suffer loss again. Pictures of his wife and the love they once shared were all over the house, but he'd yet to talk to Tori about the pain of losing his wife, Olivia's mother.

"Mark?" Apprehension formed a knot in her stomach, but she desperately wanted to get closer to him. "Tell me about your wife. You know her death wasn't your fault, right?"

He stilled, his fork hovering over his plate and his gaze downcast.

Tori swallowed against the sudden dryness in her

throat. Was she wrong to assume their lovemaking had brought them closer?

He laid down his fork and it lightly clattered against the plate. He raised his gaze to hers, a dark tinge at his cheeks. "Lauren wasn't so different than you. She was kind, determined, and sometimes impulsive…even reckless. A woman who intrigued me, excited me and I wanted her all for my own from pretty much the moment I laid eyes on her."

"You must have loved her very much." Tori's heart kicked painfully. His clear love for his wife suddenly heighten her vulnerability as she sat at his kitchen table clad in his shirt, without her clothes, heels, notebook and armor.

He cleared his throat. "I loved her more than life itself…and now I think I might be falling for you."

Shock reverberated through her. "What?"

"But that doesn't mean I am hell bent on doing all I can to protect you because I failed Lauren. I'm protecting you, to the best of my ability, because I want to. I need to believe you're as safe as I can make you." A muscle jumped in his jaw as his blue gaze burned into hers. "I know how Lauren died wasn't my fault, but it *will* be my fault if anything happens to you from here on in. I can't, I won't, allow that to happen."

"You think you might be falling for me?" Her heart pounded as she put down her knife and fork and stood, panic thundering through her. She had sex. She didn't do love. Yet, with Mark… She closed her eyes. "You can't just blurt that out and expect me to say the same in return. We barely know one another. There are things you still don't know about me. Things I don't know about you." She opened her eyes, fear she'd failed him twisting and turning inside. "Love needs to be earned, built on. You can't just say that when you don't really know me."

"What else do I need to know?"

"Well, all this with Abby? If it turns out that it's entirely my fault, what then?"

"That isn't going to happen because this couldn't possibly be your fault. You've done nothing wrong."

"Done nothing wrong?" She stared in disbelief and planted her trembling hands on her hips. "I saw the guy who took her but have given nothing to help the police. I had his scarf and it provided nothing. I've received letters—zilch. I've gone back to where it all began—nada. This *is* my fault, Mark and no one, including you, will make me believe otherwise. Whether or not either of us likes it, I am in this up to my neck and you…" She shook her head, swiped at the tears that dared to fall. "You say you're falling in love with me? No. Not now."

He stood, his gaze angry. "Why does it freak you out so much that I might be falling for you? You deserve to be loved, Tori. You deserve everything."

Her heart ached with need, but she couldn't let him—let herself—get into anything close to love. Not when her whole life could fall apart if Abby had been hurt…or worse. "Why? Because of what Brian Appleton did to me? Because I left home and never looked back until now? I don't think so. I don't deserve your love, Mark. You're too good. Too nice…too bloody male and strong. I'll change you. I'll make you see the world through my eyes and it's not a pretty place."

He came toward her, his hand outstretched but she

raised hers, warning him off. "No. Don't. I'm going to shower and then we'll go to Littledale and pretend this conversation never happened."

Irritation flashed in his eyes once more. "I meant every word and now you expect me to forget I said it?"

His face blurred through her tears. "Yes."

She fled from the kitchen. Taking the stairs two at a time, Tori stormed into his bedroom and slammed the door. She pressed her hand to her racing heart and tried to level her breathing. Not once had anyone, other than her family…other than Brian Appleton…told her they loved her. Until now.

How could she accept Mark's love when she would inevitably hurt him? How could she accept his love when he had a beautiful daughter and one day Tori's presence might endanger Olivia? She attracted screwed-up people. First Brian Appleton and now his copycat, or whoever the hell this new monster thought he was.

Loving her was dangerous. Especially dangerous for someone who she was beginning to love too.

She pushed away from the door and marched into the en-suite. Tori turned the shower on and stepped under the water. She would wash and refocus. She would go home. She would face her demons and then, only then, would she wash Mark's words from her heart.

But for now, she wanted to keep them safe awhile longer.

****

Mark stared at the lock on his front door as he listened to the shower running upstairs. The lock wasn't enough. He needed to fit an additional one. He glanced up the stairs. He'd followed Tori from the kitchen and debated whether to trace her steps to the upper floor too, but instinct told him to do so would push her farther away.

He meant every word he'd said when he'd told her how he felt about her and thought the timing perfect, considering how she'd lain on his chest throughout the night. One leg and arm flung over his body as though cradling him close, not wanting him to leave her. She hadn't moved an inch all night, her soft snoring amusing him each time he'd woken before drifting off again.

Yet now, his mind scrambled between the decision to give her time—and the suspicion she tried to tell him something significant every time she insisted she was at the center of Abby's disappearance. Tori's adamancy she was the one to blame for everything that had happened poked at his confidence he could fully trust her.

Her latest insistence of guilt had felt different to the other times she'd inferred it. This time her words hadn't been coated in fear, but with the genuine need for him to listen to her.

And now he couldn't halt the worry he had trusted her too soon…fallen for her a little too fast.

He fiddled with the lock, shoving the door with more force than intended.

Had he made a huge mistake inviting Tori into his home and practically ejecting Olivia from the place she had every right to feel the safest? It was rare that he trusted anyone so quickly or succinctly, but he'd trusted Tori from the moment she'd ran onto the playground and he'd looked into her eyes.

Why? What was it about her that justified her

immediate reliability?

Cursing, Mark marched back through the house and into his workshop.

He had little more than Tori's supposition that she was meant to see Abby pushed into that car. What if Tori had been a part of Abby's abduction all along? What if her being the concerned party was nothing more than a very thick, very dense, smokescreen? He had to think about Olivia. He'd promised Lauren at her graveside that he would always put their daughter first in his decisions, no matter what.

Had he failed to do that?

He screwed his eyes shut and battled to get a hold on whatever it was that had triggered such horrible suspicions of deceit from a woman he had made love to hours before.

It was crazy. Stupid. Out of order on so many levels.

Opening his eyes, he buried his thoughts deep into his mind and grabbed his toolbox. Reaching over his workbench, he swiped up one of the new, still packaged locks he'd bought the day before. He needed to make a start on affixing the additional lock before Tori reappeared. Judging by her usually pristine makeup and clothes, he had a good twenty minutes before they headed out.

Her appearance was the biggest aspect that differentiated her from Lauren. His wife had rarely worn makeup, and if someone would have told him the second time he fell in love it would be with a woman who loved hair, makeup and high heels over barefaced beauty, jeans and hiking boots, he would have laughed in their face.

Yet, that's exactly what had happened.

He strode back into the house to the front door. The shower had stopped running and the only noise in the empty house was Tori's footsteps as they creaked across the floorboards above him. His body itched with the need to go upstairs and make love to her. To make her listen and accept his feelings for her were very, very real—and to convince himself he wasn't a fool to feel so strongly about her.

Instead, he slashed open the new lock packaging with a knife and placed the lock above the existing one. Taking a pencil from his toolbox, he marked where the screws would need to be positioned.

The sudden opening of his letterbox made him flinch, but he finished aligning the lock, ignoring the small pile of mail as it landed at his feet.

He bent down to grab his screwdriver.

And his gaze glued to the letter on the top of the pile.

The typeface was unmistakable and his pulse beat in his ears as Mark strained to listen for Tori. The envelope was the same cream color and the address had been typed with the same black ink, but this envelope was different. This one had a postmark and this one was for him.

Mark picked up the letter as his nerves stretched and his temper rose. He took up his knife and slashed open the envelope, one hundred percent sure whoever the letter's author, they knew Tori was with him.

*Mark, Mark, Mark…*

*What do you think you're doing? Do you think I'll stand by and let you take her? Tori is mine. Has always been mine, in one way or another. Listen very carefully.*

*This is your only warning and then it won't be Abby the world is worried for, but your own dear daughter. Olivia. Such a pretty name. Such a pretty girl.*

*I want you to read my words very carefully. Take Tori home and I promise I won't hurt Olivia. I'm angry, Mark. There's no escaping how angry I am after learning you've taken my Tori.*

*Have you made love to her, Mark? I really hope you haven't for Olivia's sake.*

*Now, you give her back to me. You give her back to me, Mark fucking Bolton.*

*Best wishes,*

*Your Friend*

"Mark? What is it?"

He flinched and turned around, his anger so potent that at first he could only see the mirage of Olivia standing on the stairs, rather than Tori.

"Another letter." He held it aloft, his gaze never leaving her face as he waited for her reaction. "Only this one's for me. This one's about my daughter."

The color drained from her face as Tori descended the remaining steps. Her green eyes wide with worry and her bottom lip ever so slightly trembling. "Mark, I'm sorry. I'm sorry for everything."

"For everything?" Red-hot anger tore through his blood, misting his vision. "What do you have to be sorry for, Tori? You have nothing to do with these letters, right?"

She stepped back, almost stumbling onto the stairs. "What?"

"We have to find her. I want to know where Abby is before this sick psycho goes after Olivia."

"He said he's going after Olivia?"

"Yes, if I don't give *you* back. What the hell is that about? Who is this guy?"

"I don't know." Her voice cracked. "If I had any idea, don't you think I'd tell you? Tell the police?"

"How should I know? There's still so much I don't know about you, remember?"

She stared, color rushing into her cheeks. "Are you accusing me of something?"

The words lodged like rocks in his throat. He couldn't say them. If he did, he would lose her regardless of whether he was right or wrong.

She came toward him and tipped her head back to meet his eyes. Hers glinted with fiery determination. "I have no idea who has Abby. I have no idea why he wants me. What I do know is we need to get the hell out of here and start looking for him. Her abduction is my fault, Mark, but I am not to blame for his sick games and threats."

He opened his mouth to respond, not even sure what to say considering how his entire world had just been tipped on an axis so much worse than it was before.

She didn't wait for a response or anything else from him. Instead, she shoved his toolbox aside, opened the front door and glared. "Are you coming or not?"

Chapter Nineteen

As Tori and Mark stood outside the three-bedroom semi-detached house where Brian Appleton had held her captive, she sneaked a glance at Mark. His jaw was tight and his brow furrowed as he stared ahead at the gray slated building in front of them. His silence during the car journey had brought forth, once again, the sense she was losing something that could have the potential to make her life happier.

No man had broken through her barriers as Mark had.

His steady gaze and easy smile had chipped away her self-imposed protection and enticed her to get closer. Even the prospect of forging a relationship with his daughter didn't frighten her. Not anymore. After all, wasn't Olivia living proof of Mark's steadfast and loving virtues?

He was kind, caring, strong and protective. No matter how much Tori wanted to see something negative in him to prevent her future heartbreak, what threatened to break her heart today was the possibility her words and actions were changing Mark into someone who suspected. Who didn't trust or want to trust.

And now Olivia was being threatened because Tori was in their lives.

She took his hand. "I'm sorry, Mark."

His chest rose as he inhaled. "Me too."

Those two words gave her nothing. What was he sorry for? For ever meeting her? For allowing her into his home? She couldn't blame him for feeling that way about either scenario. She swallowed. "Won't you look at me?"

He faced her, his blue eyes dark. Pulling every ounce of her courage to the surface, Tori cupped her hand to his cheek. "Talk to me. Tell me what you're thinking."

"You really want to know?"

"Of course."

He reached up and eased her hand from his face. Tori's heart picked up speed and then calmed when he didn't release her fingers but, instead, tightened his grip. He shook his head. "Rightly or wrongly, when I received that letter this morning everything changed. As much as I believed myself to be on board with finding Abby and her abductor, now Olivia's involved, it's become personal and that means I'm in deeper than I ever was before. I didn't think that was possible considering my worry for you and Olivia was pretty bad to begin with. But now? Now, I want this guy and when I have him, I want to kill him."

Fear rippled through Tori to see such unadulterated rage in Mark's eyes. "Mark, listen—"

"How shall we play this?"

"Play what?"

"You brought us here. What's the plan?"

In an effort to lessen his pain, his fear and to help settle his fury, a confession of her feelings for him hovered on her tongue. Yet, the release of holding herself back from any form of intimacy raged a war inside. He'd told her he was falling for her and, in return, she bawled him out. He'd helped her get through some of the pain Brian Appleton had caused the first time around and seemed to be causing again. In return, she'd endangered the most precious person in Mark's life.

Once again, her courage failed.

She faced the house, her fingers still intertwined with his. "I'm going to knock on the door and find out who's living here now. Then I'll ask what they know about who has lived there since Brian Appleton. Whether he's abroad or not, someone is trying to get to me by copying what he did to me. Who's to say they aren't copying other aspects of his life?" She faced him, squinting against the mid-morning sun. "Who's to say Abby isn't in that house, in that basement, just the same as I was?"

He looked toward the house, his eyes narrowed. "That's too much to hope for but, either way, we need to know for sure. Come on."

He led the way along the front pathway, his hand still firmly wrapped around hers. Tori concentrated on leveling her breathing as she retraced the same flagstone pavement she had walked nearly two decades before. The brown wooden door had been painted a bright, sunny yellow, the age-old windows replaced with shiny, latticed ones, but still a strange menace emanated from every brick, tile and eave.

When she knocked on the door, Tori silently cursed her body's tremor. She glanced at Mark before the door swung open and a young woman in her early twenties stood on the threshold. She smiled. "May I help you?"

She was so blonde, her blue eyes so filled with

innocent contentment, that guilt slithered through Tori that she could be about to upset this woman. Tori fought the need to turn and run. "I…I…"

Mark slid his arm around her waist. "Good morning, I wonder if you might be able to help us. My name is Mark Bolton and this is Tori Peterson, we're investigating the disappearance of Abby Brady. You might have heard about it on the news?"

The young woman frowned. "Of course. Are you the police?"

Tori cleared her throat and took a step back from Mark's touch, knowing she had to stand on her own two feet. Now and maybe forever. Forcing a smile, she offered her hand. "We're not. I'm a journalist and Mark is a concerned father. You are?"

"Robyn Chamberlain." Suspicion clouded her eyes. "What can I do for you?"

Tori dropped her hand to her side. "Might we come in for a moment?"

Robyn eased the door forward, lessening the gap into her home. "I don't think so. What do you want?"

Tori glanced at Mark and he nodded. "Tell her."

Nausea churned in Tori's stomach as she faced Robyn. "Many years ago, I was held captive in your house by Brian Appleton. Maybe you've been told about it? I was rescued by the police six days later."

Robyn's cheeks reddened. "You're her? Of course, I remember your name now." She shook her head, her gaze softening. "I'm sorry you went through that."

Tori dipped her head. "Thank you."

"Even though I know the house's history, it's been ours for two years. We're happy here."

"I understand. It's just that I suspect Abby's

disappearance might be linked to mine and so…" Tori inhaled. "I'm clutching at straws, but maybe something has happened to you or the house over the last few weeks? Something you thought nothing of at the time, but in light of what I've told you—"

"I really can't think of anything. I'm sorry."

"Are you sure?"

Robyn Chamberlain frowned, her gaze darting over Tori's face. "Well…"

Tori's heart beat faster. "Well?"

Robyn slumped her shoulders. "It's probably silly to say so, but there was a woman who came here a couple of months ago and spoke to my husband. She asked if she could look around the house. When he told me, I wasn't exactly thrilled that he'd allowed her to do just that."

Tori frowned. "He let her in?"

"Yes. I guess she must have lived here at some point. She said the place was unrecognizable, whatever that meant."

Tori glanced at Mark before facing Robyn. "What else did she say?"

"She asked who'd lived here since the Brian Appleton kidnapping case." She stepped back. "I'm sorry, but I really don't want my husband and me to be involved in something that has nothing to do with us." She moved to close the door. "I'm sorry."

"Wait." Tori slapped her hand to the door, desperately trying not to alarm the woman but unable to resist pushing further with this possible new step forward. "Can you remember what this woman looked like? Was she alone?"

"I told you, my husband spoke to her. He didn't

mention anyone else. She asked who lived here before us. I think she asked if she could see the garden."

"The garden?"

"Yes. Paul, my husband, took her through the house to the back. I remember he said she seemed more interested in the kitchen than the garden though."

Tori stared. The basement where she'd been kept prisoner had ran off the kitchen. "Did she say anything else?"

"Not that I remember."

Not wanting to push her too far, Tori rifled in her bag and brought out a business card. "Please, could you speak to your husband and ask him to call me? I would really appreciate the opportunity to speak with him."

Robyn Chamberlain cautiously took the card and scanned the print. She raised her gaze to Tori's. "We really don't want our names in the paper, Miss Peterson."

"You won't, I promise."

"I don't see how we can help any—"

"You've helped so much already. This isn't about what happened to me. It's about getting Abby home to her parents. Please. Just ask your husband to call me. If he can give me a description of the woman he spoke to—"

"Do you think we should call the police?" Robyn worried her bottom lip. "You don't think this woman has that little girl, do you?"

"I don't know. It's highly unlikely." Tori forced a smile and reached out to gently grip Robyn's arm. "I'm working closely with Detective Chief Inspector Thornhill of the Barlington police. I promise you, anything significant you or your husband tells me, I will relay it to the inspector immediately."

Robyn flitted her gaze between Tori and Mark before she sighed. "Okay, I'll ask Paul to call you."

Tori released Robyn's arm. "Thank you. Thank you so much."

Turning, she walked down the pathway, the distant exchange of Mark and Robyn Chamberlain bidding each other goodbye drifting behind her. Tori waited by Mark's car, impatience humming through her. He shunted open the locks and they slid into the front seats. Without looking at her, he gunned the engine and pulled away from Brian Appleton's old house.

Tori waited until they hit a main road before she spoke. "We need to find out who that woman was and why she was there. Clearly, she posed a big enough mystery for Robyn Chamberlain to remember her husband mentioning her."

"Surely the fact her husband invited a strange woman into the house was enough to jog her memory. In my experience, that would set alarm bells ringing for half the female race."

"This woman has something to do with this, Mark. I know it. Can we grab a coffee somewhere? I want to call Cally and get her looking into who this woman might be."

He frowned. "What have you got to tell her? We haven't even got a name."

"She could be Appleton's wife. Even his daughter maybe."

"Why would you think that?"

"I don't know." She closed her eyes. "Everything is so messed up."

"Just wait until you hear from Paul Chamberlain.

In the meantime, why don't we pass by your old primary school and see if anything clicks there?"

She opened her eyes. "I want Cally to look into the women in Brian Appleton's life in case one of them came back here. We've no time to waste." She stared at his profile and softened her voice. "He's mentioned Olivia, remember?"

He snapped his head around, his gaze irritated. "Of course I remember."

Hating herself for mentioning Olivia and, in turn, refueling his anger, Tori laid her hand on his shoulder and squeezed. "Then let's find out who this woman is and what she was doing at Brian Appleton's house. Two months is ample time to plan, scheme and work out how to abduct a child. Something tells me this woman is key to finding Abby."

He glanced at her again before facing the road and pressing on the gas. "Head me in the right direction for the town center. We'll find somewhere to stop."

Swallowing against the nerves lodged like stones in her throat, Tori leaned back in her seat. "Take the next left. It's a ten-minute drive from here."

\*\*\*\*

Memories washed over Tori as she entered Quillford's Coffee Shop. As she approached the counter, she inhaled the aroma of fresh coffee, cinnamon and the sweet scent of jam and pastry. The walls were covered in sepia newspaper print wallpaper, dotted and decorated with famous stars from today and beyond. It was a hub to her formative years as a young girl dreaming of seeing her words in print one day. She'd loved this place back then and even now, despite everything that had happened to her in Littledale, the warmth of good times enveloped her.

She smiled softly, tears stinging. Her father had often brought her here for a cookie and milkshake after dance class on Saturday mornings. Each week her mother had told him off for letting her have so much sugar before lunch, and each week her father would take Tori again. She'd definitely known happiness prior to Brian Appleton. Her smiled dissolved. Yet, that knowledge offered little respite to the guilt that she was responsible for Abby's abduction.

"What are you having?" Mark placed his hand at the small of her back and leaned in close, his breath warm against her ear. "The usual?"

Heat whispered through her and her stomach knotted at the softness in his voice. It had barely been more than a few hours since they'd been in bed and he'd last spoken to her that way, but God, she'd missed it.

She faced him and smiled softly. "A latte would be great. Thanks."

"Grab a table. I'll be right over."

Selecting a booth by the window, Tori slid along the seat and stared at Mark's turned back. Never before had she wanted two things so badly—one, to find Abby and two, for her and Mark to have a chance to be together once this was all over. Was expecting two things too greedy? Too many wishes for God to grant?

She suspected the answer was yes.

Pulling her phone from her bag, she dialed Cally's number before staring blindly through the window.

Cally immediately answered. "Hi, Tori. You okay?"

Tori refocused. "I need a favor."

"Anything. You know that."

"I'm in Littledale with Mark and we've just spoken to someone who told us about a woman I think might have known Brian Appleton. I want you to forget everything you learned before and treat this as a brand new enquiry."

"Tori—"

"We can't afford to waste time on this, Cally. Please. I'm relying on you." Tori looked up and flashed Mark a quick smile as he slid a steaming, oversized cup in front of her. She closed her eyes and rubbed her thumb and forefinger into her brow. "Cally, are you still there?"

"As always."

Ignoring Cally's snippy tone, Tori frowned. "I want you to look into Brian Appleton's wife and daughter."

"Why?"

"Because I'm sure he has something to do with Abby's disappearance and, if he doesn't, someone very close to him does. We've got little chance of finding out who he was chummy with in and out of prison, but with a little digging, you should be able to find something about his family when he lived in Littledale. Will you do this for me? Please."

Cally sighed. "Of course I will, but that doesn't make me any less worried about you. Are you sure involving Mark Bolton in this is a good idea?"

Tori opened her eyes and met Mark's concentrated gaze. "I am. Yes."

"And everything's okay between you two?"

Tori smiled, her heart twisting. "Everything's great between us."

There was a moment's pause and then Cally tutted. "Oh, Tori, tell me you haven't."

Tori blinked and picked up her coffee cup, her cheeks hot. "What?"

"You know what. Have you slept with him?"

"Cally." Tori laughed. "What is this? Just do as I've asked. If you have to tell Neil, that's fine, but if you can keep this to yourself, all the better. Call me as soon as you know anything. No matter how small."

"Okay, okay. And Tori?"

"Yes?"

"Be careful."

"I will. Speak soon." Tori ended the call and tossed her phone onto the table. "Cally's on the case. Did you want to get back to Barlington?"

"Once we've taken a quick visit to your old school. I called Olivia's friend's mum where Olivia stayed last night. I want her home where I can look after her." His jaw tightened as he turned to scan the street outside. "I don't want her staying out anymore."

"I understand."

He met her eyes. "It's my fault she's in danger."

Tori took his hand. "If it's anyone's fault, it's mine. Would you rather I went home tonight? I don't want to endanger Olivia any more than I do you."

His gaze traveled over her face before he pulled his hand from hers and picked up his cup. "No, you stay with me."

"Mark—"

"I want you and Olivia at the house. No arguments."

Tori opened her mouth to protest further, but his steely gaze locking on hers over the rim of his cup silenced her. He'd told her how he felt about her and she couldn't deny how good his words had made her feel…even if she wasn't ready to say them back.

She would tell him she was falling for him too once Abby was found and her captor arrested. Then, and only then, would she know how great a danger she posed to Mark and Olivia and all that they had known before she barged into their lives and ruined everything.

Mark put down his cup. "If Cally comes back with anything on Appleton's family, we're going straight to Thornhill with it, right?"

"Of course. Why wouldn't we?"

"I don't want you to take any new information about Appleton and run with it. We have to do this the right way. We're talking about children's lives here. We can't risk anything more happening to Abby or Olivia."

Sadness gripped Tori's heart and she tightened her hands around her cup. "Something's constantly happening to Abby regardless of whether whoever has her is physically hurting her. The scars that little girl will carry will stay with her for the rest of her life whether we find her or not."

"And that's why I'm scared out of my mind now this maniac has mentioned Olivia. He's following you, which means he's following me." He looked out the window. "He could be watching us now, for all we know."

Tori followed his gaze and waited for the unease in her stomach, or the tingling at her neck, to tell her someone was out there. Nothing came. "He's not here now."

"How do you know?"

She turned. "Because I've felt him before. I know when he's close. That's how I know he wasn't around when Abby was taken. If Appleton's involved, whoever took Abby is working with him."

Mark's gaze darkened. "Any ideas who that could be?"

"No, and that's our biggest problem. I just get this feeling Brian Appleton is here…but not." She inhaled a shaky breath. "I didn't feel him straight away when he left the scarf, but I did feel something just out of reach." She blinked back the tears that pricked her eyes. "We're getting closer, Mark. We have to have faith that whoever the abductor is, he'll be caught."

He squeezed her hand where it lay on the table. "Once we leave here, we'll take this latest letter to Thornhill. We'll also tell him about our visit to Robyn Chamberlain."

"Not yet. I'd rather keep that to ourselves. If Thornhill bans me from doing anything else, I'll go crazy."

"This is as much about Olivia as Abby now. From now on, we do a little of what I want to do too. This isn't about you anymore. It's about both of us."

Hurt that he should think for one moment she didn't realize how much he was involved squeezed at Tori's heart. "Fine. You take the letter to Thornhill and get Olivia from school but, please, can you just hold off telling Thornhill about Robyn? I just want to check out one more thing."

He frowned. "Which is?"

"Trust me to do this right, Mark."

She lifted her cup and drank. When she looked at him again, he stared straight back at her with anger and

258

suspicion. Despite knowing what she was about to do was best for him, Olivia and Abby, it didn't make it hurt any less that, judging by his closed expression, she'd undoubtedly lost the first person she'd had a chance to love outside of her family.

Chapter Twenty

Mark walked down the steps of Barlington Police Station, his relief at passing over the odious letter to Thornill somewhat easing the tormenting prospect each word had held.

He slid into the front seat of his car and gripped the steering wheel. For days his mind had been filled with what could be happening to Abby—and now those thoughts mixed with what *could* happen to Olivia. Sickness merged with anxiety, and the scenarios in his head catapulted him back to the place he'd inhabited before he met Tori. A guarded, protective fort through which no one could attack or hurt. The shackles he'd locked around his daughter were fitted back in place, with a few more bolted on top for extra security.

Starting the ignition, Mark left the parking lot. He glanced at the passing houses and boutique shops, the town's green, the baroque town hall and cursed the monster—or monsters—currently ruining so many lives in this once happy town.

He glanced at the dashboard clock. Two-thirty. Just enough time to reach the school in time to collect Olivia. Once she was home and safe, maybe the gnawing anxiety in his gut would lessen. Until then, its teeth firmly tore at the flimsy confidence he could be the father Olivia deserved—a father who was there when she needed him, but also one with the wisdom to give her the space she needed to grow.

His phone buzzed on the passenger seat with an incoming call. He glanced at the lit screen. Tori. They parted about an hour before without him knowing where she was going—or more accurately, what she was up to. Maybe now she was ready to share. As soon as he reached the school he'd call her back.

He continued along the road, negotiating the increasingly heavy traffic as the time slowly ticked by before school home time. His phone rang again.

"Unknown" flashed up.

Frowning, he drove farther away from town toward the outskirts. When he was about ten minutes away from the school, his phone rang again.

"Unknown" once more.

A horrible unease rippled across the back of his neck as his mind filled with the recent letter he'd received. Checking his rearview mirror, he indicated and pulled over to the side of the road, his heart pumping. He reached for the phone just as it rang off.

"Shit." He squeezed his eyes shut and tapped the phone against his bottom lip, every nerve in his body on high alert. Now what? Did he continue to the school? He waited in the hope the caller would try again.

The phone pinged with a voicemail and he immediately called up the message.

*"Mark, Mr. Bolton, this is Karen, Principal White. Wherever you are, you need to come to the school immediately. Mark…it's Olivia. She's missing…"*

The remainder of the message went unheeded as Mark checked his side mirror and sped onto the road. His vision misted red around the edges and his knuckles ached from his grip on the steering wheel.

"For Christ's sake, move it, will you!" Cars seemed to appear from every direction, boxing him in. He punched the heel of his hand to the horn. "Get out the way!"

The usual ten-minute journey to the school took Mark five. Outside the school gates, he yanked his keys from the ignition and got out of the car. As he sprinted into the school grounds, his heart beat fast and every primitive instinct surged dangerously to the surface. His body trembled with suppressed anger and his mind whirled with a kaleidoscope of macabre images as his worst nightmare became true.

His baby was gone.

Missing.

Taken.

Once he reached the locked double doors of the school, he pressed his finger hard to the security buzzer and held it there. Seconds later, Principal White came hurrying to the door. Her fingers fumbled over and over the lock before she finally managed to pull open the door. "Mark, I'm so sorry."

Brushing past her, he frantically looked around the lobby as though the principal was mistaken and any moment now Olivia would appear with her usual snarky attitude in place and telling Mark how embarrassing it was to have her dad collect her from school.

But only stunned silence reigned.

He darted his gaze from one teacher to the next as they stood in a semicircle in front of him, their eyes wide and their hands raised to their mouths.

He snapped his attention to Principal White. "What the hell happened? Where is she?"

"I don't know." Tears glinted in her eyes and the

hand she held at her throat trembled. "Miss Leigh didn't notice Olivia missing from class until the school bell rang. We have no idea how she could have got out, or how someone could've got in. Please, Mark, I don't know what to say."

Mark stepped forward, his blood burning hot with a violent anger that pulsed in his ears and rended his heart. He clenched his fists at his sides. "Tell me you've called the police."

The screeching of tires outside snapped his gaze to the door. Two squad cars drew to a stop and four officers alighted along with Sergeant Jansen and DCI Thornhill. They marched through the open door and Mark strode forward.

He faced Thornhill. "The bastard has Olivia. He has my little girl. This stops now. Do you hear me?"

"Mr. Bolton—"

"I mean it." Mark swiped his arm through the air, slicing the inspector's attempted contact in two. "You get your officers lined up and looking for my daughter and Abby Brady right now. Two girls are missing. Two. Now what the bloody hell are you going to do about it?"

"You need to calm down." Thornhill glared, his cheeks dark. "Yelling at everyone trying to help will do no good. Now, why don't we go into Principal White's office and see where we go from here?"

"You expect me to sit around and talk about this?" Mark vibrated with the anger flowing through him. He'd failed. Olivia was out there, God only knew where, and he was standing around doing jack shit. "If you won't do your damn job, I'll do it for you."

He stormed toward the exit.

"Mr. Bolton!"

Mark held up his hand to the inspector's call. What the bloody hell could they tell him? It was perfectly clear no one at the damn school had a clue what had happened. A sharp pain sliced at his chest. He wasn't here when someone came in and took his daughter. He was out of town. With Tori…trying to find someone else's little girl whilst his own was being snatched. What if that was the plan? What if the person who wanted Tori knew she wouldn't be in Barlington this morning? That Mark would be with her, leaving the coast clear to take his most precious possession?

The only thing he was suddenly one hundred percent certain of was that Tori had nothing to do with Olivia's disappearance. She had no hand in it because there would be absolutely no gain to her. Taking his daughter would add nothing, but destroy everything they had. Olivia's disappearance was his punishment for taking his attention, his entire devotion from his daughter, in order to spend time with Tori.

His eyes stung. If God gave Olivia back, he would never make that mistake again. Not ever.

The stomp of boots behind him brought Mark to a halt and he turned. He met the determined gaze of Sergeant Jansen. "Mr. Bolton, you need to come back inside."

Mark glared. "No, what I *need* is to find my daughter."

"And in order to do that we have to work together. We have the letters you and Miss Peterson handed in. We know your daughter's disappearance is connected to Abby Brady. The best thing you can do right now is stay where the police are. The same goes for Miss

Peterson. Do you know where she is?"

Mark stared as he tried his hardest to recollect what he and Tori had last talked about, even where he'd last seen her. All his brain provided him with was flashes of Olivia at age two, four, eight, ten…

He squeezed his eyes shut. "I don't know where she is."

"Okay, come on. Let's go inside."

Mark opened his eyes and scanned the immediate area hoping to God Olivia jumped out of the shrubbery shouting, "Surprise!" He waited, but only the whistling of the October wind through the eaves of the school building answered him.

Olivia was gone and he had no idea where Tori was either.

Failure bore down on his shoulders, a heavy judgment, jolting and hindering his steps as he followed Jansen inside. Ignoring the sympathetic gazes and shocked faces of the teachers and staff as they blurred in his peripheral vision, Mark allowed Jansen to steer him along the corridor, his hand tight at Mark's elbow.

Jansen knocked on Principal White's office door before pushing it open. Inside, the principal stood at the window, her eyes wide and scared. Mark turned to Thornhill who sat straight-backed, hands folded in front of him, behind her desk. He immediately rose to his feet, his face a mask of solemnity. "Mr. Bolton, it seems that whoever we're dealing with is taking more risks as he gains confidence. I have spoken to several of the staff here and there's every chance both Abby and Olivia knew their abductor because he works at the school. A regular fixture."

"A regular fixture? Are you telling me *everyone*

who works here hasn't been questioned up until now?"

"Of course they have."

"Then what the hell are you saying?"

Thornhill's gaze turned steely. "It means my officers are speaking again to every decorator, painter and plasterer who's worked on the school renovations for the last three months. We need to go back further."

Mark shook his head, nausea coating his throat. "Olivia would never leave the school grounds with an older man."

Inspector Thornhill stared. "I'm afraid you can't be any more certain of that than I can."

****

Tori pulled up and parked just along from the street that housed Valentine Textiles. Her earlier research had led her to find out that Huw Valentine specialized in the manufacturing of children's clothing. His business instantly became as interesting to her as the guy's enthusiasm in girls' dance. Getting out of the car, she locked it and dropped her keys into her bag. Nerves leapt in her stomach and uncertainty she was doing the right thing slipped and slid inside. Whether or not this move proved to be a bad one, she intended to play it anyway.

Upon reaching the tall, wrought-iron gates outside the factory, Tori paused. She scanned the old-fashioned building. Made of red brick with three stacked chimneys that would have once upon a time choked out gray smoke against the clear blue sky, she estimated its origin to be nineteen-fifties, maybe earlier. Its windows were black and uninviting, the double doors at the front closed to intruders. She involuntarily shivered. With no idea what she'd find if she managed to get inside, or if she risked arrest, she shouldered the reality that it was down to her to do something—and that meant finding a way to look around the place owned by Huw Valentine.

Her journalistic instinct told her something didn't add up; told her Valentine knew more about Abby's disappearance. It was time to listen to her gut. Pulling her phone from the bag slung across her chest, Tori checked her missed calls for a response from Paul Chamberlain, or better still, a call from Cally saying she'd found something useful about Brian Appleton's first family.

The only missed calls were from Mark—three in total.

Frowning, she dialed his number, cursing her penchant for listening to the radio at full volume whenever she drove.

"Tori? Thank God."

"Mark, what's wrong?" Her body turned rigid. The terrified tone of his voice couldn't be misinterpreted as anything other than out and out panic. "What's happened?"

"It's Olivia. He's got her, Tori. The bastard has taken my baby just as he threatened he would. The police think she left the school with someone she knew but I can't see her ever doing something like that." His voice hitched. "Not when she knows how much I stress over her safety. She wouldn't do it. I know she wouldn't."

Anger and fear streamed through Tori's body sending her heart thundering. "Of course she wouldn't. There has to be some other explanation. Are you su—"

"He's got her. There's no doubt in my mind. I'm at the school being held under fucking house arrest by

Thornhill. Where are you?"

She flinched at his curse. "I'm paying a follow up visit to Huw Valentine."

"What?" The sound of moving and shuffling came down the line before Mark spoke again, his voice lowered. "Have you found out something else? I don't like you pursuing this alone. Not now. Who's to say this faceless bastard who's taken Olivia and Abby won't come after you next?"

Tori pulled back her shoulders and embraced every ounce of her anger. "If that happens, don't you think it will be a good thing?"

"Of course I don't. How can you even think that?"

"Because the chances are he will take me to wherever he has Abby and Olivia."

"No, this isn't a good plan. Whatever you're thinking of doing—"

"Just do everything the police advise to get Olivia home. I'll come to the school as soon as I can."

"Tori—"

She ended the call and inhaled. Determination flowed hot through her blood. This ended today. Whether she lived or died trying, no more girls would be taken…no more hurt would be endured.

Silencing her phone, Tori dropped it into her bag and snapped it closed with a decisive whip of the zipper. She lifted her chin and headed for the office adjacent to the factory.

When she pushed open the door, the first thing that greeted her was the well-known voice of a radio DJ, followed by the bump and grind of some modern dance track. She stared around the unoccupied and stuffy room for a split second before a woman of no more than nineteen or twenty emerged from a door at the back.

She smiled. "Can I help you?"

Tori stepped forward and smiled. "Yes, I wonder if I might have a few moments with Mr. Valentine? I don't have an appointment, but hope he'll be willing to see me. What I have to say shouldn't take long."

"I'm afraid Mr. Valentine won't be back until tomorrow. Maybe I could take your name and number? Ask him to call you tomorrow?"

*Where are you, Valentine? Where were you when Olivia was taken?* "Oh, that's a shame. I was really hoping to see him today. Do you know where he is?"

The young girl's smile faltered. "I'm Mr. Valentine's personal assistant. Maybe I can help you?"

Clearly Huw Valentine wasn't without loyalty from his staff, judging by the way the young girl's eyes clouded with suspicion. Tori struggled to keep her smile in place as her frustration mounted. "No, that's okay. I'll call him later. Thanks."

"But—"

"It's fine, honestly. Thanks for your help." Tori turned and headed back through the office door and out into the courtyard.

She wandered slowly as she scanned the area around her before glancing back toward the façade of the factory. How the hell could she get inside? She needed to talk to the staff. Her mind and heart were full of fear for Olivia and Abby, making Tori doubt every investigative method and tactic she'd so confidently relied on in the past.

She could not falter. Not now Mark relied on her to find his daughter...and he did rely on her, whether he knew it or not. At least, she wanted him to.

Determination to prove herself trustworthy—and worthy—of the love he so easily claimed to feel for her, Tori glanced toward the office before dashing to her left behind some parked cars and out of view.

Slipping off her high heels, she winced against the cold concrete before maneuvering on bent legs past the cars to the back of the factory. Clanging and banging from within grew louder and blended with the clacking, out of key melody, of what must have been textile machinery.

To the side, a door marked 'Storage' lay wide open.

Her heart beat faster. An open invitation if she'd ever seen one.

With a quick look over her shoulder, Tori straightened and headed for the door. She entered the outbuilding, her palms clammy. As her eyes adjusted to the darkness, she saw bag after bag, tied and tagged, and stacked on metal shelving, each labeled with a business name.

She strained her ears to any noise, or worse, any staff.

Silence.

Taking a deep breath, she stepped toward the bags. They were shelved in alphabetical order. She ran her gaze over them, hoping one of the businesses struck some suspicion or Valentine's possible connection to Abby. Nothing. Frustration and fear of discovery sped Tori's pulse as she continued along the rows of shelving.

She stopped and stared at the two tied bags in front of her.

'Barlington Primary—Christmas Costumes'

Tori lifted her hand to her mouth. Surely this small discovery was enough for the police to connect Valentine to the school…to connect him to Principal White?

She eased her phone from her bag and dialed Thornhill's number as she slipped her shoes back on and exited the storage room. She hurried back through the courtyard, not caring who saw her now she'd unearthed a possible connection between the principal and Valentine. Tori strode through the factory gates and onto the street.

"DCI Thornhill speaking."

"Inspector, it's Tori Peterson."

"Miss Peterson, you need to come to the school directly. We have every need to keep yourself and Mr. Bolton together from here on in."

"I've found something that connects Huw Valentine to the school. I'm at his factory and in the storage area there are hundreds of bags. His textile company has made costumes for the school. He must know the principal or another teacher there."

"And what are you assuming even if that is true?"

"That they could be connected to Abby's abduction."

"That's not enough of a link to even pursue a warrant. You do realize you're trespassing?"

Annoyance pinched hot at her cheeks. "So arrest me, but I recommend you arrest Huw Valentine first."

Tori tightened her grip on the phone. If Thornhill dismissed her discovery out of hand…

He cleared his throat. "I will have officers try to reach Mr. Valentine. In the meantime, I'm taking Mr.

Bolton to the station. I'd like for you to meet us there."

"I'm on my way." Tori ended the call and made for her car.

As she slid into the driver's seat and started the ignition, a small frisson of hope simmered deep inside. Huw Valentine had to be involved in some way—no matter how small. When he'd spoken with Tori at the sports center, did he have Abby Brady hidden somewhere, scared and alone? Tied up and afraid in a darkened basement waiting and waiting for his return, because even the company of her captor was better than the confused and terrified hours she spent alone.

Tears burned Tori's eyes.

*We're coming, Abby. We're coming, Olivia. Just hold on…*

Chapter Twenty-One

At the police station parking lot, Tori fought to get her emotions under control. Every time she thought of what Mark would be going through with Olivia gone…she inhaled and wrapped her arms around herself. What could she do for him? How could she stop or undo what had happened? Her heart was filled with pain for a man she had quickly come to care so much for. There was nothing she could say or do to ease Mark's distress, other than bring Olivia home. Tori squeezed her eyes shut. She couldn't even contemplate what he'd do if Olivia were still missing by nightfall.

Taking a deep breath, she stepped from her car just as her phone rang. Locking the door, she looked at the display but the number was "Unknown." Frowning, she accepted the call as she walked slowly toward the station doors. "Hello?"

"Is this Tori Peterson?"

"It is."

"Miss Peterson, this Paul Chamberlain. My wife asked that I call you."

Tori stopped at the hope of a further step forward. "Thank you so much for calling back."

"Of course. As soon as Robyn told me your visit had something to do with Abby Brady, there was no question of me not calling. I'm also very sorry for what happened to you."

Tori closed her eyes. "Thank you."

"I understand you wanted to ask me about the woman who came here a couple of months ago?"

"Yes." Tori opened her eyes and forced her mind to focus on the here and now, rather than the past…or even the future. "Did she mention her name at all? Why she was interested in your home?"

"The whole thing was a little bizarre. She didn't tell me her name, only that she used to live here many years ago and as she was in the area, would love to have a look around."

Tori frowned. "Did you believe she knew the house?"

"I did initially and saw no harm in letting her inside…not that Robyn agreed with that sentiment when I told her."

"So what happened to make you suspect she didn't know the house?"

"I got the impression she had no clue about the layout of the rooms. She urged me ahead of her into each room as though she didn't know her way. She commented on moved furniture and how lovely the kitchen was as if she hadn't seen it before which didn't added up."

"Why?"

"I know for a fact the kitchen hasn't been changed for ten years or more."

"Couldn't she have lived there further back than that?"

"I suppose, but considering her age, she would've been very young and why would you want to see a house you can barely remember?"

Tori's mind raced. Brian Appleton had lived in the

house with his first wife and their young daughter. Was her theory about the abductor being his child, the right one? Could they be looking for a woman rather than a man? The thought made the revulsion in her stomach all the stronger.

She pressed her hand to her abdomen. "How old would you say this woman was?"

"About nineteen or twenty."

Tori frowned. It was more plausible that Abby and Olivia would trust a young woman of that age than they would an older man, but it definitely wasn't a woman who forced Abby into that car. Tori swallowed. God, were the police looking for more than one person? Was that how the abductor seemed to know where Tori and Mark were at any given moment? Because there were actually two or more people involved in the kidnappings?

She glanced around the station car park. "You've been really helpful, Mr. Chamberlain. I'd appreciate you calling me if you think of anything that might be relevant about this woman and a connection to Abby Brady or myself."

"Of course…and Miss Peterson? I wish you all the best in your endeavors."

The line went dead and Tori stared at the phone. Each slowly passing second brought forth the certainty they were looking for more than one person. Possibly male and female. Taking a deep breath, Tori hurried toward the station and she was quickly ushered to Thornhill's office by Sergeant Collins.

Mark's cursing and yelling could be heard along the corridor before they even reached the inspector's door. When Collins pushed it open, Mark's voice boomed loud and clear.

"God damn it, that's not good enough. My daughter's gone, Inspector. Gone. Whether Olivia and Abby are together or not, doesn't matter to me. I want my daughter back and I refuse to stand around here not doing anything."

Tori's heart broke to see Mark looking so terrified, his eyes wide, his face red and his hands clenched. The grip of his potent, emanating fury bounced from the office walls. She stepped forward and touched his arm. "Mark."

He spun around and Tori instinctively stepped back. His normally kind blue eyes were bloodshot and unfocussed; his usually clean-shaven jaw gray and his mouth twisted in an angry line. He didn't look like Mark. He looked frenzied, dangerous and out of control.

Their eyes locked as Tori's heart thundered. She had to get him doing something before he did something regrettable; something that might inadvertently affect their chances of finding Olivia sooner rather than later.

She cupped her hands to his tight jaw. "We're leaving, okay? We're leaving right now, but you need to calm down."

"Miss Peterson…" Thornhill rose to his feet. "You and Mr. Bolton are not in charge—"

Tori kept her focus on Mark. "We can go back to my place. Cool off. Think what happens next, okay?"

"Miss Peterson? Are you listening—"

"With all due respect, Inspector…" She dropped her hands from Mark's face and turned to face Thornhill, anger and frustration making her tremble. "I have managed to discover more today than your entire force has this past week as far as I know."

He glared. "I have officers locating Mr. Valentine as we speak. I have officers at his factory. This is a highly sensitive case and having you carrying on with no regard for your own safety, or that of others, does little more than risk Olivia and Abby's lives. Police work is methodical, carefully executed and thinking of the public at all times. From what I can tell, you are acting recklessly and without thought."

"Is that so?" She reached behind her and clasped Mark's hand, needing his touch, his underlying strength to mix and blend with hers as certainty she could no longer pursue this investigation without him burned deep inside. He trembled, his frustration seeming to vibrate from his very core. "Well, in that case, I'll leave it to you to visit Brian Appleton's old house in Littledale."

Thornhill glared. "What are you talking about now?"

"I went there this morning and spoke to the current residents, a Mr. and Mrs. Chamberlain. A young woman of around twenty years old went to the house a few months ago asking questions. I think that woman was Brian Appleton's daughter. Where is she? Do you know? What about his ex-wife?"

The inspector's cheeks reddened, his eyes blazing with undisguised fury. "We have no reason to go after Appleton's ex-wife and daughter. They've built a new life for themselves in Devon. Unless there is a substantiated reason to think they might know something about the abductions, I have no cause to talk to them. You might be involved personally with these abductions because of what happened to you, Miss Peterson but you cannot expect us to rush headlong into a situation based on your suspicions. In my world, I need a valid reason to question people. Whereas you—"

"Go off as I want to, without having to slash my way through miles and miles of restricting police tape. Damn right I do." She tugged on Mark's hand and stole her other arm around his waist. "We're leaving."

Mark stiffened in her grasp and Tori lifted her face to look at him. His skin was ashen as he faced the inspector, his blue eyes ice cold. "Find my daughter, Inspector, or so help me God, someone, somewhere, will live to regret your epic failure should anything happen to her."

Dread and fear rippled through Tori's blood. Mark's tone was almost catatonic…as though he had been taken over by a dangerous and invisible force. She needed to get him out of there and back to her apartment, before something happened that they'd never forgive themselves for.

****

Mark followed Tori up the stairs of her apartment block wondering how the hell he managed to put one foot in front of the other. Anger, violence, and revulsion swirled in a maelstrom through his body. His knuckles and jaw ached with tension, his mind a mess with the imaginings and actions he feared and craved in equal measure. Tori had promised him once they were inside her apartment, they would make a plan. A plan that enabled them to hunt a predator down and bring Olivia and Abby home.

She pushed open the apartment door and flicked on a lamp just inside the hallway. "Let's pour a drink and

278

figure things out as calmly as possible."

He closed the door and faced her. He stared into her eyes, lower over her perfect nose and dangerous lips. "We have to get her home, Tori."

Her eyes glinted with tears. "We will."

"I can't think about the alternative." Red-hot fury simmered in his gut and his pulse beat at his temple. "She's all I have and she's not going to be taken from me. Not ever."

A lone tear slipped onto her cheek and she swiped at it. "Then let's get to work."

She took his hand, leading him into her living room and switched on the light.

The sight in front of them drew Mark to a halt. Tori gasped.

Abby Brady sat as still as a statue on Tori's settee.

Her eyes were wide with fear and she visibly shook. Her hands and ankles were free of constraint, but she somehow looked trapped, confined and unable to move. The way she was dressed and left for them to find would undoubtedly be as cruel and terrifying to Tori as it must be for Abby.

Mark's heart beat fast, his anger flowing through him at the macabre clothes this precious child wore. It was an outfit more suited to Marilyn Monroe in her heyday. The full nineteen-fifties skirt, complete with netted petticoats and satin slashed neck top, turned his stomach…but it was the lipstick on Abby's mouth and the shadow on her eyes that made him want to rip whoever had dressed her this way in half.

He slipped his hand from Tori's and slowly approached the settee. He sat next to Abby, careful not to touch or frightened her. "Are you okay, sweetheart?"

She lifted her sad gaze to his and shook her head, her bottom lip trembling.

Mark glanced at Tori. Her eyes were as wide and fearful as Abby's and the color had drained from her face. At last she blinked and her paralysis broke. She stepped forward and dragged a leather beanbag from the side of the settee to sit on it in front of Abby. "Now, where have you been, little lady?" Tori's smile trembled as she slowly reached for Abby's hand. "We've been looking for you everywhere."

"Can I go home now?" Abby stared at Tori, tears sliding gently over her cheeks. "I want to see my mummy."

"Of course you can, sweetheart." Tori's voice cracked. "I'm going to get my phone and call her right now, okay?"

Mark glanced at Tori as she stood, their eyes locking in meaningful battle against whoever had done this. The child had been left in Tori's apartment. Her abductor had been in Tori's home and touched whatever he or she chose to touch.

Clenching his jaw, Mark nodded before forcing a smile and turning to Abby. "Would you like a drink? I bet Tori has some lemonade."

She shook her head. "I want to go home."

"I know you do and we're going to get you home as soon as we can, okay?"

Tori returned with her phone and sat on Abby's other side. She dialed and closed her eyes.

As Tori spoke to Susan Brady, Mark cleared his throat, desperate to distract Abby from what she had been through, yet equally as desperate to find Olivia. "Abby? Can you tell me about the place you've been?

Who you were with?"

Although he knew the police should ask his questions, each minute, each second, was another where Olivia could be enduring God only knew what. He hoped and prayed that all this sicko wanted to do was dress girls up…the alternative couldn't be thought about.

"Is the lady talking to mummy called Tori?"

Abby's softly spoken question broke through his contemplation and Mark re-focused. "It is. Have you heard that name before?"

She nodded. "The lady who looked after me loves her."

Mark glanced at Tori. "Loves Tori?"

Abby nodded.

Tori put down the phone and smiled at Abby. "Okay, your mum is on the way, sweetheart. I had to call the police too, but you're not to be scared. They just want to make sure you're all right."

"Mummy's coming?"

"Yes, she is."

Abby gave a tentative smile before it faltered and she stared down at her skirt, plucking and picking at the shiny material. "The lady told me you were pretty." Her gaze inched over Tori's face before she reached up to touch Tori's hair. "She said you had red hair and green eyes like me. Yours are way prettier than mine."

Mark flicked his gaze to Tori. She stared back at him, her smile too wide before she faced Abby. "She said that? Was she nice?"

Abby shrugged. "Sometimes. When I let her dress me up without fidgeting. Mummy says I fidget sometimes. The lady wasn't nice when she left me at home with the man. He was moody and didn't want to talk to me so he locked me in the strange room with all the funny clothes."

Mark stomach knotted with suppressed rage as he fought not to curl his hands into fists.

"The lady said she was going to marry you one day so I thought Tori was a man." Abby looked from Tori to her skirt, plucking over and over as she talked in one long stream. "She said mummy wouldn't miss me and wouldn't cry, but I think mummy's been crying. The lady said she'd give me back, but she didn't, not for a long time. She sang to me, which was sometimes nice, but I didn't like the words very much. Mummy sings nice songs, not like the lady's."

Mark frowned. "What were the songs, Abby? Can you remember?"

She shook her head. "I think my granddad would like them."

"They were old songs?"

"Uh-huh."

Tori reached for her phone and smiled. "Did they songs sound a little like this one?" She scrolled her finger back and forth over the phone and then Sinatra's voice filled the room. "Like this?"

Mark held himself rigid. Sinatra. The first letter. He slowly turned from Tori to Abby, every muscle in his body straining with the effort it took to act as though hearing the track, understanding the possibility of what it meant, hadn't funneled deep into his mind like the sharpened point of a damn screwdriver.

Another sign of Appleton's involvement. The fifties. The housewife. The music.

Abby closed her hands over her ears. "Turn it off.

Turn it off."

Tori immediately silenced the music and embraced Abby. "I'm sorry, sweetheart. I'm so sorry. It's all gone. No more music."

She looked at Mark over Abby's head, her eyes shining with tears and mouthed "Appleton's daughter."

Mark nodded. Tori knew as much about Brian Appleton as anyone else unfortunate enough to be selected as his victim. The dressing Abby up and the old songs were enough to make Tori believe this girl endured an experience too similar to Tori's for her abuser to be anyone else other than someone emulating Appleton.

There was every possibility that person could be Appleton's abandoned and rejected daughter. The little girl he'd severed all contact with once he was released from his insulting and pitiful prison sentence. Instead the bastard chose to move abroad and create a new family and identity, maybe leaving behind a now adult daughter whose resentment had burgeoned into evil.

The buzz of Tori's intercom sliced through the thick tension and Tori stood, giving Abby's hand a quick squeeze. She strode to the intercom. "Hello?"

"It's Susan, Tori. Do you have her? Do you have my baby?"

Tori smiled. "She's right here."

"Oh, thank God. The police are here too."

Tori pressed the buzzer. "Come on up."

Tori stepped away from the intercom and faced Abby. "Mummy's coming, sweetheart."

The harsh rapping at the door echoed through the apartment and Mark stood. When Abby stood too and slipped her hand into his, he stared at the top of her head, holding her hand as firmly as he dared. Was it wrong to relish the burst of euphoria that rushed through him that this little girl needed and wanted to know he was right beside her, when he couldn't be beside his own child?

As Tori hurried to the door, Mark fought the mixed joy and anticipation of seeing one child safely reunited with her parents—and the horrible pain of being separated from Olivia. Susan Brady rushed into the apartment ahead of her husband and the police, her expression evolving from terror to sheer joy when Abby ran from Mark into her mother's arms.

Susan and Simon Brady planted kisses all over Abby's painted face, seemingly oblivious to its vileness. Mark didn't blame them. He would do no different if Olivia walked through the door. He closed his eyes against the turmoil that raged a war inside him. When he got Olivia back, he couldn't give her the gift of Lauren's arms, the tenderness of her kiss. All he had was himself and who knew if that would be enough for Olivia after this? What if his little girl wanted so much more now she knew her dad wasn't enough to protect her from harm?

He opened his eyes and faced Tori. With a tilt of his head, he gestured for her to join him across the room. He took her elbow and steered her away from the police and the chattering and crying of the ecstatic Bradys. In the far corner of Tori's living room and confident they were out of the police's earshot, Mark looked deep into Tori's eyes and saw exactly what he expected. Fear, vengeance and loathing.

Tori's dark green eyes stormed like a violent and angry ocean. "He dressed me the same way, in practically the same clothes. We're looking for Appleton's daughter. It can't possibly be anyone else."

Mark trembled with the need to rush from the apartment, to find his baby and bring her home. "I feel like I'm dying, Tori. Dying, or ready to kill someone."

Her eyes shone with tears. "We'll find Olivia. I promise."

"Have you ever seen a picture of Appleton's daughter?"

She shook her head. "Never. I've got no idea where to start looking for her either."

He glanced toward Thornhill as he and Sergeant Jansen asked Abby questions. The strain of the past days showed on the inspector's face, now lined around the eyes and mouth so much more prominently than when they'd first met.

"What about the police?" Mark frowned before meeting Tori's eyes once more. "They must have a picture on file?"

She looked over at the gathered group. "They will, but I can't imagine they'll have an up-to-date one so all we have to hope now is Thornhill takes my instinct about this and runs with it." She faced Mark once more. "If he doesn't, then he can't blame us when we go *recklessly* off on our own again, can he?" She looked past his shoulder. "It's Olivia we need to worry about."

"I have to find her, Tori. I can't stand around here anymore."

"Hey." She cupped her hands to his jaw and stared deep into his eyes. "We know who we're looking for now. There's every chance she'll return Olivia as she has Abby. She wants me, Mark. If using me as bait is what it takes to get Olivia home, that's what we'll do."

Lifting his face from her hands, he squeezed his eyes shut. "I can't let you do that, Tori. Don't even suggest it."

"Look at me. Mark, please."

He opened his eyes. Distress ripped through him, fear and loathing mixed and burned. "It's too dangerous."

"Listen. We stay focused, okay? We have more details now. We know there are two people involved. The woman is Appleton's daughter, I'm sure of it. Between us and the police, we'll bring Olivia home." She shook her head. "No more superhero stuff. The villains are too great in number for anyone to fight them all. Believe me, I've tried."

"This time, everything we do, we do together." Angry tears burned behind his eyes and Mark wrapped his arms around this wonderful woman, he pressed his lips to her hair. "And when I find who's responsible for touching my daughter and Abby…"

"You'll let me have five minutes with her first." She pulled back, her gaze inching over his face. "You're an amazing dad, Mark."

He turned to look at Thornhill, unable to respond to Tori's statement when he had so badly failed Olivia. There was nothing amazing about him. Not while his daughter was still missing. "Even if the police only have a picture of Appleton's daughter when she was young, with all the digital enhancing stuff they use nowadays, they should be able to get a good idea of what she looks like now. It has to be worth Thornhill having that done, at least." He narrowed his eyes toward the inspector. "We'll wait until he's finished with the Bradys and then it's Olivia's turn."

Chapter Twenty-Two

After showing the reunited Bradys, Thornhill, Jansen and the female police liaison from her apartment, Tori closed the door behind them and faced Mark. He stood in the center of her living room, his face so still and set, it looked carved from the wood he worked with every day.

She walked toward him and took his hands. "We're making steps. At least now, Thornhill has agreed to look at Brian Appleton's daughter."

He inhaled. "And what about us? Do you really think I can wait here for news as Thornhill just suggested?"

"No, I don't…and there's no way I'm sitting here doing nothing either."

"Right answer." He slid his hands from hers, pushed back the fallen hair from his brow and walked across the room. He stared out the window, his shoulders high and stiff.

Helplessness slithered through her. What now? What could they do next?

Mark abruptly turned around. "I'm going back to the school."

Manic determination shone in his eyes. Every second Olivia was missing would be torture to him. Worry for him and Olivia made Tori's heart race with fear…no telling what Mark's love for his daughter would make him capable of. "To do what?"

"You found a connection between the school and Valentine. Thornhill has officers looking for Valentine, but he didn't mention the principal. I think she's too far down his list to be seen as a suspect. I'm going to go talk to her myself."

"I really don't think they're involved. Maybe their connection is an innocent one. We should just focus on Appleton and his daughter."

"I have to do something."

Tori's heart ached to see such anger, frustration and pain in his gaze. She had no right to stop him doing anything he wanted. She crossed her arms. "Okay, then go see the principal. What will you say to her?"

"I don't know, but with the costumes you found, we know they at least know of each other…maybe more."

"Okay, go talk to her. Find out whatever you can. Ask her anything and everything you can think of until you are a hundred percent convinced either of her guilt, or that she had nothing to do with these kidnappings." She walked toward him and gripped his hand. "We have to know either way."

He exhaled, his angry gaze lingering over her face. "And what about you? What will you do?"

"I'll stay here in case whoever had Abby decides he or she is going to deliver Olivia back here too."

"Do you think that could happen?"

The hope in his eyes and the flush of color at his cheeks twisted at Tori's heart. She desperately wanted to say she did, but false hope was the last thing Mark needed from her. She lifted her shoulders. "I don't know, but we can pray, can't we?"

He brushed past her and picked up his jacket. "Can I take your car?"

"Of course." She walked him to the door. "While I wait, I'm going to talk to Cally and see what she's managed to find out about Brian Appleton's family. Neither of us will stop working until Olivia's home."

He pulled her close. He held her firm and tight, his arms filled with a desperation that yanked hard on her heart. She slid her hands to his waist and pressed her head into his chest, pouring every ounce of her will and tentative love for him into their embrace.

His lips gently brushed hers as they parted.

Tears stung her eyes, but she forced a soft smile. "I'll talk to you soon, okay?"

He nodded before turning and leaving her apartment.

Tori closed the door and leaned her back against it, her heart aching and her mind whirling. There was little chance of Olivia being delivered back anytime soon. Whoever had taken her, would be enjoying their power.

The way Brian Appleton had. He'd sit gleefully watching the news as he continued to hold Tori in his home without detection. He'd make her wear dresses with frills and nets, bows and ribbons, drink wine and they'd eat take out as though they were lovers in conspiracy. Tori breath caught and she pressed her hand to her stomach.

It was all a game. An illusion. She would not be fool enough to believe a narcissist who preyed on children in order to get what they wanted would ever play by any rules other than their own. The letters she and Mark had received showed the abductor's escalating fury. This game could go on much, much longer.

Whoever the opponent, they wanted *her*—which meant she had to do whatever it took to entice them from their lair to claim their prize.

She strode across her living room to a small writing desk and her laptop. Firing it up, she typed in Brian Appleton's name on a search engine.

Fighting the need to turn away from the images that appeared, Tori scanned the links to several press websites before selecting the most respected. She scanned the copy for any indication of Appleton's first family when he'd lived in Littledale. His ex-wife's name was Lucy nee Weir, but his daughter's name was withheld due to her young age at the time. How was she supposed to act on her supposition about Appleton's eldest child without a name or picture? The skepticism in Thornhill's eyes had done nothing to boost Tori's confidence he would carry through on his word to pursue Brian Appleton's daughter.

The inspector had seemed adamant Tori looked in the wrong place, which meant he would follow up his own thoughts before hers.

Behind her on the coffee table, her phone vibrated.

Tori rose, her mind still embroiled in a way forward with regard to Appleton's daughter. She accepted the call. "Hello?"

"Tori?"

Tori stiffened. "Olivia?"

"You need to come and get me." Olivia's voice cracked. "I'm at the mall."

"The mall? But—"

"He left me here. Tori, please, come. I'm scared."

"I'll be right there. Whereabouts are you?"

"He told me to sit on a bench in the food hall. I'm by the pizza place."

"Okay, don't move. Everything's going to be all right. I'll be there as soon as I can."

"He said I had to tell you not to call my dad and that he'd be watching." Her voice broke a second time. "Please don't make him mad because then he'll tell *her*."

Nausea rose bitter in Tori's throat. "There's two of them?"

"Three, but I haven't seen the other man. They just argue about him all the time."

*Three?* Dread clutched at Tori's stomach. "Okay, be brave. I'll be there before you know it."

Tori ended the call, her body trembling. She snatched her keys and purse from the kitchen counter and left the apartment, her phone clutched in her hand. She raced to her car and slid into the driver's seat. Just in case Olivia called again, Tori set her phone to speaker with fumbling fingers. She shoved the keys into the ignition and pulled away with a screech of tires.

She gripped the steering wheel. How could she not call Mark? He'd never forgive her once he found out she'd spoken to Olivia and not told him.

But she couldn't risk angering whoever watched his daughter and have Olivia's pick up go horribly wrong. She'd seen enough TV programs to know the drill. Keep to the villain's code of play or take a gamble with the victim's life.

Cursing every traffic light, crossing and car that dared to drive in front of her, Tori made it to the mall in record time. Screeching to a stop in a vacant spot, she yanked the keys from the ignition, snatched up her purse and phone and got out of the car. Running into the mall, she sprinted to the escalator, then the next and the next until, at last, she burst into the heaving food hall.

Mothers with strollers, groups of teenagers and men in business suits rushed or lingered everywhere. Tori stood on tiptoes trying to see over the hundreds of heads surrounding her. Cursing, she frantically shouldered her way through the crowd with muffled apologies as she stepped on toes and knocked purses from their owners' hands. Her heart beat painfully behind her ribcage and perspiration beaded cold at her hairline.

At last, she reached the pizza place and frantically scanned the benches and seating area.

Olivia wasn't there.

"Don't do this to me." She murmured, weaving amongst more and more people as she strode around the seats. "Don't do this to me, please."

"Tori, over here."

She spun around and tears leapt into her eyes. Olivia sat rigid on a bench, partially hidden from view by a plastic fir tree. Tori froze. Olivia was dressed in the clothes that Tori had been wearing the day Appleton took her. The clothes the police never found.

"Oh, my God." The words whispered over her lips as Tori hurried toward Mark's daughter. "You bastard."

Olivia stood and rushed into Tori's opens arms. Closing her eyes, Tori pulled her close and squeezed her small body. "It's all right. Everything's all right now. I've got you."

She pressed a kiss to Olivia's dark hair and rocked her as the girl's sobs wracked her body.

Tori scanned the area around them. Appleton had to be here somewhere. Only a blur of unfamiliar faces, too absorbed in their own lives to notice, or care, about the plight of the young girl crying in Tori's arms.

"You're safe now," Tori whispered. "I'm going to take home to your dad, okay?"

Olivia continued to cry, her sobs slowly lessening to whimpers until she pulled gently back from Tori's embrace. Her wide, blue eyes, so similar to Mark's, stared into Tori's. "I didn't think you'd come."

"What? Of course I would."

"I've been so horrible to you."

"Hey." Tori pulled Olivia close once more. "You've been fine. Absolutely fine. Come on, let's go. Your dad's going to be so happy to see you."

"Is he okay?"

"He will be now. Come on."

Tori slid her arm around Olivia's shoulders and steered her toward the escalator, all the while, searching for Brian Appleton…or someone who looked like him. Despite the years since she'd last seen him, there was no doubt in her mind she would recognize him. As her fingers touched the clothes that had once been hers, everything that happened to her came crashing back hitching Tori's stretched nerves tighter.

Once they were safely inside her car, Tori put her phone on speaker and dialed Mark's number. She pulled away and headed straight for the police station. Thornhill needed to have the clothes Olivia was wearing analyzed as soon as possible. Who knew if a tiny, incriminating piece of DNA could be lifted from them? They had no time to waste and she hoped Mark understood that when she told him where she was going with Olivia.

He picked up on the third ring.

"Tori? Do you have news?"

Tori looked at Olivia and winked, indicating she should talk. Olivia smiled for the first time since Tori found her. "Hi, Dad."

"Olivia? Oh, thank God. Are you all right?"

"No, I want to see you."

"I'm on my way." His voice cracked. "Where are you?"

Tori took a breath. "I'm taking her to the police station. We'll meet you there."

"What? Why aren't you bringing straight to me? What happened? Where did you find her?"

"At the mall. Olivia phoned me, Mark, said whoever had taken her specifically warned for me to come alone. I didn't want to risk anything going wrong. I'm sorry." Tori swallowed against the dryness in her throat. He sounded so angry, so distant…so unlike the Mark she was falling for. "Meet us at the police station and we can talk some more. I had to do this without telling you. I'm so—"

"Don't, Tori. Just don't. You have no idea what it's like to have kids, so just don't. I'll see you in just a few minutes, Olivia. Okay? I love you."

The line went dead and Tori fought her tears.

The severance between her and Mark had been clear in his every word.

"My dad didn't mean that, Tori. He's just scared, that's all."

Tori forced a smile as she stared ahead. "I know. Everything's fine. Don't worry."

When Olivia leaned across and pressed a kiss to

Tori's cheek, she gripped the steering wheel hard and tried not to think about the future that could've been possible without Brian Appleton in her past…or her present.

**** 

Mark raced into Barlington Police station, his heart pounding as hysteria mixed with relief that Olivia had been found and was all right. His head a mess and his heart even more so, he headed straight to the reception desk. The duty sergeant looked up from the paperwork in front of him. "Ah, Mr. Bolton. Come straight through, your daughter is being looked after by Constable Louise Ryland."

The seconds ticked by like minutes in his desperation to hold Olivia in his arms. Mark followed the desk sergeant through the door into the main station. The sidelong glances and stilled fingers of the policemen and women at computers or standing did nothing to ease Mark's tension.

An office door ahead of the sergeant opened and Thornhill emerged, his face grave. "Mr. Bolton."

"Where's my daughter?"

"She's in my office waiting for you."

Mark brushed past him into the office. Olivia stood and rushed toward him. He closed his arms around his most precious possession, her cheek pressed to his chest where it belonged. Relief pounded on a painful slash through his chest. If he'd lost her, if anything would've happened to her…

He squeezed his eyes shut and murmured words he hoped with soothe her soft whimpers. Eventually, she pulled back and that was when he noticed her clothes. Why was she dressed in what were clearly police issue sweatshirt and pants?

He looked at Thornhill. "Why is my daughter dressed like this? How dare you order her clothes from her without my permission."

"Miss Peterson signed her agreement, Mr. Bolton. We needed to test the clothes Olivia was wearing for possible DNA evidence. Why don't you take a seat? There have been a few developments since Olivia was found."

Sickness rolled through Mark's gut. Whoever had taken Olivia had touched her. Touched her clothes. Her skin.

Olivia eased back from Mark's arms and with his hand firmly clasped around hers, he led her to one of the three chairs in front of Thornhill's desk. The inspector looked to the female officer who had risen to her feet when Mark entered the office. "Thank you, Constable Ryland. You may return to your work."

The young woman smiled at Mark and smoothed her hand down Olivia's arm. "You'll be okay now, Olivia. I'm very proud of you."

Tears burned behind Mark's eyes. Through his mist of anger, he hadn't even thought to tell Olivia the same thing…or even ask if she was okay. Shame pinched hot at his cheeks as he looked into Olivia's eyes for the first time since he'd seen her that morning.

"Are you okay?"

She nodded.

"Are you hurt?"

She shook her head.

Mark curled his free hand tightly around the arm of the chair. Every instinct in his body screamed to bolt from the station and track down whoever dared to touch her.

Olivia's big, blue eyes sought his. "They took Tori away, Dad."

Mark stilled. "What?"

"The police. They took Tori."

Unease knotted Mark's gut and he faced Thornhill. "What's she talking about? Where's Tori?"

Olivia touched his arm. "I went with the man because he said he'd take me to Abby."

Mark stiffened. "What man, sweetheart?"

"The man at school. He was there to fix the roof."

Mark slowly turned to Thornhill. "It was one of the workmen and you missed that since Abby was taken? For crying out loud."

Thornhill glared. "Why don't we just focus on the here and now?" He turned to Olivia, his gaze softening. "Olivia has been fantastic. She sat down with an artist and all available units have a description of this man as we speak." He met Mark's gaze. "Whoever he is, he's working with a man and woman. Olivia has also seen the woman face to face and we know she's the ringleader in both Abby's and Olivia's disappearance."

Mark dragged his gaze from his daughter's beautiful blue eyes and tried to focus on Thornhill. "As Tori suspected. This is Brian Appleton's daughter you're looking for, right?"

"I think after questioning Miss Peterson, we are—"

"Wait. You questioned Tori?" Mark glared. "In what capacity?"

Thornhill held Mark's gaze, his lips tightly pressed together.

Disbelief swept through Mark, hitching his anger. "As a suspect? Are you crazy?"

"Miss Peterson was the person who found both girls, Mr. Bolton."

"And?"

"And we had to make sure she is innocent of any wrongdoing. She was at the school when Abby was taken. She was later found in her apartment. Then she is dating you and Olivia goes missing."

"And that led you to question her? For God's sake, she told you she was in the middle of all this because of what happened to her. Instead of focusing on that, you throw her into an interview room?" He shook his head, his body trembling with the strength of his fury. "Where is she now?"

"As far as I know Miss Peterson is still being questioned by Sergeant Jansen. If she's not and has chosen to leave, we cannot keep her here against her will. She would only have been able to leave once we are satisfied she's not involved in any way with what has been happening. We had no choice but to question her, Mr. Bolton. The clothes Olivia was wearing were the same ones Miss Peterson wore when Appleton abducted her, although they were never located at the time."

Mark swallowed. "The same clothes?"

"Yes."

Further words lodged in Mark's throat. The last time he'd spoken to Tori he hadn't thanked her for finding Olivia, but accused her of knowing nothing because she didn't have children of her own. Now, the police had insinuated she was somehow involved?

"Dad?"

He faced Olivia.

"Tori isn't to blame for any of this. The man at the

school told me he could take me to Abby so I sneaked out by asking to go to the toilet when we were going for PE. I guessed it would be awhile before Miss Leigh noticed I was missing. This is all my fault, not Tori's."

Mark gripped her hand and lifted it to his lips, pressed a kiss to her knuckles. "You did what you thought you could to help find Abby, sweetheart. That makes you good, not bad. Okay?"

Tears slipped over Olivia's cheeks. "And now you're mad at Tori too."

"No." Mark shook his head, his heart beating fast. "I'm not mad at Tori. I don't think I'll ever be mad at Tori after she brought you safely home, do you?"

"She's so brave, Dad. I don't know what happened to her, but it must've been bad for the police to want to talk to her. She's kind and she's beautiful. You should really, really like her, Dad. I do."

Mark swallowed and turned to Thornhill. "So what happens next?"

The inspector looked to Olivia. "Why don't you tell your dad what you told me?"

Olivia inhaled a shaky breath before speaking in a rush, her eyes wide. "I got in the man's car and he drove me away from school. He made me put on a blindfold and then we drove some more."

Mark fought the sickness inside him as he tried to concentrate on what Olivia was saying. His baby girl had got into a stranger's car of her own free will; had allowed someone to blindfold her all in the name of saving Abby. Should he be proud? Flip out entirely? Or just accept that no matter what he did, Olivia would always have a mind of her own.

"Go on, I'm listening." He winked in an effort to

allay some of the fear in her eyes. "What happened next?"

Her shoulders relaxed. "Then he took me to this house, took off the blindfold and told me to knock on the door. He stood at the gate, waiting."

"He didn't go in with you?"

"No. He stayed outside. A lady answered the door."

Mark swallowed. "Did you know this lady?"

"No, but Tori does."

"Tori knows her?" Mark stilled. "How do you know?"

"Because the lady knew all about her and you. She said that you stole Tori from her and she didn't really want me, but you had to be shown who was in charge. She said once she has Tori, everything would be okay."

Mark snapped his gaze to Thornhill. "You knew all this and let Tori walk out of here? Who's to say this woman won't come after her? Hurt her? You must understand what knowing about this woman will do to Tori? She took my daughter, for crying out loud. Tori will go after whoever this is alone if she has to. She won't think about the dangers to herself, or just how bloody reckless it will be to act alone. Everything that's happened affects her more deeply than either you or I will ever imagine, Inspector."

Thornhill's gaze turned steely. "I'm confident with the description Olivia has given us, it's only a matter of time until the culprits are caught. We're doing our jobs, Mr. Bolton. You have no need to be concerned on that score. We also believe the property where your daughter was taken isn't too far out of town. The drop-off at the mall suggests that something either spooked the kidnappers and they wanted Olivia out of the way. Or else, they came to their senses. If it's the latter, there's every chance they could make a run for it. I have all officers working on finding a possible address."

Olivia shook her head. "You're wrong."

Mark faced her. Olivia stared at Thornhill. "She gave me back because she doesn't want to do anything else to stop Tori loving her."

Olivia said the words in such a matter of fact way; with such simplicity, Mark's stomach turned. Whoever this woman was, she was dangerous if she could convince Olivia that her actions were in any way understandable.

She turned from Thornhill. "Can we find Tori now, Dad? I think you should tell her it's okay that she didn't call you before. It wasn't her fault."

Mark rose to his feet. "You're right. Let's get out of here."

Thornhill stood. "Rest assured we'll find these people, Mr. Bolton."

"Yeah?" Mark glared. "Well, it had better be in the next hour or so, because if Tori has already left and is in any way hurt because of your failure to arrest someone..." Mark shook his head. "You call me as soon as you know anything."

Grasping Olivia's hand, Mark strode through the station to the front desk. He addressed Sergeant Collins. "Is Miss Peterson still here?"

"She left about five minutes ago once she found out you had arrived and were with your daughter."

Dread rippled through his blood and Mark glanced toward the station doors. "Did she say where she was going?"

The sergeant shook his head.

"Damn it." Mark marched toward the doors and shoved them open.

As soon as he and Olivia were sat in his car, he tried Tori's number.

It went straight to voicemail.

He cursed.

He couldn't blame her if she never wanted to speak to him ever again. Mark started the ignition. He had to find her or else suffer the consequences for the rest of his life.

## Chapter Twenty-Three

Tori tried and failed to avoid Cally's wide-eyed stare across their desks. "They questioned you?"

"Yes." Tori sighed. "I'm a little shaken up by it, but I'll be fine."

"That's diabolical."

"What is? The police were doing their job. Admittedly, not a very good one, but their job all the same."

"How can you joke about this?"

Tori struggled to keep control of the frustration rolling around inside her. "The last thing I'm doing is joking. If I'm honest, I'm madder than I've been in my whole life. I find Olivia, I find Abby and then I'm punished for it."

"You're shaking."

"No, I'm not." Tori pulled her trembling hands from her keyboard into her lap. "I'll be fine. I just need to figure out what to do next."

"I'll tell you what you're doing next." Cally stood and hitched her purse onto her shoulder before she picked up her phone. "You're coming home with me."

Tori frowned. "What?"

"I mean it." Tears glinted in Cally's eyes. "You shouldn't be here like this. It isn't right."

"I appreciate your concern, but I need to work."

"Fine. Then we'll work at my house."

"We can't." Tori shook her head and tapped a few keys on her computer. "I have to find the woman who held Abby and Olivia. She's after me, not them. Who's to say she isn't going to come at me with a damn gun the minute I walk out of here."

"If you really think that, you need to come home with me right now."

"Why?"

"Because she probably knows you're here. She'll wait for you to be alone. You shouldn't be alone. Not anymore. In fact, why don't you stay at mine tonight?"

Tori stopped typing and looked up. "Why would I stay at yours?"

Cally slumped. "Because, Tori, I'd like to think you are coming to see me as a friend as well as a colleague. I'm worried about you."

"And that's very sweet of you, but—"

"I'm not being sweet, I'm being practical. Stay. Please. We'll do everything we can to find this woman and then later, I'm going to cook you dinner and you're going to relax."

The seriousness in Cally's gaze was so unlike her that guilt pressed down on Tori that she'd contributed to making her young protégée so upset. Tori forced a smile and winked. "Is this some sort of girlie sleepover?"

Cally wiggled her eyebrows, her eyes lighting with humor. "If you like."

Tori laughed. As much as the sound felt alien and inappropriate, it was wrong that Cally should be so worried. Tori turned back to her computer. "Look, how about I accept the dinner, but I'm not sure I'll stay the night. I could certainly do with getting out of here for a while." She glanced around at her colleagues, met the eyes of several before they hastily looked away. "I feel like the entire office is watching me."

"Then let's go now."

"Now?"

"Why not?" Cally came around the desk and stood sentry at Tori's chair. "Ready?"

"Fine." Defeated, Tori packed up her laptop and picked up her purse, dropping her phone inside. "Let's go."

They walked through the office, their colleagues' gazes burning holes in Tori's back. They'd nearly reached the elevator to take them down to the lobby when Greg came running toward them. "Hey, where are you two going?"

Tori exchanged a look of impatience with Cally before slowing turning around. "I need to get out of here for a while."

He frowned and glanced between her and Cally. "Everything okay?"

"Everything's fine."

"Everyone knows you were questioned by the police, Tori. What happened?"

"Nothing." She shrugged, feigning nonchalance. "They just wanted to clear me of any suspicion since both girls were found in my care. They're satisfied I had nothing to do with their disappearances and, hopefully now, the police will be busy going after the right people."

"People? As in more than one?"

"There's two men and a woman involved. It looks as though one was in charge of enticing Olivia and Abby from the school, the other…" She shook her head, frustration burning. "I don't know what the other one's role is…and the woman? It seems she wants me."

He glanced from Tori to Cally and back again, confusion etched on his face. "She wants you? Why?"

"Greg, I don't want to talk—"

"You heard her." Cally slipped her arm around Tori's waist, her eyes like daggers as she glared at Greg. "Just stop looking for gossip and get back to work. I'm taking Tori back to my place. I'll look after her."

Too tired to talk anymore, Tori let Cally lead her from the office and out into the open air. The bright autumnal sunshine hitched the headache starting at her temples. "I don't feel too good."

"And that's why we're going to get you home. Give me your keys."

"But—"

Cally lifted an eyebrow and held out her hand, palm flat. "No more arguments. You're going to let me help you for once. You're always looking after everyone else. It's my turn to look after you now."

Tori passed over her keys, suddenly grateful for Cally's friendship. Maybe she should've given Cally more credit before now. She'd been working at the paper for six months and, in that time she'd gone from shy, but hardworking, to being a lot more confident and astute in her reporting.

As she slid into the passenger seat, Tori smiled. As well as letting down the guard around her heart—no matter how much she might regret it if Mark wanted nothing to do with her anymore—it was time she thought about easing out the hand of friendship too.

She turned to Cally. "Thanks for this. My head's a

mess so I really appreciate you looking out for me."

"And what about your heart?" Cally frowned, concern darkening her gaze. "I don't suppose things are working out as you expected with Mark? Not with all this upheaval going on."

"You can hardly label his daughter getting into a stranger's car as upheaval. I don't blame him for turning on me. This is my fault, no matter which way I look at it."

"That's so not true." Cally started the car, her eyes narrowed as she stared through the windscreen. "Sometimes people can be blind to what's going on around them. So you didn't recognize the signs that you could be danger? Don't you ever think that maybe the signs weren't there? That there really was no danger at all?"

"How can you say that? Two girls were taken."

When Cally turned, her eyes were kind. "And they were brought back. It's over, Tori. All's well, that ends well."

"Maybe." Tori shifted back into the seat, exhausted but at the same time grateful for someone else, literally, taking the wheel. "But I can't relax until these animals are caught. I need to know why something that happened to me years ago was brought back alive again. Those girls were innocent victims in all this."

"All will become clear eventually, I'm sure. Now sit back and relax. When we get to my place, we'll work out what happens next, okay?"

Tori returned Cally's smile, but how was she supposed to relax with a trio of dangerous and unpredictable perpetrators still running free? Add the fact Mark clearly blamed Tori for Olivia's abduction, and Tori's heart hurt as though it lay like an open wound in her chest. She pulled her phone from her bag and her heart skipped to see a missed call from Mark since she'd left the station.

"He called." Her heart picked up speed. "I didn't think he would."

Cally pressed on the gas and drove toward the parking lot exit. "Who?"

"Mark. I need to call him back." She hit the return call button.

"Do you want me to wait here until you've finished your call?"

"There's no need—"

Mark picked up on the second ring. "Hey."

Cally cut the engine.

Tori smiled. "Hey. How's Olivia?"

"She's doing amazingly well considering."

"I'm proud of her. She did good, even if she did take one hell of a risk in an effort to find Abby."

"Where are you now?"

"At the paper. Although I'm leaving to get away for a while. Cally and I are going back to her place to see what we can find out about the woman who held Abby and Olivia, if not the men as well. There must be something we're missing."

"Are you staying at Cally's for the night?"

Tori glanced at Cally as she stared ahead, seemingly deep in thought. "It's been discussed."

"Will you? For me? I need to know you're with someone tonight. I want to spend time alone with Olivia, but tomorrow…" He exhaled. "We need to talk."

Tori's heart kicked painfully as her fragile hope

they would work things out splintered. 'We need to talk' only ever meant one thing. She forced a smile. "Sure. We'll talk tomorrow."

"You'll stay at Cally's?"

"Yes."

"Okay. See you soon."

The line went dead and Tori turned to Cally. "Is that offer of a bed for the night still open?"

"Of course." Cally grinned and restarted the car. "We're going to have so much fun."

Tori pulled her bottom lip between her teeth to stem any snarky response. Suddenly, Cally's over-enthusiasm only enhanced her need to be back in Mark's arms.

****

Mark carried a huge bowl of popcorn and a large bottle of Coke into the living room. Olivia sat on the settee in her favorite Dalmatian all in one pajamas, her hair still damp from her bath and her legs crossed. Her thumbs moved in a blur over the lit screen of her phone, the opening credits of *The Goonies* paused on the TV. He fought the urge to ask her who she texted. His protectiveness bubbled in his blood, but the last thing he wanted was reinstate tension between them.

It felt so good to have his little girl home. It had been far too long since they had spent contented time together this way. Her brief disappearance had somehow banished the push/pull between them, leaving behind a learned journey that maybe they'd both desperately needed.

"Here we go." He put the popcorn on the table in front of the settee and twisted off the top of the Coke. "Do you want to pass me those glasses?"

"Sure." She finished her text and reached for the glasses she'd brought in earlier. "Here."

Mark filled the glasses and held one out to her. "You okay?"

She took the glass, her eyes averted. "Sure."

The need to push her for more squirmed inside, but Mark pursed his lips against his questions. She was getting to the age where she would make her own choices, regardless of his guidance—and he needed to accept that being a parent was also about letting your kids make their own way and their own mistakes.

He'd just prefer that Olivia had heeded the lesson about accepting rides from strangers a little more closely.

He cleared his throat. "So, shall we watch the movie?"

"Uh-huh."

Mark sat beside her and ran his hand over her hair. "You know I love you, right?"

She glanced at him, rolled her eyes and pointed the remote at the TV. "Always, Dad."

The screen flickered to life and Mark eased back into the cushions, crossing his ankles on the coffee table in the hope Olivia would take his posture as relaxed, even if he was still so tense, so desperate to ask her more questions, that there was little chance he'd be able to concentrate on the film.

They watched in silence for a few seconds before Olivia pointed the remote at the TV and paused it. "Do you know what was really strange about the woman I was with?"

Mark fisted his hand, crushing the popcorn in his palm. "What?"

"The more I think about it, the more I think I've seen her before."

"Did you tell the police that?" Mark tried to control the adrenaline rushing through him and not risk scaring her. "What did she look like?"

"I didn't tell the police because I didn't think I knew her, but now I think I saw her the day Abby was taken. The woman was with Tori. At the school…maybe not. I don't know." Her eyes grew wide with worry. "I could be wrong."

"How was she dressed?"

"Kind of old-fashioned, but in a cool way."

"Like the olden days?"

"Yeah. Was it her? The lady with Tori?"

Mark stared, the day passing through his memory on a camera-like roll of photographs. Cally. Only Cally had been with Tori that day. "Could I borrow your phone, hon?"

Suspicion clouded Olivia's gaze. "Why?"

"I left mine in the kitchen." He raised his eyebrows. "I'm not going to steal it, Liv."

She reluctantly handed him her phone and set the movie to play again. Mark drew his gaze over his daughter's profile before turning his attention to the phone. He called up a search engine and entered the name of Tori's newspaper.

He scrolled through to the staff.

There were pictures of her editor, Tori, and a few of the other reporters, but no one else that she'd specifically mentioned to him. Where was Cally? Greg?

Unease rippled through him as he turned to Olivia. "Could you pause this a second, Liv?"

She pointed the remote at the TV and faced him.

"What's wrong?"

"Hopefully nothing." He ran his gaze over her face, uncertain how to pursue the questions he needed to ask without alarming her. "Are you sure this woman's name was never mentioned in front of you? You have no idea who she is?"

She shook her head, her body rigid.

"Okay. It's okay." He pulled her into his arms and kissed her hair. "I need to make sure Tori's all right. Would you be okay to go to Michelle's for a while?"

"Uh-huh."

"Great. I'll ring her mum while you go and get dressed."

"Okay." Olivia got up from the settee and raced from the room, her hurried footsteps stomping up the stairs.

Mark immediately pushed up from the settee and stormed into the kitchen. He grabbed his phone from the windowsill and dialed Tori's number.

It went straight to voicemail.

His heart picked up speed. If his suspicions were right, he had insisted Tori stay the night with Brian Appleton's daughter…and Mark had no idea where Cally lived. He tried Tori a second time. No answer.

"God damn it." He dialed Thornhill.

"DCI Thornhill speaking."

"Inspector, Mark Bolton." Mark stuffed his hand into his hair. "I think the woman we're looking for is Tori's co-worker, Cally. I've no idea of her surname or her address. Tori isn't answering her phone and she's with Cally as I speak."

"Slow down, Mr. Bolton. What has led you to think she's the woman we're looking for?"

"Olivia thinks she might have been held by the woman who was with Tori the day Abby was taken. That woman was Tori's colleague, Cally. Like I said, I could be wrong, but Tori's not answering her phone and I'm worried."

"I'll get someone to head over to the newspaper and see what we can find out there. You stay where you are in case Miss Peterson calls."

The phone went dead.

Mark stared at it, his mind racing. Over his dead body would he stay put. He pocketed the phone, snatched his keys from the kitchen table and strode into the hallway. He called up the stairs. "Liv? You ready?"

She emerged on the landing and ran down the stairs, her eyes wide with worry. "Have you found, Tori?"

"Not yet, but I will. Let's go."

Chapter Twenty-Four

Tori smothered a yawn with the back of her hand. "I still think we should've stopped by my place so I could pick up an overnight bag. It seems silly for you to have to drive out again later."

"I don't mind." Cally smiled as she negotiated the rush hour through Barlington's High Street. "We could always swing by your house and then grab a takeout if I'm too tired to cook once we're done working."

"I suppose. I don't want you go to any trouble for me, that's all."

"It's no trouble. I like to do things for you."

Tori resisted the urge to roll her eyes as Cally drove farther and farther toward the very edge of Barlington. The girl was sweet, but independence had been Tori's middle name for as long as she could remember. Which was what made her growing need to be around Mark all the more worrying. Through the time they'd spent together, she'd grown to like having him near, having him to lean on.

The townhouses and shops gradually dwindled as they neared the quieter side of town that led toward the greenery and villages foreign visitors deemed so quintessentially English.

Tori frowned. "I didn't realize you lived so far out of town. This is quite a commute every day."

"It is, but worth it." She glanced at Tori and

blushed. "I've followed your career for a while and wanted to work with you more than anything."

"You have?" Tori smiled, surprised by Cally's admission. "Well, that's really nice to hear. Hope the real me hasn't disappointed you too much."

"Oh, God, no. Well, not now anyway."

Tori laughed. "But I did before? Gee, thanks."

Cally grinned as she stared ahead. "You know what I mean. Sometimes, you can be a bit, I don't know…"

"Pissy? Impatient? Sarcastic?" Tori raised her hand. "Guilty as charged." Her mind's eye filled with Mark's face and she smiled. "But at least now I seem to warming to a more preferable state of heart and mind."

Cally glanced at her. "In what way?"

Tori dropped back against the headrest and closed her eyes, absorbing the joy of having Olivia and Abby home with their parents, safe and well; of knowing even if Mark didn't want her, at least his daughter was back with a father who loved her more than life itself. "Now, I wonder if there might be more happiness for me out there than I ever thought possible before."

"Before Mark?"

Tori opened her eyes and smiled. "Yes. Before Mark."

When Cally gave no further response, Tori turned. Cally's jaw was tight, her color a little pale. Tori glanced at Cally's hands on the steering wheel. Her knuckles shone white.

She frowned. "You really don't like him, do you?"

"Who?"

"Mark."

Cally shrugged. "I don't know him."

Impatience simmered inside Tori and she fought to

keep it in check. "He makes me smile, Cally. In my world, that means a lot."

"It's not that I don't like him."

"Then what?" Tori raised an eyebrow as her temper cooled—a little. She didn't want to be that snappish person anymore. Mark had shown her there was more to a person's life than their history. "Well?"

Cally sighed. "It's just that *you* barely know him. Considering how you met, your relationship with him seems a little too intense." She glanced at Tori, genuine worry in her eyes. "I know what happened to you and you hear about cases where victims lean on people who help them. They end up falling into some sort of misplaced love. I can't help thinking that what's happening with you and Mark."

Tori huffed out a laugh, discomfort that Cally might be right rippling through her. "Misplaced love? That's ridiculous. I'm not in love with the guy..." Tori's cheeks burned. *Liar.* "He's just the best person, the most genuine person, I've met in a long time. Anyway, why shouldn't I grab a chance at some romance? Don't I deserve that as much as the next person?"

"Of course you do. We all do." Cally's cheeks turned pink. "I'm sorry. It's none of my business."

Tori turned to the side window, not trusting herself to say more. How could Cally be so judgmental about Mark when his daughter had been kidnapped like Olivia was someone else's property to take? How could she not see that Mark had been through a horrific, nightmare ordeal that no parent should have to face?

Cally turned the car into a deserted cul-de-sac of pretty houses, their gardens neatly tended, their front doors each painted a different color of the rainbow. Yet, as inviting as the small street looked on the outside, it didn't feel quite as it should. The houses displayed something close to TV show perfection but the darkened windows and the street—silent of children or activity—shrouded Tori with inexplicable unease. She turned and sneaked a look at Cally.

She stared straight ahead, the color in her cheeks high and her shoulders stiff.

A few seconds later, Cally pulled into a driveway in front one of the houses and cut the engine. "Here we are."

Tori peered through the windscreen at Cally's house. It was pretty big for someone on a trainee journalist's wage. Tori raised her eyebrows. "I expected you to be renting an apartment or something. This looks big enough for a small family."

"Oh, my dad pays the mortgage."

"Your dad? Lucky you."

"Uh-huh." Cally leaned over and her hair brushed Tori's leg as Cally retrieved their purses by Tori's feet. Cally straightened and smiled. "Come on. Let's get inside and get to work. I've got your purse."

Frowning, Tori got out of the car and followed Cally to her front door. As Cally put the key in the lock, Tori looked left and right along the street. It was so quiet. Like a lull before the storm.

"Tori?"

Tori started and turned, plastering on a smile. "Sorry."

Cally waited inside the house, her fingers curled around the edge of the door. "You were miles away."

"It just seems so quiet here. I suppose that comes

from me living and working in the center of town."

Cally smiled and held the door wider in invitation. Tori stepped over the threshold into the hallway and Cally closed the door behind her. Tori stared at the array of pictures covering almost every square inch of the cream-painted walls. The smiling faces of Elvis, Marilyn Monroe, Bobby Darin and a few others Tori didn't recognize stared back. Foreboding inched up her spine as she looked from the checkered black and white floor tiles toward the open kitchen door at the end of the hall.

The sliver of cupboards and utensils she could see through the partially open door were like something lifted from a housewives' guide, circa '58.

Tori closed her eyes and withdrew into herself as claustrophobia threatened.

Cally?

All this time?

The walls drew in closer and the floor seemed to tilt this way and that.

When a lock, then a second and a third, were thrown into place behind her, Tori didn't as much as flinch. Her body turned numb as she closed down.

Just as she had with Cally's father.

Tori's peripheral vision blurred and turned gray, but she fought back the urge to faint with all her might.

*Mark. Think of Mark. Think of Olivia.*

Cally came forward, her high-heels clicking on the tiled floor. She moved behind Tori and her suddenly sickening floral perfume infused Tori's nostrils as Cally's breath brushed against Tori's ear. "Now you know the lengths I've had to endure to get you here, I hope you're going to be nice. I love you, Tori. So much."

Tori slowly regained her equilibrium as she drew on the inner strength that had got her through the years since her abduction. The panic and terror eased.

When she'd fought, Brian Appleton had liked it. When she surrendered, he became uninterested...almost bored. He didn't hurt her. He ignored her.

Tori slowly opened her eyes as Mark's invisible arms came around her and held her close. He pressed a lingering kiss to her crown, pushing his strength and resilience deep into her head and heart.

She softly smiled and turned to meet Cally's gleaming gaze. "I had no idea you felt that way about me."

Cally smiled, her cheeks flushed and her eyes bright with excitement. "You're not mad?"

"How could I be mad?" Tori laughed and looked around her. "You've told me you love me and your house is beautiful."

"And what about me?"

Tori struggled to keep her lips from trembling. "You?"

"Aren't I beautiful too?"

"Of course you are. That's why I never guessed how you felt about me. You're so young and pretty, Cally. So out of my league."

"Oh, Tori." Her blush deepened. "Let's go into the kitchen. I baked some muffins this morning. We can have them with some tea. Please tell me you know how to bake too? Now we're together you can stay home all day and bake, and clean and do whatever you like to the house. Does that sound good?"

"That sounds amazing."

Cally laughed and clutched their purses to her chest. "We're going to be so happy together."

Tori stared at her purse, visualizing her phone within. She raised her gaze to Cally's. "Could I have my purse? I need to use your bathroom." She grimaced. "Women's…you know."

"You have your period?" Cally's face fell. "Oh, I'm sorry. I have plenty of sanitary towels upstairs. First door on the right." She turned and headed into the kitchen, Tori's purse still clutched firmly in her hand.

Tori squeezed her eyes shut. She would not be a victim again. She was in control. This time she would either die trying to escape…or kill her captor with her bare hands.

She walked upstairs and peered into each of the upstairs bedrooms. When she reached the master bedroom, Tori froze.

Laid out on the bed was a pale-pink baby-doll nightdress and matching frilly knickers. Mule slippers on the floor, neatly set out at right angles to each other.

Tori's stomach convulsed and she slapped her hand to her mouth as sickness rose.

*Not again. Please God, not again.*

As helplessness threatened, she fought to hold onto her rage rather than give in to the fear and terror that filled her lungs, threatening to tear a scream from her throat.

She had to get out of here.

Tori hurried into the bathroom and locked the door. She flitted her gaze over the pink enamel bath and strew of nineteen-fifties toiletries and trinkets. It was as though she had stepped into Brian Appleton's home all over again. Yet, the situation felt worse, more gruesome, and more inappropriate with time having moved forward so many years.

Embracing the anger and the need to survive, her heart pumped with determination. She tried the bathroom windows. Tears burning her eyes as she pushed and shoved at the handles.

It was hopeless.

She was trapped, caught and caged once more.

No, she would not surrender. Never.

Frantic, she opened a cupboard suspended on the wall, looking for anything she could use as a weapon. Bottles and tubes of every shape and size, but nothing sharp, nothing of any use.

There was a knock on the door and Tori froze.

"Tori? Are you okay in there?"

Tori swallowed the lump in her throat. "I'll be out in just a second."

"You sure you're okay?" The handle moved as Cally tried it. "I've poured us some wine."

"Sounds great." Tori looked around the garishly tiled walls and stopped. "I'll be right out."

"Come into my bedroom when you're done. I have something to show you."

"Okay."

Cally's footsteps faded. Tori moved to the toilet and pulled the flush.

She scanned the bathroom once more and her gaze fell on a glass bottle on the windowsill. It was heavy and reassuring in her hand as she pulled back the lock and opened the door.

The bottle slipped from her hand and thudded against the carpet.

Cally glared, the silver, jagged edged knife in her

hand glinting. "You shouldn't have taken so long. I knew you were up to something. I just knew it."

"I—"

"Shut up. Just shut the hell up."

Tori's stomach rolled and her heart beat fast. "Cally, this is crazy."

"Crazy? What's crazy is that you don't see me, Tori. You don't see me, but you will. You will see me through a lover's eyes." She came forward and gripped Tori's elbow, her breath close to Tori's ear. "We're going to make love and then you'll see how much you want to be with me."

Tori stumbled as Cally dragged her toward the master bedroom, the tip of the knife pressed so hard into Tori's side, her blood seeped warm against her skin.

Brian Appleton had been just the beginning. He'd never drawn blood…

\*\*\*\*

On the way to Olivia's friend's house, Mark dialed through to Tori's newspaper office. Sickness rolled through him as he gripped the steering wheel, the phone ringing over and over. It neared six, but judging by the hours Tori told him she'd kept at the office prior to Abby's disappearance, chances were someone was still at work there.

At last, someone picked up.

"Barlington Gazette. Neil Rose speaking."

Ignoring Olivia's stare as it bored into his temple, Mark cleared his throat. "Mr. Rose, this is Mark Bolton. I'm trying to get hold of Tori, but she's not answering her phone."

"Aren't you the guy Tori hooked up with since

Abby Brady went missing? How's your daughter doing?"

"She's doing great. I'm proud of her." Mark sneaked a glance at Olivia and winked.

"Glad to hear it. Tori left a while ago with Cally. Have you tried Cally?"

"I haven't got her number, but Tori said to meet her at Cally's later if I missed Tori at the office. Do you have her address? I've stupidly deleted it from my phone notes."

"I can't really give you—"

"I wouldn't normally ask but with everything that's been happening…"

"Fine, fine. Cally lives at thirty-one, Candleford Close just outside Barlington. Do you know it?"

"I'll find it. Thanks."

"No problem. Wishing the best for you and your daughter." Neil paused. "I've got to go, someone's knocking at the front door. Oh shit, what do the police want at this time of night?"

The line went dead and Mark turned to Olivia. "Can you see if you can find Candleford Close on the GPS?"

"Are you going to get Tori, Dad?"

Mark gripped the steering wheel tighter. "Yes."

"But if she's with Cally, the woman I stayed with, she might hurt you."

"I won't let that happen." He glanced at her before reaching across the space separating them. He gripped Olivia's hand. "Her entire focus is Tori. I don't have any choice but to do this, Liv. I can't leave Tori there, knowing what I do."

"Then call the police."

"I already have. They're at Tori's office now." He forced a smile and squeezed her fingers. "Chances are they'll be right behind me, heading for Candleford Close. There's nothing for you to worry about. I won't do anything stupid. As long as you're safe at Michelle's, I'll be happy, okay?"

He glanced at her again. Olivia stared back, her eyes wide and scared before she blinked and her gaze filled with trust. "Okay."

She slid her hand from his and pushed buttons on the GPS with the mind-boggling assurance that kids of her age had over Mark's generation. She located Cally's street and the GPS' metallic, female voice filled the car.

Ignoring her directions for now, Mark pressed on the accelerator, speeding his journey toward Olivia's friend's house. They arrived in record time.

Walking her to the door, impatience rippled through Mark as he shifted from one foot to the other. At last, Michelle's mum, Diane, opened the door. "Mark, are you okay?"

"I'm fine. Thanks for having her at such short notice."

"No problem at all."

Olivia reached onto her toes beside him and pressed a hurried kiss to his cheek. "Love you, Dad. Call me when you can."

Mark smiled softly as his baby brushed past him and Diane into the house.

He shifted his gaze from Olivia's retreating back to Diane. "Guess kids are a lot more resilient than we give them credit for. I've met someone recently who has proven that more than she realizes."

Diane smiled. "Would this be Tori Peterson, by any chance? Olivia has told me about her. It's good, Mark. I've hated you being alone all these years."

Not wanting to deal with reminder that he ran a huge risk of losing Tori as he had Lauren, he cleared his throat. "I've got to go. Olivia has an overnight bag, but I hope to collect her in the next couple of hours."

"Take all the time you need. She'll be fine."

He nodded and jogged to his car.

He'd already wasted far too much time.

Starting the car, he pressed a few buttons and the GPS re-engaged. He followed the system's directions and quickly sped through town toward the outskirts. It came as no surprise when he turned onto a quiet cul-de-sac. There was no way Cally could've gotten away with locking up children without raising the neighbor's suspicions in a busy street. He squinted toward the dusk-shadowed doors and their numbers. When he reached number twenty-seven, two houses away from Cally's, he cut the engine and killed his sidelights.

He inhaled a long breath and scanned the street. There were no official police vehicles or unmarked cars that could be the police on stakeout. He focused on Cally's house and studied its exterior, his heart pumping with adrenaline. It looked to be a standard three-bedroom semi-detached, with a side access to the back.

It would be a bad move to knock, which meant he had no choice but to break and enter. He couldn't give a crap what kind of trouble that might mean for him down the line. He had to get Tori out of there.

God only knew how far Cally had gone in the hours Tori had been with her. He just hoped and prayed

Cally hadn't physically hurt Tori…or worse.

As for the emotional and mental wounds Cally's actions would undoubtedly rip open for Tori again, he would be there for her. Hopefully, forever.

Mark got out of the car and slowly walked to the back, hoping Cally was distracted enough not to notice him along the street. Opening the car's trunk, he removed a screwdriver and shut the trunk as quietly as humanly possible. He locked the car and slipped his keys into his front pocket.

Gripping the screwdriver, his blood pumping, Mark made his way along the street. He passed Cally's house and waited. The living room curtains were open. He stared toward the darkened window, but detected no movement. He squinted toward the upper level, where a bedside lamp glowed amber in the front bedroom.

He closed his eyes and inhaled in an attempt to slow his heart rate and steady his focus. If he acted on the rage sweeping through his blood, it could mean a mistake of fatal proportions. He looked along the street toward the cul-de-sac's entrance. Still no sign of the police.

Pulling back his shoulders, Mark swept through Cally's gate, past the front door, and into the alley that ran along the side of the house to the back. He pressed his spine to the house's brick wall, straining his ears to any sound coming from the back garden. When nothing but birdsong greeted him, he slowly moved along the wall to the rear.

He crouched low and made his way to the door and tried the handle.

Locked.

Moving farther along the wall, he slowly

straightened to peer through the kitchen window.

The yellow, gingham curtains hanging at the windows were the softest aspect of the stark, bright yellow room. The appliances were pristine white; everything fifties retro, from the big vintage refrigerator to white Formica table and weave-backed chairs.

Everything was eerily spotless…unlived in.

Instead of presenting a picture of domestic perfection, the whole look was creepy.

He pulled back and looked at the upper windows. One was larger than the other, clearly the bigger of the two was a bedroom; opaque glass indicated the bathroom. No signs of activity in either.

Creeping back to the door, he took his screwdriver to the lock. The seconds ticked by like minutes in his head until he managed to remove the lock and ease the door open.

Once inside, he stilled.

The twinned sound of female murmuring filtered through the kitchen, followed by heavy and rapid footsteps on the second level above him. Mark glanced toward the ceiling and send up a silent prayer that what he was about to do would mean Tori's rescue, rather than risk to her safety.

He walked through the kitchen to the stairs.

Tori's tone was hard, but the tremor beneath was clear. "Just let me go, Cally. You're not thinking straight. Do you want the same to happen to you that happened to your father?"

"My father did everything wrong. He took you. You came to me."

"I didn't come to you. I thought we were friends. That you were offering me a safe place to relax while the police hunted down the person who wanted me. If I thought for one minute that person might be you—"

"Shut up and take off the rest of your fucking clothes, Tori. Don't make me mad."

Fury catapulted through Mark, his blood boiling from the manic threat in Cally's voice. All rationale left his mind as he stormed the remainder of the stairs and along the landing. Slapping his hand to the partially open door, he shoved it back with such force it thudded against the wall.

The first thing he saw was the blood seeping from Tori's side, staining the top of her white panties as she fought with Cally. Hands and nails slapped and clawed, hair was pulled and screams heard. He lunged forward just as Cally managed to escape Tori's hold. She came toward him, the knife in her hand raised and her eyes wide and glazed with manic fury. "You bastard. How dare you come into my house. You son of a bitch!"

He caught her wrists and whipped Cally's arms behind her back, the knife falling to the floor as he charged her face first onto the bed. She writhed and wriggled beneath him but he held her fast. Blood pumped in his head and blind rage threatened to erase sensible thought. "Call the police, Tori. Call them now."

"Let me punch her. Just once."

"Go. Now."

He sensed her hesitation and turned. She stared at Cally with such venom, Mark feared Tori's next move. Cally screeched and moaned beneath him like the trapped animal she was. He held her fast. "Tori, it's over. Ring Thornhill. Go."

She blinked and at last focused on him. "Let me hit

her. This is about me and her, Mark. Let me show the bitch *I'm* in charge and have been for my entire adult life."

He shook his head, despite the desperate wish to comply with his lover's command. "Go. Now."

With another glare at Cally, Tori turned and took off downstairs.

Mark leaned his full weight on Cally and hitched her wrists higher. She yelped and wriggled some more. Holding her tight, he leaned in close to her ear. "You'll pay for this. You'll pay for taking my daughter, for taking Abby and for daring to bring back the nightmare your father started for Tori."

"I love her, you idiot. I fucking love her."

He tightened his grip on her wrists, reveled in the throb of her blood beneath his hands. "You don't know what love is and where you're going, you never will."

Epilogue

*Two weeks later*

Tori glanced at Mark and Olivia on either side of her and inhaled. Hand in hand, the three of them had become a unit that Tori could never have predicted, nor hoped for. Her fears of commitment and trust stubbornly lingered, yet were embedded further inside and losing their strength and hold on her every day. She wanted Mark and Olivia in her life so much and so far, since Cally's arrest, they didn't seem in any hurry to leave Tori and her past behind them.

She looked at the façade of Barlington Police Station and squeezed their hands. "Let's hope we don't ever have to make this visit again."

Mark tugged on her hand. "Hey. It might have been us who got Cally, but it was Thornhill and his team who tracked down her associates. There's no way he's going to let them go again. They won't see the light of day for a long time."

Tori swallowed, she desperately wanted to believe him—to trust him—but Mark's words did nothing to quash the dread that had gnawed at her since Thornhill had summoned them there earlier.

The inspector's tone had been far from encouraging. It had been full of warning.

"I think he's going to tell us something we're not

going to want to hear." Tori looked at Olivia. "Are you sure you want to come in with us?"

She nodded. "Cally took me away from Dad. I want to know that isn't going to happen again."

Tears pricked at Tori's eyes. "It won't, sweetheart. Please believe that."

"It happened to you again."

Words failed her as Tori looked into the young girl's eyes. How could she deny Olivia's matter-of-fact statement? She had been taken again, albeit in an entirely different way.

She exhaled. "Maybe, but look at me now. What Cally did hasn't destroyed me, it's made me stronger and it brought me you and your dad." Tori looked to Mark. He met her gaze, his eyes a storm of fear and frustration. She smiled. "So maybe everything isn't as bad as it seems."

His gaze lingered on hers before he looked past her to Olivia. "Everything's going to be okay, Liv. Once we're done here, how about we go into the travel agents?"

Olivia slipped her hand from Tori's and stared wide-eyed at Mark, color darkening her cheeks. "We're taking a holiday?"

Tori's stomach knotted as she tried to keep her face impassive and not show the pain of Mark and Olivia leaving—even for a little while.

Mark smiled. "Would you like that? We can go wherever you like."

"Can we go to Washington? See the White House?"

"Sounds good to me."

Tori forced a smile. "Well, let's get this over with

so you two can start making your plans."

She slid her hand from Mark's and walked ahead of them, her heart aching as she pushed open the station's double doors and walked inside.

Sergeant Collins put down the phone at the desk as Tori approached.

"Ah, Miss Peterson, good to see you again. I hope you've recovered as well as can be expected from your ordeal?"

Tori forced a smile. "I'm getting there, as is Olivia."

The sergeant looked to Tori's side at Olivia. "You're a brave girl. You should be proud of yourself."

Olivia smiled. "I am."

"Good." Sergeant Collins' smile faltered as he pressed the buzzer beneath his desk. "Come on through and I'll take you to DCI Thornhill."

Unease rippled through Tori. A flash of apprehension, maybe even sympathy, had shot through the sergeant's gaze before he'd turned away. The dread in her stomach gathered weight and Tori breathed deep.

Avoiding the stares of the other police officers, they followed Sergeant Collins between the desks that until recently Tori hadn't had the necessity to see. Now, Barlington Police Station felt as familiar as her living room. Aware of Mark and Olivia behind her, Tori straightened her spine and lifted her chin. They needed her to be strong. They all deserved to be happy from now on—hopefully together.

Thornhill rose from behind his desk as they entered his office, his hand outstretched to Tori. "It's nice to see you again, Miss Peterson."

"Thank you."

He shook Mark's hand and then Olivia's before nodding toward the chairs in front of his desk. "Take a seat. All of you."

As they sat, the tension in the room thickened and Tori clenched her hands in her lap and prepared for further bad news. From the gravity of the inspector's expression and the way his steady gaze bore into hers, Tori sensed he hadn't summoned her here to say Cally, Greg and their associate were likely to be sentenced to life imprisonment.

His entire expression screamed of having to relay bad news.

He cleared his throat. "Okay, well, I asked you to come in because I wanted you to hear the latest from me, rather than on the news this evening."

In her peripheral vision, Mark shifted in his seat and Olivia reached for her father's hand.

Tori clenched her joined hands tighter so she wouldn't reach for Mark's other hand.

DCI Thornhill looked at Mark and Olivia, before turning his entire focus on Tori. "Miss Martine Appleton, aka Cally Seymour, has been charged with abduction along with her associates, Greg Falmer and Ian Green. Miss Appleton has also received the added charge of child cruelty against Abby Brady and Olivia as well as attempted grievous bodily harm for the injuries she sustained to you during your final altercation with her."

A little of the tension eased in Tori's shoulders. "So she'll be imprisoned? She'll stand trial?"

"We're not certain of that yet."

Tori stiffened. "What? But you just said—"

Mark squeezed her hands. "Let him finish, Tori."

Thornhill's jaw tightened, his frustration clear in his eyes. "She has given a full confession, but I wanted to prepare you for the possible ruling that she might not be mentally fit to stand trial."

Tori pursed her lips and intertwined her fingers with Mark's as she trembled. "Go on."

The inspector held her gaze. "After accompanying you to the school several times when you picked up your niece, Miss Appleton chose Abby primarily because of how much she looks like you did at the same age. After her father's arrest, Miss Appleton's mother took her daughter away and severed all ties with her husband which led to Miss Appleton obsessing over her father's case and, in turn, you. She has told us she wanted you because her father wanted you. She believes she's in love with you and orchestrated it so she got a job working with you at the Gazette. When you didn't return her feelings, she arranged Abby's abduction and hoped, because of what happened to you, you would feel compelled to find Abby."

Mark slid his hand from Tori's and stood. He shoved his fingers into his hair and paced the room. She reached across his vacated seat and offered her hand to Olivia. The young girl's eyes shone with tears as she rose from her seat to sit next to Tori, her gaze turning to her father.

Tori faced Thornhill. "And then she took Olivia to punish Mark? Because she knew I was falling in love with him?" Mark's gaze burned into her temple, but she kept her focus on Thornhill…pretended not to be affected by Olivia laying her head on her shoulder. "Am I right?"

The inspector nodded. "Yes."

Tori swallowed as her temper simmered. "So what happens now?"

Thornhill leaned forward and placed his forearms on the desk, his gaze somber and determined. "We'll find a way to get them, Miss Peterson. All three will pay for their crimes. Trust me."

"Trust you? I hate to point this out to you, but Mark and I had a hell of a lot to do with catching these monsters."

Thornhill glared. "We worked night and day, Miss Peterson. Unfortunately, our leads were nowhere near as strong as yours because you were the lynchpin in this case from the very start. It is hardly fair to dismiss police efforts when—"

"When she has every right to do so?" Mark stood beside her and slid his arm around Tori's shoulders. "Miss Peterson, Olivia and I will leave you in peace, Inspector. We'd appreciate being kept informed of everything that happens from here on in."

Tori trembled beneath Mark's grasp. Did this mean he was pleased that she'd finally admitted aloud that she was falling for him as he had confessed to her weeks before? Did they stand a chance of staying together after everything that had happened? She dragged her gaze from the inspector's and faced Mark.

He winked. "Let's get out of here."

Tori rose, her heart beating fast with hope of a brilliant, new, love-filled future. She faced Thornhill and held out her hand. "Do want you have to do to ensure justice is served, Inspector. Abby Brady deserves that and so does Olivia."

He nodded and shook her hand, his gaze softening. "And so do you. I'll be in touch."

Tori walked out of Thornhill's office ahead of Mark and Olivia. Her head ached and her stomach was knotted. So much had happened. So much had changed inside her. But was that a good place for her, Mark and Olivia to go forward?

They emerged through the station doors into the parking lot.

Tori continued to walk ahead toward Mark's car, uncertain and unsure what to say or do now that she'd voiced her feelings for him when all he wanted right now was to ensure Olivia was happy and had a holiday she so desperately deserved.

"Tori?"

She halted and briefly closed her eyes before facing him.

He stood with his arm around Olivia's shoulders. "I vote for Disneyland, Olivia votes the White House. You get the casting vote."

"Why me?"

Olivia grinned. "Because you're coming with us."

Tori's heart picked up speed. "What?"

Mark slipped his arm from Olivia and closed the space between him and Tori. He gently placed his hands on her waist and dipped his head to brush his lips across hers. "We've got a chance here, Tori. Do you trust me enough to take it? I want you to be with Olivia and me. I hope you want that too. For the first time in five years, my heart is someone else's for the taking. What do you say?"

Tori blinked and the tears she'd held inside for so long escaped. "I say yes. A million times, yes."

He grinned and pulled her close, his mouth covering hers.

When Olivia muttered, "Ugh" behind them, Tori smiled against Mark's lips and fell with every part of herself into the life she'd always dreamed of.

**A word about the author…**

Rachel Brimble lives in the U.K. with her husband, two teenage daughters, and a beloved Labrador. She is a member of Romance Writers of America and the Romantic Novelists Association. When she's not writing, she is reading, knitting, or walking the beautiful English countryside with family and friends.
www.rachelbrimble.com
www.rachelbrimble.blogspot.com